The Reisman Case

Andrew Diamond

Cover design by Lindsay Heider Diamond. Woman's silhouette licensed from Stock Unlimited. Thunderbolt and fingerprint licensed from Deposit Photos.

ISBN (Paperback): 978-1734139242
ISBN (e-book): 978-1734139235

For Addie, who always means what she says.

Freddy—

At the bar, you asked me to lay out the details of the Reisman case from beginning to end. I told you that would be too long a story to tell in one sitting, too involved a tale for that noisy setting.

I've had time since then to write it all out. A full case report, which I submit to you here.

I made some decisions along the way, as I'm sure you've heard from Anton, that might have seemed reckless. That's what you do when the stakes are high and the outcome matters more to you personally than to any other player in the game. I've always had faith in my abilities, and I've never fully trusted others to do things right, certainly not to my own high standards, and certainly not when it's *my* life on the line. Roscoe Lehmann was right when he said the best motivation is to have some skin in the game.

The risks paid off. So what if Anton was horrified? Lawyers are trained for caution, and caution wasn't going to help me in this case.

You've heard of those ride-alongs where cops give civilians a first-hand view of the streets? Well, I'm going to put you in the passenger seat of my mind and show you the case as it unfolded before me. You'll get the facts as I found them, and you can make of them what you will. I respect your experience and abilities. I'd like to know if you would have acted differently in my position.

You asked how all this started. It started as all our troubles start: unremarkably, on a day that looked like any other, under circumstances I would not have remembered if the case had not played out as it did.

If I had known what this case would turn into, I never would have accepted it. No one walks into a burning house.

—Claire

1

You know what I used to do. Due diligence for corporate buyouts. I'd go into a company, interview people, run through the books, dig into their intellectual property and production processes, pick apart the management structure and organizational psychology. The goal was to expose hidden risks before the purchaser finalized the deal.

It was corporate detective work. I was good at, I enjoyed it, and it paid well.

Then six months ago, when my life was falling apart, I got sucked into a world of trouble not of my own making. An old friend bequeathed me some information I didn't want. Simply having it made me a target. I met some very nasty people, got locked in The Friday Cage and had to think my way out.

That experience woke me up. It gave me a taste of what I really wanted to do. The world is full of bad people, and someone needs to keep them from hurting the good.

I enrolled in criminal justice courses at American University. To pay the bills, I picked up a contract with the Securities and Exchange commission, reviewing documents in a securities fraud case.

That was dull work. My life consisted of subway rides between Woodley Park and Union Station, hours of combing through tedious documents, and more hours of pointless meetings. Outside of work, I studied, and when I wasn't studying, I was wrapping up my grandmother's affairs. Selling her house, her car. Establishing a trust to pay for her dementia care.

It wasn't much of a life.

In mid-July, the contractor that had placed me in the SEC asked if I wanted to renew for three more months. I was looking for an excuse to say no, waiting till the last minute when I had to give them a firm answer, hoping that something more interesting would come along. I wanted distraction, something to take me away from the responsibilities of work and family and study, something other than myself to occupy my mind in that lonely apartment.

The night before I had to give my final answer, I got a call from Roscoe Lehmann. Did I have a few days to look into something for him? I asked him what kind of investigation he needed and he said he'd rather not discuss it over the phone.

"Come to my house tomorrow morning. I'll give you the details in person. It's a simple case, bread and butter work. It shouldn't take more than a few days."

I wanted to ask how he'd found me and if he knew I wasn't licensed yet, but I decided to save those questions for our meeting.

At the close of the call, all I could think was, Well, here's my distraction. I told Lehmann I'd see him at 10:30 the next morning.

After I hung up, I told my employer I wouldn't be renewing the contract right away. I'd need a week or two off. That was fine with them.

I understood why his name sounded familiar when I Googled Roscoe Lehmann. He owned a company that sold appliances—refrigerators, dishwashers, dryers. I'd seen his trucks around DC since I was a girl, big white box trucks with the green Lehmann Appliance logo, though there seemed to be fewer of them now than when I was young.

I found Lehmann's house on Zillow, a six bedroom in Potomac worth two and a half million. He had owned it since it was built in the mid-eighties. I guessed he'd have to be at least sixty-five.

He was obviously a private man. No social media, no photos of him at charity fundraisers or any of the other events where the rich from Potomac tend to show up. He'd lost a son some years back, but other than that, his name didn't show up in the news.

Before I left the next morning, I had a mental picture of the person I would meet: an older man with money who had withdrawn from the mainstream of life into quiet and solitude. A discreet man who, if he ever had cause to hire an investigator, would want to keep it on the down low, would want to talk face-to-face so he could assess the quality of the person he was hiring.

That all fit with the way I liked to work. I looked forward to meeting him.

2

He lived in that part of Potomac where huge stone houses sit behind iron gates and the rolling lawns stay green even when the rest of the county is brown with drought. Mercedes in every driveway, next to the Land Rover or the Porsche, and landscaping trucks on every other block because in his neighborhood, even the bushes have servants.

Lehmann's house was at the end of one of the older streets, a two-story brick mansion with a two-car garage and an asphalt drive. The shaggy grass gave the yard a disheveled look, like stubble on the face of a man who'd been up drinking all night. Every other lawn on the street was freshly cut.

The rough asphalt drive had faded from black to grey. Tiny weeds and tufts of grass peeped up through gnarled cracks that bulged like varicose veins.

I wondered if Lehmann was down on his luck, or too depressed to maintain the property. Or maybe he was just cheap.

The grey GMC Yukon in the driveway had Florida plates. Maybe he's a snowbird, I thought. If he doesn't live here full time, why should he care if it's all ship-shape?

I parked behind the SUV, cut the engine, and took a photo of the Yukon's license plate because—why not? Better to have information you don't need than to be missing information you do. If I got curious later, and I knew I would, I could look up his Florida address, find out what kind of mansion he had down there.

I checked myself in the rearview, turned it back, rubbed my hands on my slacks, and thought, "Okay, let's see what Roscoe Lehmann wants."

It was hot, and the car was in the sun, so I left the windows down. I wore navy slacks and a white sleeveless top. I would not have worn that in the shape I was in last winter, but I'd regained all the weight I'd lost. I was healthy again, and on a broiling July day, I didn't want to sweat any more than I had to.

The only thing I took from the car was my shoulder bag, which held a laptop, phone, pen and paper, and a few other items.

I stopped at the Yukon before going to the door. The SUV was spotless inside and out. Much better maintained than the property. What did that say about the man? I wasn't sure.

I tucked the observation and the question into my mental case file, ascended three slate steps and rang the bell beside the heavy wooden door.

You don't notice when a house has a portico over the front door, but you notice when it *doesn't* have one. You notice when it's July and that sweltering DC sun is beating down on you.

I could see where the portico had once been attached to the house. Slanted lines above the door showed it had a pitched roof, and two faded squares at the corners of the stoop showed where the support posts had stood. He'd had it removed, but there didn't seem to be any work in progress to replace it.

Beads of sweat were forming on my scalp and on the back of my neck. I checked my watch. Ten thirty-two. I rang again.

Through the windows on either side of the door, I could see the dark stain of the floors, the deep red border of the Persian rug, and the bottom of a stairway that ascended to the right. I wondered if Lehmann himself would answer or if he'd send a servant.

When I drew back from the window, I felt someone watching me. Whether it was real or not, I didn't know. It was a hard feeling to shake after what had happened six months earlier. First one man had been following me and then another.

Even after they'd been locked up, I continued to look over my shoulder. The only analogy I can give to people who haven't been stalked is that the aftereffect is like getting off a boat. The rational part of you knows you're on solid ground, but you still feel the rocking sea in your bones.

My paranoia flared up now and then, and I had to make a conscious effort to tamp it down.

Time, I told myself. Time will erase this feeling, if I let it.

But even now, months after those men had been put away, I was acutely sensitive to the presence of others. I still carried the stun gun in my shoulder bag. I still couldn't give myself permission to relax.

A motion in the window above caught my eye. One side of the curtain fluttered shut, as if a hand had just let go of it.

Then the door in front of me opened. The man on the other side, sixty or so—a few years younger than I had guessed in my musings the night before—seemed to startle at the sight of me.

"Hello," I said.

I put on my friendliest smile, extended my hand. "I'm Claire."

He shook off his surprise with some effort. Almost unwillingly, I thought. His hand was clammy, his grip half-hearted.

"We had an appointment. 10:30. Remember?"

"Yes, I remember." His face was tan and lined from years of sun. Florida, I thought.

His blue suit was expensive and well-tailored, more like the spotless Yukon than the shaggy lawn, but it was too dark for the summer heat. Who would go outside in that? Maybe all his business was indoors that day.

"Come in, won't you?" He moved aside to make way.

The air inside was twenty degrees cooler. He closed the door behind me and it took a few seconds for my eyes to adjust to the darkness.

"Sorry, Roscoe Lehmann. I should have introduced myself. I don't know where my head is today. I didn't forget about you, Claire. I just lost track of time and..."

He stopped and stared at me, appraising my features with the calculating interest of a car dealer evaluating a trade-in.

"And?" I said.

Again, he had to force himself to stop staring. "I'm sorry. Would you like something to drink? Iced tea? Lemonade?"

"Lemonade sounds good."

"Great. Let me show you to the office."

He led me down the hallway toward the rear of the house. Between the living room in front and his office in back, a stairway ascended to the right. Three dark wood steps led to a landing before the stairs turned left and went up to the second floor. A large, discolored square marked the spot where a painting had been removed from the landing wall. It must have had a substantial frame. The two heavy-duty wall anchors that had supported it stared out like empty eyes from a blank, forsaken face.

I wondered if Roscoe Lehmann was in the process of moving his wealth to the Sunshine State. Maybe the painting was a favorite, or a piece of great value. An original by some famous artist.

A faint, familiar smell lingered on the steps. Oribe. An expensive shampoo. I used to use it when I was earning a big salary. You don't forget that scent. It told me someone else was in the house.

After we passed the stairs, Lehmann said, "Right here." He showed me into the office. "I'll be back in a minute with your drink. Sit wherever you like."

The room had a heavy feel: wood paneling, mahogany desk, intricately patterned Persian rug. One wall held a shelf of leather-bound books, the kind you know the owner didn't read because all the spines were the same dull brown with titles debossed in gold. Western literature's greatest hits, priced by the foot to decorate a library or a den. Framed watercolors showed the fish and waterfowl of the Chesapeake Bay.

Two green leather-upholstered chairs stood before the heavy desk. It could have been a stage set for the office of a 1940s banker. The green chairs would be for loan applicants.

Behind the desk, an Aeron chair broke the illusion. An ergonomic intrusion from the twenty-first century to ease a rich man's aging back.

Huge French windows overlooked the back yard, which extended fifty or sixty yards to a stand of trees. The pool was empty except for two feet of brown water at the deep end. The leaves must have been steeping since autumn. They had sunk to the bottom and turned black. Sparse grass clippings on the surface gave the water a tinge of green.

On the outside, the property had the feel of a once-flourishing man now in decline. Inside, it was clean and well furnished, but quiet and lifeless; dark, with high ceilings that made it feel empty despite the rich furnishings.

It lacked the warmth of a home, felt more like a second home, or an interior decorator's set piece, meant to be looked at rather than lived in. The ticking of the clock on the shelf added a dimension of loneliness, as if time were winding down to its inevitable end. The heavy decor didn't fit with the bright scent that lingered on the stairway. A woman who spent that much on shampoo would never let her pool fall into such a state.

"Ah, the pool," said Lehmann, handing me a tall cool glass. "I *will* get around to that. I will! Take a seat if you'd like. Unless you prefer to stand."

"Thank you," I said.

I took one of the loan applicant's seats. Lehmann took the Aeron behind the desk. I sipped my drink—which was both too sweet and too sour—and looked for a spot to put it down. There were no coasters, and I didn't want to stain the wood. Lehmann put his drink on the old-fashioned blotter, and I did the same.

"You want me to cut to the chase?" he asked.

"Sure."

"I had a feeling. You have that look. Straight to the point. You know what I do, right?"

"You sell appliances."

He smiled. "That's not how I would put it. I own the company. We have warehouses in Maryland and Virginia. We sell to builders and consumers. We... Okay, I don't need to give you the whole pitch. The reason I called you, I think one of my employees is stealing."

"Any idea who?"

"I have a very definite idea."

"You know how much he's taken? Sorry, is this person you're thinking of a he or a she?"

"He. As for what he's taken, I'm not exactly sure."

"He has access to company accounts?"

"No. He works at the warehouse."

"So, he's taking merchandise? Not embezzling?"

"That's my suspicion."

"But you don't know what he might have taken? Don't you track inventory?"

The question seemed to catch him off guard. Or maybe it was just the sharpness of my tone. Neither should have bothered him. We had already established that I'm straight to the point, and who moves merchandise without tracking inventory?

"I do track inventory," he said, "but it's a little more complicated than that. Say, for example, we get a delivery. The supplier says it was signed for on such and such date and twelve items were delivered. Somehow, we only have eight. Where did the other four go? They were never even scanned into our tracking system to be counted."

"So, you think it's someone on the receiving dock?"

"Yes."

"Do you have security watching them?"

"The warehouse has a guard, but he works for the property owner, not me. He's up and down Rockville Pike, patrolling half a dozen properties. So, no. No one is watching him at this point."

"What about cameras?"

"They don't cover every inch of the warehouse. Things move around a lot. A guy with a dolly moves an item off camera, maybe it shows up again, maybe it doesn't."

"Okay. So, you think your employee is stealing. What do you want me to do?"

"Follow him. See if you can catch him hauling anything in his pickup. Find out if he rented storage space to stash things. Find out if he's selling online. See if he's spending beyond his means. He makes fourteen dollars an hour."

"He married?"

"What difference does that make?" Lehmann asked.

"A single man might get by on fourteen dollars an hour. A married man can't pay the rent on that."

"He's single."

"Dangerous?"

"Is he dangerous?" Lehmann repeated the question slowly, as if he wasn't sure how to answer.

"It's a simple question," I said. "I'd like to know before I run into him."

"Shouldn't you make that determination on your own?"

"I should and I will, but I want to get your take on him first. How long has he been working for you?"

"Two months."

"Did you know him before that?"

"No. And as for dangerous, I'm not sure how to answer. He's..." Lehmann paused to search for the word. "Delicate."

"How do you mean?"

"He's a loner. Pathologically shy. Which is part of the reason I asked you here."

I heard a thump on the floor upstairs. Lehmann glanced up quickly and scowled.

"I'm sorry, *what* is the reason you asked me here?"

"Jacob is too wary," he said, "and too shy to let people close."

"I don't need to get close to him to figure out if he's stealing."

"Oh, but you do. He's painfully shy. You won't learn anything about him without—"

"He doesn't sound like the kind who would steal. Thieves are bold or desperate, not shy."

"There's something else though."

"Uh-huh. I could tell."

I could also tell that Roscoe Lehmann had just shaved his beard. The skin on his lower cheeks and chin was lighter than his upper cheeks and forehead, like it had been shielded from the sun. Red spots and dry white flakes were signs of razor burn.

"I don't think this person is motivated by simple greed," Lehmann said. "I think he might be harboring some resentment. Maybe some kind of vendetta. As I said, he's..."

He searched once more for a word. He could have said "delicate" again, after all the trouble he'd gone through to dredge up that vague and useless adjective, but something compelled him to dig deeper this time for an even vaguer description. "He's not quite right."

"Okay, I asked you if this person was dangerous." My tone was sharp, impatient. I try to control that, because I know how it puts people off, but Lehmann's evasiveness came off as less than honest.

"And I would say no," Lehmann said cautiously. "Not toward you."

He leaned forward and smiled with the overly reassuring manner of a salesman trying to reel in a customer. His smile was too ready, too eager, flashing beneath eyes that too obviously kept score of my reactions.

"Not toward *me*?" I asked. "Why not toward me?"

"I just think that the attention of a woman—"

"No," I stood and looped my bag over shoulder. "I'm not in this business to give anyone *attention*. Especially not some delicate man who *isn't quite right*."

Lehmann rushed around the desk and got in front of me. "Please!"

"Hire someone else. Or just fire the guy if you want to be rid of him."

"For what cause?" Lehmann pleaded. "Until I can prove he's stealing—"

"You don't need cause. Maryland is a right-to-work state. You can hire and fire at will."

I tried to step around him, but he blocked my way.

"But if there *is* something wrong with him," he pleaded, "if he does hold some kind of vendetta and I fire him—"

"So, you *do* think he's dangerous? You've only known him two months. What could he possibly have against you?"

"I don't know. And I don't care. But if you can prove he's stealing, I can get him arrested."

"You don't think *that* will piss him off? I'm sorry. This isn't for me."

This time I did step around him, but he cut me off at the double doors of the office.

"You don't get it," he said, grabbing my arm. "Once the cops have him—"

"Take your hands off me."

Lehmann let go. "—they'll see what state he's in. They'll put him back in the institution."

"Okay, this is going from bad to worse." I gave him a hard look. "You bring me here with a story about a stealing employee, and now he's a madman who needs to be locked up again. Unless he can get the attention of a woman."

"No, no, no. You're misinterpreting."

"Misinterpreting what? Those are your own words. Get out of my way."

I walked past him, turned left in the hall and headed back toward the front door.

"Claire, wait!"

"Sorry. We're done."

"Okay, just do this much for me. Follow him. Look for clues. A storage space. Spending beyond his means. Evidence left in his truck. Just get me that. That's all. I'll take care of the rest."

I stopped at the front door and thought about it. This would be my first case, if I accepted it. I didn't have an investigator's license, but it was a simple job, and it would give me some practice. Follow, observe, gather evidence, write a report.

Lehmann stood beside me with the nervous air of a dog that didn't want to be left.

"Okay," I said. "First condition: if this guy shows any sign of being a psychopath, I'm out. You find someone else to follow him."

"Fine."

"Second, you pay me for three days up front, and if I have to bail on the assignment because your friend is nutso, I keep the money."

"Fine. And if you're nervous about—you really shouldn't be because he's painfully shy—"

"And he has a vendetta."

"Possibly, but that would be against me, not you. If you're worried, then only talk to him in public, where there are people around to see."

"I'd do that anyway."

"Talk to him on the loading dock, in the warehouse if you want, but don't let on there's any kind of investigation."

"Why would I do that? If I'm investigating the guy, I'm not going to tell him."

"No, I mean if you talk to the other workers, don't let them think you're an investigator."

"Why not?"

"I hired one once before and things got ugly. The guy was aggressive and threatening. It caused a lot of resentment and hurt morale. I don't want that again."

"I don't work like that," I said.

"So do we have a deal?"

"Aren't you going to ask my rate?"

"What's your rate?"

I hesitated a split second longer than I should have.

"Two thousand a day," I said. I didn't want the job, so I named a price I knew he wouldn't accept.

"Deal."

For a moment, we stood staring at each other, neither one knowing what to do next. At last, I told him I'd start when he signed a contract and paid me.

"I can pay you now," Lehmann said. "We don't need a contract."

I shook my head. "There is no *we* without a contract."

"Do you have one with you?"

"Of course."

"All right," Lehmann sighed. "Come into the kitchen. The light's better in there."

I laid two copies of a contract on the marble top of the kitchen island. I had spent several evenings drafting this months before and had reviewed it with a lawyer. A standard terms-of-service agreement between investigator and client. Even though I didn't have a license, I had my paperwork ready ahead of time so I could hit the ground running the day a license came through.

I filled in the daily rate we had agreed on and wrote a brief addendum spelling out the terms we'd discussed. If the subject of the investigation turned out to be dangerous or threatening, I could opt out and keep the money.

Lehmann watched me write with the eager anticipation of a dog watching its owner scrape the remains of a steak into its bowl.

He flipped to the last pages and signed both copies. I don't know why he thought I wouldn't notice that. No successful business owner signs a contract without reading it.

Lehmann excused himself and went upstairs, to get his checkbook, I assumed.

Alone in the kitchen, I tried to assemble a picture of the man's life from the scene around me. The sink was dirty, but the stove was spotless, which told me he probably didn't cook. Three boxes of cereal sat on the counter, all opened, beside one of those old-fashioned coffee grinders that you crank by hand. I didn't see a coffee maker anywhere.

Lehmann returned after a minute with a manila envelope.

"What's this?" I asked as he handed it to me.

"Your pay."

The envelope was stuffed with cash.

"A simple check would do."

"Cash is cleaner."

"Not for me."

"We have a contract," Lehmann said. "And that's legal tender. Take it."

Who keeps six thousand dollars cash in their house? Or gives that kind of money to someone they just met? I didn't ask aloud. I just gave him a curious look, an invitation to explain himself.

He read the invitation and ignored it. My doubts didn't matter to him. I took that as a slight. One more point against a man I trusted less and less since the moment we met.

"Professor Williamson recommended you very highly," he said.

I'd meant to ask him how he'd heard of me. Funny he had thought of it himself just then. Williamson taught Foundations of Criminal Justice Systems at American University, one of two classes I had taken in the spring.

Lehmann picked up his copy of the contract, folded it in half and stuffed it into the pocket of his suit.

"Make sure you take photos," he said.

Why would you bother telling me that, I wondered. Do you think I'm stupid?

"Of course," I said politely. "They're all yours when the case is done."

"And write your notes by hand."

"What difference does it make how I write my notes?"

"I don't want you sending reports electronically."

"Is someone snooping on you?"

"That's a separate issue and none of your concern." A cold rebuff delivered in a reassuring tone, with a courteous salesman's smile.

I extended my hand, polite and professional, but decidedly more cool than warm for this man I neither liked nor trusted. "Okay, Mr. Lehmann. I'll call you later with some questions."

Again, his hand was clammy and limp. Totally at odds with the eager smile and dark brown eyes that looked on me with too much familiarity.

A minute later, I was rolling up the windows in the BMW, cranking the air conditioning, wondering how much of the story Lehmann wasn't telling me.

I pulled a printed page from the envelope of cash and looked over the photo and details. Jacob Reisman was twenty-five years old, but he looked closer to forty. Chubby face, balding, with a wispy blond comb-over and the dark-ringed eyes of a chronic insomniac. Lives in Rockville, MD. Drives a twelve-year old blue Chevy 1500 pickup. His address and license plate number were right there at the top of the page.

I put the paper on the passenger seat and released the emergency brake. My accountant's sense told me the same thing my gut was telling me. Something was wrong with this setup. How many appliances would this thief have to steal to justify a six-thousand-dollar investigation? Why not spend five hundred bucks for a few extra surveillance cameras and catch him in the act?

But I had signed an agreement. I wasn't going to back out of my first case before the ink on the contract had dried. I have always looked at quitting as the lowest form of failure, a humiliation you can hide from everyone but yourself. And part of me was curious. What was this case really about? If it involved more than thievery, I should be able to figure it out. And if I couldn't, I was in the wrong business.

I pushed the shift into reverse and checked the rearview to see if it was safe to back up. A fluttering motion drew my eyes to the second-floor window. The nails on the hand that pulled the curtain shut were painted red. A woman's hand, small and slim like my own.

3

Lehmann's warehouse was off of Crabbes Branch Way in Rockville, a putty-colored box with corrugated metal siding in a light industrial park that was also home to a sign maker, a sheet metal works, and an auto body shop. I drove up there the morning after we spoke.

I was supposed to be an insurance inspector from The Hartford, inspecting warehouse conditions to calculate a rate adjustment. Lehmann called ahead to tell them I'd be coming. I had a clipboard with a convincing looking inspection checklist with The Hartford logo at the top of each page.

When I pulled into the side lot, I found Reisman's truck parked in the shade of a cherry tree. The loading dock was around back, and the warehouse had no side windows, so I could look at the blue Chevy without being watched.

In the bed, I found razor-cut scraps of heavy-duty cardboard and a couple of plastic straps used to wrap large appliance boxes. I took photos of those, and of the interior of the truck, which was spotless. No garbage, no stains, not even dust on the dashboard.

The outside of the truck was clean, except for some dents and scrapes near the top of the tailgate, as if it had banged down on a concrete loading dock. I photographed that as well.

Walking into the warehouse felt familiar, like the old days of due diligence, when I walked into companies to interview people, document processes, check the books and inspect facilities. This was just another day at the office, except for my regrettable choice of clothing.

I wore a brown suit (not my color) because I was supposed to be representing a conservative industry. It was one of those muggy July mornings when the air is so thick you can see the haze. Cicadas were buzzing in the trees, nature's soundtrack to DC's timeless molten summers, and I was sticking to my clothes before I reached the concrete steps of the dock.

A man who I guessed was in his twenties was pushing a washer on a dolly into one of Lehmann's box trucks. Beside him, another man made notes on a clipboard. He had the air of a supervisor, so I approached him. I had forgotten to ask Lehmann his name. My fault. I usually arrange every detail of an encounter like this beforehand, because I don't like to look unprepared, and I don't like surprises.

The man looked up as I approached. He was six feet tall, powerfully built, a black man, maybe forty, with a bushy beard and a friendly face. He had an air of intelligence that told me he was going to be helpful.

"I help you?"

"Are you the supervisor?"

"Carl Graves."

He leaned forward and extended his hand. He had the firm shake of a confident, purposeful man.

"Claire Chastain."

My name didn't seem to register, so I added, "From The Hartford."

Still nothing.

"I'm here to do an inspection. For your insurance. Didn't Roscoe Lehmann call you?"

"No, but that don't mean nothing." He had an easy smile.

My impression so far was that Lehmann ran his business like he kept his home. Not ship shape. It didn't surprise his employees when he let things fall through the cracks.

The twenty-something guy came off the back of the truck with an empty dolly and Graves pointed out three large boxes to be loaded next.

"The two Whirlpools first," he said. "The Bosch goes in last, gets dropped first."

Turning back to me, he asked where I wanted to start my inspection.

"Let's start in the back with the fire exits."

The warehouse was as plain as you'd expect: concrete floor beneath bright blue-white lights; high, exposed metal rafters; the same corrugated metal walls inside as out. The only remarkable thing about the place was the amount of empty space. They could have run the whole operation from a building half the size. That's the sort of thing I'd note in my report to a corporate buyer. Move the fulfillment center to a smaller warehouse to cut costs.

"Not a lot of inventory," Graves said. "But that's good for insurance, right? Plenty of room to maneuver. Fewer accidents. Last thing you want is you're wrestling a fridge onto the dolly and you back into a wall of dishwashers. How many claims we have last year?"

"I don't know. I'm an inspector, not an adjustor."

I estimated the space between rows of appliances—ten feet—and made a note on my checklist.

Graves told me he'd been with Lehmann for eleven years.

"Roscoe's good people," he said. "I like to know who I'm working with. Like them to know me too. Some bosses ain't like that. You ain't nothin' to them. They don't even know your name. But Roscoe's a good guy. We think alike. 'Bout business, anyway. The family stuff, I stay out of. Eleven years ago, this warehouse was full."

He swept his hand toward the empty space.

"We had twice as many trucks. Business been goin' down since Lowes and Home Depot took over the country. They're eatin' us alive. Even Best Buy's sellin' appliances now. It's like, how you gonna compete with them? They're nationwide. Got a billion dollars to throw into ads and inventory. We got two warehouses. Maryland and Virginia. Both of 'em used to be full. Now it's—well you got eyes. You can see it."

As we made our way back toward the loading dock, he told me the high-end items in Lehmann's showroom near Montgomery Mall had good profit margins, though not as good as the old days. The national chains had driven prices down.

"Most of what we move here is builder's grade. That's code talk for piece of shit. When a builder puts a kitchen in a new house, the fridge, stove, the washer just gotta work till the buyer signs the contract. After that, they don't care. Margins on builder's grade ain't hardly enough to keep you afloat, unless you move a lot of it, and that's us. Hustle, baby, hustle! Everyone up here's bustin' their ass, 'cept old Three Times."

He pointed toward a pale, pudgy, slow-moving man with a bad combover. This was my first glimpse of Reisman. He was pushing a washing machine on a small electric forklift called a walk-behind. I could see from twelve feet away that his knuckles were white on the control handle. Long strands of golden hair were plastered with sweat to the top of his bald head. The anxious concentration on his face made him look like an overgrown child afraid of losing control of a machine that couldn't have been going more than two miles an hour.

Lehmann had said he was delicate, and now I understood. The walk-behind was hardly moving, there were no obstructions in his path, and there was no way the washing machine could fall off. But to see the anxiety in his face, you'd think he was pushing a baby stroller along the edge of a windy cliff. Just watching him made me tense. The way he held his breath, I wondered if he might have some developmental disability.

The impatient driver standing at the back the truck said, "Yo, step it up, retard. I ain't got all goddamn day."

Reisman lowered his head like a dog expecting a blow.

"Ease up, Lenny," said Graves. He had a confident, easy manner with the other employees. "Half a minute ain't gonna kill you."

Graves led me over to the desks at the side of the loading dock. When Reisman was out of earshot, in the truck's cargo box, I asked Graves why he called him Three Times.

"He checks everything three times. Give him a manifest to load a truck, he'll check the item number once on the page, then he'll check it on the box. Check it on the page, check it on the box, make sure they match up. Three times when he picks up, and three times when he gets it on the truck. Makes the drivers crazy, but since he came on, they never have to come back in the middle of the day to swap out a fridge. He makes sure every item on that truck is the *right* item.

"Some of these guys," Graves shook his head, "they don't care what they load. Paper says three dryers, they grab the first three they see. If it's wrong, that's the driver's problem. Three Times is slow, but he don't make mistakes."

The two desks at which we stood belonged to Graves and Reisman. They were heavy wood, like nineteen forties government surplus. Each had a keyboard and monitor and stacks of papers. The easygoing Graves didn't mind disarray. Soda cups from Subway, coffee cups from Starbucks, ragged stacks of printed orders bleeding into each other.

Reisman's papers were sorted into three piles, each meticulously stacked, with the edges flush, as if they'd been pressed into place against a ruler. Watching him come off the back of the box truck stewarding the immense responsibility of the empty walk-behind, I got the sense that if someone knocked his papers out of order, he'd go into a panic and wouldn't be able to work again until they were all set straight again.

I asked Graves to point out the security cameras. The coverage was better than Lehmann had led me to believe. I didn't see how anyone could move goods in or out without being seen. Unless some of the cameras didn't work. When I asked Graves if any of them were broken, he shrugged.

I didn't want to raise suspicions, so I led Graves slowly toward the matter I was there to investigate.

"In a typical year, how many claims do you file for goods damaged in the warehouse?"

"In this warehouse?" He thought for a second. "One? Maybe. I don't know about Virginia. You'll have to ask them."

"What about worker injuries?"

"Don't you all have that info? You're the insurer."

"We do. I just want to know whether the warehouse supervisor is on top of his game."

He smiled. "I could tell you, but I'll let you ask Jake. He does the paperwork now. Might make him feel important to answer some questions from the likes of you."

"What about theft?" I asked.

"Ain't no theft here."

"You sure?"

"What do you mean, am I sure? I run this place. This stuff is heavy. You can't just put it in your pocket and walk out."

"Who would file the reports if merchandise went missing?"

"Jake." Graves looked at me funny, like he was trying to make out my deeper motive.

"And would you know if he'd filed a claim?" I asked.

"He'd tell me. Anytime he does anything new, he asks me twelve times to check his work. Man's terrified of making a mistake."

"He's never filled out paperwork for missing merchandise?"

"He would have asked me how to do it. Why do you ask?"

"Just checking."

Maybe my questions were too direct. The way Graves was eyeing me—I remembered what Lehmann had said about hiring an investigator, how it made the employees mad. I didn't want Graves reading my face because I wasn't sure what it might show. I made some notes on my clipboard to look occupied.

"You mind if I sit here for a while and finish my write-up?" I asked.

"Take all the time you want. I gotta talk to the man over here."

As Graves walked toward the truck, Reisman was coming the other way, toward me.

"Yo, Jake, that's Ms. Chastain. Insurance lady. Say hello."

Graves spoke as if instructing a child. Without looking up, Reisman mumbled a weak hello at the floor as he shuffled toward his desk. This was the pathological shyness Lehmann had warned me of. I couldn't explain the cardboard and plastic straps in the back of Reisman's truck, but I also couldn't imagine this man being bold enough to steal anything.

He sat at his desk, stared into his monitor, clicked the mouse, and the printer on the desk where I sat whirred to life. While he waited for the pages to come out—and there were quite a few—he did everything he could not to look at me. He checked his monitor, straightened his already straight papers, turned to look at nothing in the rows of boxed appliances behind him.

When the printer fell silent, he looked at it twice but didn't get up. He couldn't get to it without coming close to me. His evasiveness and general air of anxiety told me he feared contact. There was something childish and pitiful about him, like a boy who'd been scolded too many times and then turned inward on himself to try to hide from the world.

I picked up the papers and brought them to him. I knew he wouldn't take them from my hand, so I laid them on the desk neatly, making sure they didn't touch the other piles he had so carefully arranged.

"Thank you," he said softly.

"You're welcome, Jake."

Maybe I shouldn't have said his name. He looked at me, alarmed. His eyes widened and his nostrils flared as if he'd come face to face with a mortal threat. I could feel his panic. For a second, I had the strange feeling that he knew me, that he recognized me from somewhere. But why should he be scared?

I was sure I'd never met him before, but could he have met me? And if so, what could I have done to make him fear me? His forehead and upper lip were sweating.

Delicate isn't the right word for him, I thought. He's damaged. Something hurt this man, and it must have happened early, before he understood how to defend himself.

I put out my hand, not out of professionalism or even courtesy, but from instinct. I wanted him to trust me.

I told him my name. His handshake was weak and timid.

This is not a thief, I told myself. This is not a thief, and this investigation is not about stolen goods. Something else is going on here.

"How long have you worked here?" I asked.

"Two months."

He was looking directly at me now. His stare was like a child's, unselfconscious, full of curiosity, a strange and sudden shift from the fear of a moment before. Was he sizing me up? Trying to place me in his memory?

"You like it?" I asked.

"Best job I ever had." He turned his attention back to the computer. A few seconds of eye contact seemed to be all he could handle.

"Where else have you worked?"

"Nowhere."

Why would Lehmann hire a man with no experience, I wondered. A twenty-five-year-old who had never worked?

"What do you like about working here?"

"Carl."

"Carl Graves?"

"He's a good person."

He looks out for you, I thought. He sticks up for you when the drivers are rude. You are not a thief. There's no way in the world you're a thief. But who are you then?

"What do you do outside of work?" I asked.

"Go home."

"That's it?"

"That's it," he said. "What do you do?"

I had to think about that. I study. I exercise. Visit my grandmother in memory care. Obsess about my past, worry about my future, wish I wasn't so alone.

"Go home," I said.

"Where are you from?" He kept his eyes on his monitor, but I could tell he was anxious to keep me engaged. A loner, too nervous to be around other people, he was probably starved for human interaction.

"DC," I said. "And you?"

I knew he had lived in California. It was on the fact sheet Lehmann had given me.

"No, what company?" he said. "I saw you walking with Carl, writing notes."

"I'm from the insurance company."

"Geico?"

"Hartford."

"Why are you here?"

"Just doing an inspection. Making sure conditions and procedures are up to standards."

"So, we're going to change then?"

"Nothing's going to change." I had the feeling change made him nervous.

"I mean, to Hartford?"

"What—um..." That caught me off guard. "What do you mean?"

He opened his drawer and pulled out a stack of papers. "I'm the form master," he said proudly. He slid the papers onto the desk in front of me.

"Claims go to Geico."

I looked at the Hartford letterhead I had forged on my bogus checklist. The letterhead I'd made after asking Lehmann who his insurer was. Why would he have told me the wrong company?

4

When I pulled out of the warehouse lot, the air conditioning in my car was blowing hot, my pants were stuck to my legs and my blouse was stuck to my back. It was close to noon and I was hangry.

I drove a couple hundred yards, then pulled into the lot of another warehouse and picked up my phone. The call to Lehmann rang six times and then went to voicemail. His voice commanded gruffly, "Leave a message."

What kind of greeting is that, I wondered. Not business friendly, that's for sure. No name, no "Sorry I missed your call." And the impatient tone wasn't in keeping with the oozing salesman character Lehmann projected in person. Maybe he didn't like people calling his cell.

"Hi, Roscoe, this is Claire. You told me the wrong insurance company. Do you understand how that puts me at risk? You said you didn't want anyone to know about this investigation, and then you let me go in there with the wrong cover. If you don't even know your own insurer, you have bigger problems than some guy stealing washers. I told you if I don't like the smell of this, I'm out. Well, I don't like the smell. Call me back, will you? I have some questions."

Maybe I should have eaten before I made that call. Maybe I should have waited till the AC cooled me off. It wasn't very polite, I admit, but when I start to question the competence and honesty of the people I'm working with, I want answers.

I dropped the phone onto the passenger seat and looked up just in time to see Jake Reisman's blue truck pass by.

"Well, well, well," I muttered as I pulled onto the road behind him. "Let's see what you're up to."

I followed him to Burger King and waited in the lot as he went through the drive-through. After that, we drove north on Frederick Avenue into Gaithersburg. Eight minutes and four turns later, Reisman parked in the lot of a self-storage facility.

I watched from across the street as he exited the truck. He had a funny way of holding the Burger King bag, away from his body, like it was something dirty, like a kindergartener carrying a skunk. I photographed him as he leaned into the bed of the truck and raked his arm from side to side. When he straightened up, I could see the plastic straps dangling from his chubby hand. I got photos of that as well.

He walked to the side of the building and stuffed the plastic straps into a garbage can. Something fell out of his hand and he bent to pick it up. A sliver of cardboard, maybe. That went into the garbage with the rest.

Reisman peered into the can the way people look into mailboxes to make sure their letters went down. He withdrew his hand, and the garbage door slapped shut. Then he checked it again.

I remembered the nickname Graves had given him. "Come on," I thought. "One more time."

Sure enough, he looked again.

After the third check, Reisman was satisfied. He walked to the roll-up door of the storage bay at the near end of the building, then looked over his shoulder. A jury looking at the photo I snapped at that moment might have concluded he was up to no good. Or they might have thought he was overly anxious or paranoid. Why does someone look over their shoulder before entering a building?

He pulled a key from his pocket, looked over his shoulder again, then stepped sideways from the roll-up door to the regular door.

No, open the big one, I thought. I want to see inside.

Reisman put the key into the lock, looked over his shoulder one last time, then went in.

After ten minutes, I began to wonder what he could be doing in there. If the cavernous appliance warehouse was hot, this little storage box had to be sweltering. Who in their right mind would want to sit in that airless oven when the July sun was at its peak?

The building had no number and I'd lost track of what street I was on, so I checked the map on my phone. I wrote the street name by hand into my notebook, as Lehmann had asked. While I was at it, I noticed the map showed a storage facility closer to Lehman's warehouse, just a block past the Burger King where Reisman had picked up lunch.

Why didn't he go to that one, I wondered. Why drive all the way up here?

I spent the next twenty-five minutes writing up what I had observed of Reisman at the warehouse. Shy indeed. Painfully anxious and childlike. Makes no effort to defend himself against abuse. Responds to kindness. Loyal to and fond of Carl Graves. Check the video from your loading dock cameras, Roscoe. It costs a lot less than a detective and gives better evidence.

Reisman finally emerged with a Burger King cup in one hand, the crumpled white bag and a manila envelope in the other. The envelope had a white sticker in the middle, an address label maybe, but there was no way I could read it from across the street. He locked up and headed to the garbage can he had visited on his way in.

Even from a distance, I could see the back of his white shirt was soaked. From the shoulders to the waist, his pink skin showed through a U-shaped patch of wetness.

Reisman pushed the crumpled bag into the garbage can. When his hand came out empty, he panicked. He dropped his cup and turned around as if looking for someone to help him. He put his hands to his head, like a little boy in distress. In the urgency of that gesture, I could feel his anxiety. Part of me wanted to calm him, this child whose fears were so out of control.

He turned back to the garbage can, wrestled the lid off, and set it down carefully on the pavement. Then he stood looking for a long time into the bin.

Can he not find it, I wondered. Or is he just scared to put his hand in?

Reisman looked over his shoulder. Once, twice, three times. He reached into the bin, withdrew the manila envelope and pinned it to the ground with his foot. There was no breeze. The stifling summer air was dead calm, but Reisman wasn't going to take the chance of letting his prize blow away.

He picked up the rectangular garbage lid from the pavement, hugged it to his chest like a toddler with an oversized toy, then replaced it atop the bin.

He was clumsy and graceless, leaning his whole body into the operation instead of just using his arms.

He knelt to the pavement and picked up his drink cup and the lid that had popped off with the straw in it. Those went into the garbage—he triple-checked to be sure—and then he picked up the envelope. I watched him pinch open the metal clasp and check the contents, as if they might have escaped when he wasn't looking.

The more I saw of this man, the more he pained me. How can anyone go through life with such paralyzing anxiety? Why should anyone have to?

My phone rang as Reisman walked back to his truck. Caller ID said Lehmann.

"Hello, Roscoe."

"Sorry about the insurance. We have general liability, fire, flood, theft. I have so much on my mind these days—"

"Hey, your friend Reisman *does* have a storage space."

"Does he now?"

"He's an odd one though. I can't figure him out."

"Neither can I."

"Why'd you hire a guy with no work experience? I can't imagine him coming off well in an interview."

"That's exactly it," Lehmann said. "The way he came off, I hired him out of pity. I didn't think he'd last, but he doesn't make mistakes and the warehouse supervisor likes that."

"That's what I heard. Listen, he's pulling out of the lot. I'll talk to you later."

Of all the due diligence cases I ever handled, there was only one where I knew on the first day that the buyer shouldn't purchase the target company. One look inside told me everything was wrong. I could have gone back to the buyer that day and told them to back out, but my job was to produce a thorough report that laid out all the facts so they could make their own decision.

This case had a similar feel. Reisman wasn't a thief. He was too nervous to even believe he'd thrown out his garbage correctly. But my job wasn't to tell Lehmann what I thought. He had paid me for three days' work, and unless I found a reason to exercise my right to back out, I'd give him a full report with three days' worth of observations and photos.

What Lehmann did with that report, and why he really wanted it was beyond my concern.

On a personal level, however, I still felt uneasy about one thing. Lehmann said Reisman had been in an institution before and suggested that he wanted to force him back into one. Why? Reisman didn't seem dangerous to me. He did seem capable of managing his life in the outside world, even if every action of every day was fraught with angst. If Lehmann had some ill intent toward this unfortunate man, I wasn't going to write anything in my report to justify inflicting harm on him.

Reisman was a turtle without a shell, a creature whose evolution had gone awry, developing anxieties and compulsions that magnified his fears instead of the normal healthy defenses that would have protected him.

But why did he need a storage space? Why would he spend his lunch hour roasting in there? And what was in the manilla envelope that he so feared to lose?

5

At 5:30 p.m., I watched from across the street as Reisman walked from the warehouse to his truck. He stopped twice along the way to pick up garbage in the lot: a paper cup and a plastic grocery bag. He carried them into the truck with him, started the engine, pulled to edge of the lot and waited almost a full minute for cars to pass before turning onto Crabbes Branch Way.

He could have turned earlier. There was space enough between the passing cars for him to go, but his pathological caution wouldn't allow it. He had to wait until every threat had cleared.

He kept the windows up too. In the afternoon heat, the air conditioning would have taken a while to cool. Most drivers would open the windows, but Reisman seemed more content to roast than to risk exposure to the outside world.

I had a good idea where he was going. His apartment was on the sixth floor of a building near the Shady Grove Metro. He had told me himself that after work, he simply went home.

But then he surprised me by heading south, not north, off of Gude Drive onto Rockville Pike. For the next twenty minutes, he enraged southbound commuters by driving fifteen miles an hour under the speed limit. Finally, he pulled into the Best Buy near Country Club Road.

He got out of the truck with the garbage he'd picked up from the warehouse lot, put the cup and bag into the overstuffed trash can outside the store entrance, pushed it down three times, and then went inside.

The store was big enough and busy enough for me to follow him in. From the entrance, I saw two employees greet him like a regular.

I stalked about the camera aisle and then among the headphones, watching as he examined a new iPhone, eavesdropping on the conversation between him and the salesman at his side.

"You want me to go through it again?"

Reisman shook his head.

"Okay, Jake. Everything's the same as yesterday. Screen size hasn't changed. Same operating system, memory, battery, camera. You want some time alone with it?"

Reisman nodded, looking at the phone, not at the man.

"Think you'll be ready to pull the trigger today?"

Reisman shook his head. No.

"All right, buddy. I'll leave you to it. Let me know if you have any questions."

Reisman picked up the phone, swiped at the screen, studied the price card on the counter, put the phone down, and then put his hands to his temples as if in aguish.

Again, I felt pity for the man. What would life be like if every decision was so agonizing?

After a few minutes, I left him to his dilemma and returned to my car.

Forty-five minutes later, he came out empty-handed.

Back into the hot truck, windows sealed, he headed north to Mission BBQ. I watched from the burger grill next door as he drove around the building repeatedly, like a dog turning in circles before it lies down.

On his fourth lap around the lot, I started to wonder what was wrong. His normal number was three. Why had he exceeded it?

On the sixth lap, the last parking spot in a row of nine opened up. That was the one he'd been waiting for. Two others had been open, but apparently they wouldn't do.

Reisman entered the store just after 7 p.m. and came out eight minutes later. I followed him back up Rockville Pike to his apartment near Shady Grove. He parked, and then walked from his truck to the entrance carrying his dinner well out in front of him.

What goes through his mind, I wondered. Is he afraid there's grease on the bag? That it will get on his pants? He can't be that picky about his clothing. He certainly doesn't mind sweating through it.

I counted eighteen floors in his building. With its simple brick exterior, this wasn't a luxury complex, but it was close enough to the Metro to be expensive. More expensive than fourteen dollars an hour could afford.

After deliberating for a few minutes, I decided to go inside. Sleuthing, I was beginning to understand, could be just as boring as the government contract I didn't want to go back to. You sit on your ass for hours at a time waiting for information you know is there. But you can't just ask for it. You have to wait for it to appear.

The sofas and tables in the lobby were clean and well-kept. Behind the desk, a concierge in a blue blazer stared into a computer monitor. The wall of cubbies behind her was stuffed with mail. The building had hundreds of units.

The concierge never looked up. I walked to the elevators unnoticed, got out on six and followed the scent of barbecue to apartment 607. I stood at the door for a few seconds and listened. No sound inside. Maybe Reisman didn't watch TV.

Two units down, the hum of a fan drifted through an open door. I looked inside. The apartment was empty and the carpet had been pulled up. A man wearing headphones stood on a step ladder with his back to me, sticking blue painter's tape in a neat line above the open window. The fan beside him sucked in air from the hall and blew it outside into the July heat.

"Hello?" came a woman's voice from the hallway behind me.

"Oh, hello." I turned to see a pale, heavy-set woman of fifty or so wiping her hands on a black apron dusted with flour.

"That one won't be ready for a while," she said. "There's a one-bedroom on fourteen and two-bedroom on eighteen."

"You work here?" I asked.

"No. Just nosy."

She had come from the apartment next to Reisman's. Her door was open and the painter's fan pulled the scent of baking bread from her kitchen into the hall.

"You live next to Jake?" I asked.

"Jake's an odd one. Keeps to himself."

"So I gathered."

"And how do you know him?" The prying tone of her question matched the measuring look in her eyes. Maybe she had admitted she was nosy because she knew she couldn't hide it.

"I met him at work."

"Oh?" Fake innocent tone. "Where does he work?"

I got the sense she already knew.

"At an appliance warehouse."

Her eyes raked over my brown slacks, the white top, the awful conservative suit I'd worn to look like an insurance inspector.

"*You* work in a warehouse?" she asked.

"Insurance," I said. "They're one of our clients."

"Oh? Was there an accident? Jake didn't get hurt, did he?" Wide eyes, hand to heart, feigned tone of concern. Who did she think she was fooling?

"No. Just a routine inspection. Do you know..." I lowered my voice. "Does Jake ever have visitors?"

Her eyes gave me a second up and down, a re-assessment that said, You're not interested in *him,* are you?

"Oh, no," she said. "He hardly leaves his apartment. Hardly makes a sound. I hope the new neighbors are as quiet. *You* don't look like the noisy type. If you're looking for a one-bedroom..." She glanced pointedly at the empty apartment. "I certainly wouldn't object to having quiet on both sides."

With that, she wished me a good evening and went back to her apartment.

I wanted to ask about rent. I was sure this place was beyond the means of anyone earning fourteen dollars an hour. I could ask the concierge in the lobby.

On my way to the elevator, I stopped outside Reisman's door. The sun coming through his west-facing window broke into three golden segments in the crack beneath the door. The shadows dividing those segments came from the feet of the man standing on the other side, the man whose eye was darkening the peephole. The shadows moved silently away, and the fisheye lens flamed with gold.

I wondered how much of the conversation he had heard.

6

The next day, on a hunch, I parked across from Lehmann's warehouse just before noon. Reisman, as expected, drove out of the lot on time and followed the same route to Burger King and then to the storage facility. Once again, he put garbage in the can and checked it three times before moving on.

I understood now that the cardboard and plastic bands I had seen in his truck the previous day came from his habit of picking up trash in the lot around the warehouse.

He went to the locked door of his storage space, carrying his lunch and what looked like the same manila envelope from yesterday.

I photographed him as he looked three times over his shoulder before unlocking the storage room door. This time, he saw my car, but I don't think he could see me inside. He winced, as if the glare coming off my windshield had blinded him.

I wondered if he even registered what he saw when he went through these compulsive motions. Was he actually worried about someone watching him, or did he just have to complete the routine out of superstition?

Again, he stayed inside through most of the hour, came out soaked in sweat, put his garbage in the can and returned to the warehouse with the envelope.

I left him there and drove to a coffee shop near Shady Grove to use the Wi-Fi.

According to Lehmann's fact sheet, Reisman had moved from California. Lehmann didn't say where in California, but it didn't take long to find out. San Luis Obispo. A beautiful town just off the Pacific Coast Highway. Why would someone move from an idyllic town with a mild year-round climate to sweltering, traffic-choked Rockville? Why would someone so anxious and ill at ease move across the country at all? That's a stressful undertaking, even for a healthy person.

I found Reisman's old address on a public records site. I could see the list of towns he'd lived in for free, but if I wanted more, I had to pay and sit for ten minutes drumming my fingers while the site searched court records, property records, vehicle registrations and the like.

Aside from his current apartment, Reisman had only one address in all the public records. Google street view showed a small apartment building, perhaps four units, in disrepair. The white stucco was chipping. The black iron rails on the balconies leaned dangerously outward, and weeds had overtaken the yard.

Reisman had one relative, Brinley, at the same address, deceased four months ago at age fifty. I paid for Brinley's full dossier, which gave me enough information to put together a sketch. She was Reisman's mother, single, with a revoked driver's license. She'd lived in the apartment over twenty years. Before that, she'd been in Los Angeles. She had a shoplifting conviction in her forties. No LinkedIn profile. No other social media. If she had ever held a job, I couldn't tell where.

A little more searching led to the number of the rental agency that managed her apartment building. When a woman answered, I asked first about the property, and then about Reisman. If he had lived there his whole life, there was a good chance they'd know him.

"Reisman?" the woman repeated. "Jake?"

"Yes."

"Hold on."

I thought I heard alarm in the woman's voice.

In a moment, a man came on the line. "Is Jake Okay?"

"Jake's fine. Who am I speaking with?"

"Ramirez. Mario. Where are you calling from?"

"Maryland."

"And he's alright?" The man let out a sigh of relief. "Every time I get a call about him, my heart jumps. He still employed?"

"Happily employed. Seems a little nervous though." His initial expression of concern told me that might be a good lead-in to get him talking.

"Oh, you don't know the half of it."

The next few minutes told me Mario Ramirez had been waiting to unload for some time about Jake Reisman.

Reisman's mother was mentally ill. Maybe schizophrenic. She refused to seek or accept treatment. A social worker helped her keep her disability paperwork up to date. The government checks kept her and Jake afloat. The apartment was Section Eight housing. They took care of each other, but she kept Jake on a short leash.

"She was a slob, and he was always cleaning," Ramirez said. "If it wasn't for him, the apartment would have been a nest of rats and roaches. Those two hardly ever went out. She convinced him the world was dangerous and he should stay inside. Not that he needed much convincing. I think the nervousness is in his genes. But he was a mama's boy. The ultimate mama's boy. When she died, I was sure he'd fall apart. Like one foot in the grave, no reason to go on. Instead, he gets up and moves across country."

"Did he say why?"

"No. He didn't even tell me he was going. I mean, not that he owed me or anything. But I used to go by and check on them. Bring 'em something from the store, a pie or a cake. He just cleaned the place out, dropped the key in the rental box and left. I'll tell you something though, he wouldn't have done that without a reason. He gets an idea in his head and he holds onto it. Like, obsessively. Sometimes he'll tell you about it, sometimes he won't."

Ramirez asked about Reisman's job, his apartment, whether he had any friends. He asked how I knew him.

"I was doing an inspection for his employer's insurer, looking for potential liabilities in the warehouse. Workers can be liabilities. I was curious about him because he had no past experience."

"I had no idea insurers were so thorough."

They're not, I thought. Not when they sell you a policy. Only when you try to collect on it. I need to learn to lie better.

"Did Jake ever get into trouble?" I asked.

"Never," Ramirez said. "Never ever. He's so damn cautious—hey, you mind if I ask you a personal question? It might sound a little off base."

"Shoot."

"You feel some kind of sympathy for the guy? Some pity?"

That caught me off guard. I wondered for a second if something in my tone had conveyed that. I didn't think so.

"Why do you ask?"

"Just a sense," Ramirez said. "It's hard not to. He's a good guy, but you gotta draw a line with him. His mind is actually pretty sharp, but emotionally, he's helpless. He's a mama's boy who lost his mama. If a woman shows him an ounce of kindness, he's drawn to her like a moth to flame."

"I wasn't planning on cuddling with him, but that's good to know. You've been very helpful."

"I don't believe that insurance bullshit."

"You're also very perceptive."

"You a social worker?"

"I'll leave that to your imagination."

7

At six pm, I was idling in the lot in front of Best Buy, waiting for the creature of habit to appear. Something delayed him that day, and he didn't show until 6:15.

From the air-conditioned front seat of my BMW, I watched him reenact yesterday's routine. Reisman walks to the store entrance, stops at the garbage can, though this time he has nothing to deposit. Salespeople greet him at the iPhone display. Reisman studies the phone. Picks it up, puts it down. Picks it up, puts it down. Reads the spec card on the counter, picks up the phone again.

I took a couple of photos, noted his time of arrival in my notebook, and sketched out the details I had gleaned from my call with Ramirez.

I decided I'd try to get a look inside his apartment that evening. All I'd have to do is get him to answer the door, chat for a few seconds with the door open and see for myself that the place wasn't stocked with stolen refrigerators.

Then I could tell Lehmann there was nothing incriminating in there. The last thing to do would be to get some photos inside the storage space. I wasn't sure yet how to do that, but once I'd confirmed it was clean, I could close the case, write it all up, give Lehmann my notebook and photos, and be done with it.

While Reisman was agonizing over the iPhone, I wondered how I was supposed to give Lehmann photos without direct electronic communication. Upload them to a photo sharing site and give him the password on a slip of paper? Or just print them all out at Walgreens?

Another BMW, blue like mine, was idling in the next row of the lot. From behind, I could see water dripping onto the asphalt, condensation from the air conditioning. Another woman waiting for another man inside the store. That was the story that started to form in my mind. I imagined her husband was buying a new computer, discussing technical specs with the salesman, geeking out a little too much over RAM and graphics cards while his wife kept the car cool and thought about dinner.

She looked like me. Or so I imagined. At one point, she turned and leaned toward the passenger seat, as if to pick something up. I saw her in profile. A face like mine. Hair like mine.

In the tedium of the long wait for Reisman, I imagined I had crossed paths with another me, with the Claire who had made different choices, who was married and settled. My husband would come out in a few minutes and we'd go home together, eat dinner together and talk about our day. I wouldn't have to eat alone. The bed beside me would be warm, and when I awoke in the middle of the night, it would not be to silence, but to the sound of another person breathing in the dark.

But I had chosen a different path, intentionally or not. I had my opportunity and I wasn't ready. I wasn't her and I didn't want to be. As lonely as I sometimes felt, the thought of having to share my bed made me feel crowded, resentful almost. Can't I have my space? Isn't there some way I can have my space and not be lonely?

I haven't worked that one out yet, and I haven't met anyone interesting enough to make me want to try.

I wondered if the other me had compromised, if she had settled for Mr. Convenient, Mr. Here-and-Now, or if she was as picky as I was.

These thoughts were going too far. I shook them off, looked into the store where Reisman, a chubby immobile fixture at the Apple display counter, agonized over his phone. A man unable to make a simple decision.

What a waste of time and money, I thought. If there was ever a less likely thief... I could probably just ask the guy to show me his storage space and he'd do it.

I actually thought about doing just that. Just walk up to him as he left the warehouse for lunch.

"Hey, Jake. I saw you have a storage space. Can you give me a tour?"

He'd be paralyzed with fear. And then he'd probably say Okay.

Because he was lonely. If I was lonely, he *had* to be.

Then I remembered Ramirez's admonition about showing kindness to that solitary man. *Like a moth to flame.*

The last thing I needed was a compulsive mama's boy obsessing over me. Like gum on the bottom of my shoe.

I came up with a better idea for getting into the storage space. If I could get into Reisman's apartment (to look for Lehmann's stack of missing refrigerators), I might be able to take pictures of his keys, then use one of those apps that copies keys from photographs.

I found three apps in the Play Store and downloaded all of them while I waited. One was linked to a key printer just a mile up Rockville Pike. Snap the photo, send it to the printer, and pick it up in ten minutes. The trick would be to get Reisman's keys away from him.

At ten past eight, Reisman was still in the store, still obsessing over the phone. He had moved away from the display each time other customers approached, and then he returned when they left. It was like he wanted his baby all to himself. Some alone time with his electronic girlfriend. The sales staff walked around him as if he were part of the display.

At 8:16—wait! What's this? He flagged down a sales rep, followed him to a locked glass display and then to a register.

A decision! Hallelujah! I marked the time in my notebook and thought maybe I should mark the calendar too. Such a momentous event!

I put the car in gear and left the lot.

Reisman would take a few minutes to check out. Then he'd go to the barbecue place and circle the building until his special parking spot opened up. Then order, pay, drive home. That would take twenty minutes, minimum. I'd be there before him, taking another look at the empty apartment two doors down.

I'd hear him coming down the hall or smell the barbecue, walk out just in time to run into him. Ask for something. Water, or a sink to wash my hands, something to get into his apartment.

He would know this wasn't a coincidence. He had seen me through the peephole the previous evening. I didn't care. By this time tomorrow, I'd turn in my report and be done. Roscoe Lehmann would be out six thousand dollars, and Jacob Reisman would go back to his routine.

Unless, as Lehmann feared, his nervous employee really did nurse some kind of grudge or vendetta. If he did, I thought, I might be able to pull it out of him. But honestly, I couldn't see this guy holding any ill will toward anyone.

8

The painters had finished taping and had begun painting the vacant apartment. They left the door open. The box fan they'd jammed into the window blew paint fumes into the muggy Rockville sky. It also sucked air in from the hall. I smelled the barbecue before I could hear Reisman coming.

I waited a few seconds, then stepped into the hall and walked head-down toward him. When I almost ran into him, I looked up, pretending to be surprised.

"Oh, hi Jake."

He held the Best Buy bag in his left hand, the barbecue in his right. As before, he held the food away from him, like he feared getting grease on his pants.

"Hello, Claire." He didn't seem at all surprised to see me.

"You live here?"

"Just like I did last night."

I knew he had seen me through the peephole the evening before, had heard my conversation with his nosy neighbor. By now, with twenty-four hours left on the case, I didn't care if he suspected me. I told him I'd been checking out the apartment down the hall.

The sound of our voices provoked the busybody. Her door opened and she poked her head out.

"Hello, Ms. Jasenko."

"Hello, Jake."

She gave me a funny look, pulled back into her apartment and shut the door.

"You don't like your apartment in DC?" Reisman asked.

Had I told him I lived in the city? I couldn't remember.

"There's more space out here," I said. "Would you mind... May I have a glass of water?"

He shifted both bags to one hand and pulled his keys from his pocket.

"It's not bottled," he said.

"That's fine. I'm just really thirsty."

"You shouldn't drink tap water."

He unlocked the door.

"I don't mind."

"It goes through pipes underground. Some of them might be lead. I have iced tea."

He swung the door open. Except for a table strewn with papers by the far window, the apartment was immaculate. I imagined he was a compulsive cleaner in his vast spare time.

The black leather couch looked new. There was no wear on the white and green rug. The coffee table was glass, and the end tables were stained cherry with matching black ceramic lamps. The table by the window was of a darker wood, polished to a high sheen. Except for the lamps, nothing quite matched. All of it was new, high quality, expensive.

After watching his agony over the purchase of the phone, I wondered how many weeks it had taken him to buy all this, how much of his energy it must have sapped. The furnishings were clearly beyond the means of a man earning fourteen dollars an hour. Reisman couldn't have inherited anything other than anxiety from a schizophrenic mother who had never worked, so the money must have come from somewhere else.

"You can have a seat if you want," he said. He put his keys and the new iPhone on the messy table by the window and carried his barbecue into the kitchen.

"I have to get a plate," he said. "And paper towels."

I went immediately to the table and made a quick inventory. An Apple laptop, pricey and new looking. Lots of papers strewn about. Not like him to be disorderly, I thought. A framed photo of a hummingbird. A hammer. A hole in the drywall above the table.

He must had hit too hard on a hollow spot when he tried to drive in a nail to hang the photo. Drywall dust on the papers. Drywall dust on the manilla envelope with the white label. This was the envelope he'd carried from the storage space two days in a row, the treasure that he worried might blow away if he didn't keep it pinned to the pavement while he put the lid back on the garbage can. There was no address on the label. Just "Jake R."

Beside the envelope, his keys.

I looked toward the kitchen. Reisman was out of sight, pulling a glass from the dishwasher for my iced tea, or a plate for his barbecue.

"Sorry about the mess," he said. "I knocked a hole in the wall this morning, and then I was late for work."

I heard him open a cabinet, put in a glass. Then another. And another. He was unloading the dishwasher. If this was part of his routine, he'd do the whole thing before he got around to his plate and my iced tea, and he'd probably have to arrange every glass, dish, and fork to his precise standards.

I pulled my phone from my bag, turned the speaker off so the camera wouldn't click, and separated Reisman's keys so I could photograph them one by one.

I imagined Jake recoiling in horror after knocking that hole in the wall. Maybe retreating to his bedroom for an hour.

"You like your tea sweet?"

"Just a little."

I snapped one photo, then another, glancing toward the kitchen each time. Maybe he washed his hands fifty times after making that hole in the wall, trying to scrub away his mistake. Two more photos of keys, then three of the tabletop. I could zoom in later, at home, see what those papers were about.

"It's sweet out of the bottle, but I have more sugar if you want."

"The bottle is fine. Nice television."

I was beside the couch when he returned, examining the sixty-inch flat screen. A new Samsung. How do you swing that on fourteen dollars an hour? On top of rent and whatever you paid for the furniture, the new Mac, the new iPhone? It was the Eleven Pro. More than I would spend on a phone.

"I don't watch it," he said. He meant the TV. "It makes me nervous. Except golf and Bob Ross. Here's your iced tea. It's lemon. I didn't tell you that. Do you still want it?"

"Thank you." I smiled, then inwardly regretted it. *Like a moth to flame.*

"Why are you following me?"

It was an innocent, straightforward question, posed without accusation or suspicion. He might have once asked his mother in that same tone why the sky was blue.

What's the point of pretending, I thought. He has the simple, direct instincts of a child.

"Mr. Lehmann has been worried about you." I would have to tell Lehmann I said that.

"He's a very nice man. I tell him I can take care of myself. But I think he's a worrier. You worry when you love people."

I wasn't sure how to respond to that. Did he really think Lehmann loved him? Because Lehmann had given him a job? Had he grown up so deprived of healthy adult attention that he mistook a job offer for a sign of love?

"Mr. Lehmann takes care of his people," he said earnestly. "He took care of Carl when Carl got hurt and couldn't work for two weeks. He gave me a job when no one else would. Not even the library in S-L-O."

S-L-O? It took me a second. San Luis Obispo. I wondered what Reisman meant when he said Lehmann "took care of Carl." I don't think Lehmann nursed him back to health. Carl probably just collected worker's comp, which was his due under the law.

"Not the library and not even the grocery store," Reisman added. "Do you see the theme?"

"That people wouldn't give you a chance?" I really didn't know what he was getting at. He was standing too close after handing me the iced tea. I would have thought that his anxiety made him sensitive to personal space, but it didn't. Not with me, at least. Maybe my smile had been too encouraging. I took a step back.

"Shelves," he said. "I couldn't work at Chipotle because hungry people make you rush, and I get flustered. In the grocery, you fill the shelves when no one's there. In the library, you put the books back. There's no rush. People aren't watching you, making you hurry. Mr. Lehmann gave me a chance, and I didn't let him down. Do you want some barbecue?"

"No. Thank you, Jake." He had inched toward me as he spoke. He was staring at my hair, like he wanted to touch it, twirl it around his finger and tell me in his childlike way that I was pretty. I stepped back.

"I can't eat until you leave," he said. "Are you leaving? You don't have to. But if you're going to be here long, I have to take the sandwich out of the box, so it doesn't get soggy."

I sipped the iced tea he had given me. I wasn't thirsty, but not to have tasted it would have been rude.

"I do have to get going," I said. "Thank you for the drink."

I had gotten what I came for—a look inside and photos of his keys—and now I wanted to get out. But the way he looked at me, like a lost dog in search of an owner... He was a pit of need no one person could fill. He seemed too happy that I liked my tea, too responsive to my earlier smile, he stood too close and was too earnest in his childlike attraction. He didn't seem to understand how uncomfortable he made me feel, how his behavior would make anyone uncomfortable.

I put the tea bottle on the end table. He took a half step closer. His stare was open and direct, filled more with a child's curiosity than a man's desire. Again, I thought of Ramirez's warning. *If a woman shows him an ounce of kindness...*

"If you're going to move in," he said, "you should wait till the paint fumes are gone. They'll give you a headache."

"Jake, I have to go." I took a step toward the door, then remembered my bag was on the table by the window. The table with the papers and the keys and the hammer and the drywall dust. The table was on the far side of the room, opposite the door. I'd have to pass him to get there.

When I stepped toward it, he stepped toward me. We both stopped.

"When I first saw you," he said, "I thought you were someone else."

He let that hang in a creepy, uncomfortable way. How was I supposed to respond to that? I wished he'd finish the thought.

He wouldn't, so I prodded him. "You thought I was someone else?"

I didn't think there was anything encouraging in my tone, but he inched closer.

I looked again at my bag on the table.

"Not an inspector," he said. "Not from insurance. If someone would have asked me who you were, I wouldn't have said an insurance lady. Do you like my apartment?"

His fascination with me was strong enough to overcome his anxiety. There was no trace of fear left in him. The nervous child was now a staring, chubby, awkward man. He was sweating, but still his creepiness felt more pathetic than threatening.

"It's a lovely place, Jake. Did you pick out the furniture yourself?"

Get the bag, I told myself. *Get your bag and get out. There's no need to be polite any longer. He's just weird and he needs to figure out on his own how to interact with people. With women, anyway.*

"I couldn't," he replied. "I made the salespeople tell me what to buy."

"You bought all of this?"

I wanted to make sure he wasn't renting. If he had actually paid for furniture he clearly couldn't afford, Lehmann would want to know. It meant either Reisman had some additional source of income, or he had spent himself into debt.

"Do you think the super will be mad?" he asked.

His eyes had a strange pleading look, as if he was seeking reassurance. I had no idea what he was talking about or how his mind flitted from one subject to the next.

"The super?"

Get the bag! Get out!

"About the hole in the wall." He pointed to the hole above the table, where he'd meant to hang the hummingbird picture. "Do you think they'll kick me out?"

"They won't kick you out. They'll send someone up to patch it."

I stepped around him toward the table. He turned, keeping his face to me, and I instinctively turned too, like prey keeping track its predator. My throat had begun to tighten and my back was to the table.

He moved closer. The needy look in his eye made me nervous. What would he do, if he had the guts to do anything? All I could see was him trying to hug me, like a child burying his face in his mother's breast. The thought of his sweaty flesh, his pudgy neediness, revolted me. Maybe it showed in my eyes, because he suddenly looked wounded.

"Do I look like the kind of person you would hate?"

"Um, Jake? Jake, you need to back up." I stepped back, two steps. I knew exactly where the hammer was on the table behind me. In a second, it was in my right hand, behind my back. My left hand picked up my bag, looped it over my shoulder.

"If you just met me," he pleaded, "and you were as pretty as you are—you're very pretty, Claire—would you hate me before you even got to know me?"

He had a strange look in his eye, like this wasn't a hypothetical question, like he was talking about something specific. I began to wonder if he'd inherited his mother's schizophrenia.

"Jake, you're scaring me."

"I don't mean to," he whined. "But this is what happens. You don't know me, but I'm a nice person. And we're just talking. But I make you nervous and you back away. Would you say mean things about me to my face? Would you hate me?"

"I don't hate you, but you need to back off. Now."

"Sorry." He took a step back. "It's just, when I look at you, I don't see the kind of person who would tell me they wanted me to die. I don't understand people who say things like that."

"I didn't say that to you, Jake, and I never would. It's not the kind of thing I'd say to anyone."

I kept my eyes on him as I moved sideways past the kitchen, back toward the exit.

"You're scared of me," he moaned.

"You're scaring me," I warned.

He followed every step I took, keeping a distance of a few feet, just out of striking range of the hammer. I wonder if he knew I had it.

"I'm sorry," he said. "I don't know how not to."

No, you don't, I thought. He looked sad. A sad, lost, horribly lonely man.

"I'm going to leave," I told him. "I'm going to back up to the door, and I do not want you to move."

Reisman nodded. "I didn't mean to scare you." He put his hands behind his back and leaned against the couch to signify he had no intention of making a move.

"You need help, Jacob."

"I know that. I wish you weren't scared of me. I would never hurt you. Never in a million years. I want you to have something."

He lurched from the couch so suddenly it startled me. But he didn't come toward me. He went the other way, to the table by the window. He picked up the manilla envelope.

"Take this," he said.

"What is it?"

He approached me slowly, tentatively, so I wouldn't feel threatened.

"I want you to have this."

"Stop there," I said.

He stopped a few feet away. He had to lean forward to pass the envelope to me.

"You'll see I'm not a bad person," he said. "All I ever wanted is in there, but it's something I can't have, so I have to let it go. Take it. Dr. Horowitz says half my troubles come from not letting go, and I need to let go of things or I'll never get better. Take the envelope. I'm letting go."

I leaned forward, took the envelope, my eyes fixed on him the whole time. My rational mind told me he wouldn't try anything, but my animal instincts were on high alert. All I wanted was to get out of there.

I twisted the knob behind me and slid out into the hall. "Goodbye, Jake."

His eyes were welling as I tossed the hammer onto the floor inside. I pulled the door shut and ran. I didn't want to wait for the elevator, so I took the stairs. My mind raced as fast as my feet down six flights of steps.

No wonder Lehmann wants him locked up, I thought. *Once the cops get their hands on him, they'll see what state he's in. They'll put him back in the institution.*

Maybe Lehmann is on a mission of mercy. Maybe Jake Reisman shouldn't be working, wasting all that anxiety and worry on petty things. Maybe he should spend some time in a hospital, focusing one hundred percent on repairing that damaged psyche, building some confidence and social skills.

As much as the guy creeped me out, I felt for him. Life is hard enough, even for the most high-functioning people in the world. To be that anxious, that sensitive, that lost... Why should anyone have to suffer that?

The stairs came out in a far corner of the lobby. So much was going through my mind, I don't remember walking out, just the blast of hot air that hit me outside the door, the waves of heat coming up off the asphalt, the sound of cicadas in the twilight.

I would write up our encounter back home in my apartment, but not until tomorrow. Not until my nerves had settled.

I drove all the way to DC before I felt safe again. I turned off Wisconsin Avenue onto Garrison Street and went into Rodman's parking lot, checking my mirror for signs of Reisman's blue truck. I knew he hadn't followed me, but I still had to confirm it a dozen times. His anxiety had seeped into me. I could smell it on myself like the grease that seeped through his bag of barbecue.

I sat quietly for a moment to calm myself. Closed my eyes, took a few deep breaths, listened to the idling engine and felt the cool air from the vents wash over my face.

Then I turned on the overhead light, opened the manila envelope and dumped out the pages. *All I ever wanted is in there.*

The sheets slid into my lap. Photos of women cut from magazine ads and clothing catalogs, glued to printer paper with a child's glue stick. Dozens and dozens of women. They all looked like me. Same hair color, same hair style, same eye color, same complexion, height, and build.

What the hell?

Seriously! What in the *hell* was all this?

I picked up my phone and dialed, fingers shaking, heart racing in fury. When Lehmann picked up, I said, "I told you if this guy's a psychopath, I'm out. Well, I'm out. Goodbye!"

9

I spent the next morning running errands and taking care of chores I'd been neglecting for weeks. I owed Lehmann his notes and photos, and I wanted to put this case behind me before the day was done. But I was in no hurry to see the man. I took my time in the grocery store, the bank, the dry cleaners. I cleaned my bathroom, scraped the ice out of the freezer, bruising and gouging my knuckles along the way. Then I thought about the facts of the case as I sat waiting for an oil change.

I couldn't explain Reisman's storage space, or how he paid for that apartment on fourteen dollars an hour, unless his psychological problems qualified him for housing assistance. I couldn't explain how he could afford the new furniture, but neither could I imagine the overanxious Reisman stealing enough to pay for it all.

If Lehmann had a thief, it wasn't Jake Reisman.

Regarding Lehmann's other concern, whether Reisman had a vendetta against him, I was sure he didn't. If anything, Reisman was grateful to Lehmann. *He gave me a job when no one else would.* He even seemed to harbor the delusion that Lehmann loved him. How his twisted mind came up with that was more than I wanted to know.

Reisman could come off as creepy even to people he liked, as I had learned the night before. Maybe Lehmann had had a similar encounter. Maybe he had rejected Reisman's oozing, needy affection and somehow started to believe Jake resented him for it.

I lingered after lunch in the small kitchen of my apartment, composing my final write up.

Subject is functional, but emotionally and psychologically stunted. Somewhat unstable, perhaps unsound. Mentioned he's in therapy with a Dr. Horowitz. Specifically mentioned his problems with "letting go," which is characteristic of an obsessive type.

I picked up my phone and looked at the photos I had taken in his apartment. Zooming in on the papers on his desk, I saw a document with the letterhead of a psychiatric institution. Reisman's name was near the top, listed as "Patient." The date on the page was ten weeks ago, two weeks before Reisman started working at Lehmann's warehouse. The rest of the page was covered by other papers, so I could glean no further information from it.

I added to my handwritten report:

Mother was mentally ill, possibly schizophrenic. Passed away four months ago. Reisman drove across the country and then appears to have been institutionalized.

He seems to be a person of deep feeling, forming quick attachments to those who show him common decency. Fond of supervisor Carl Graves, who sticks up for him. Also grateful to you, Roscoe Lehmann.

I'm not a psychiatrist, but it's possible that someone so quick to develop warm feelings may be equally quick to feel betrayal. A trained professional could give you better information. Check with his doctor, Horowitz. Though he is legally bound by patient privacy laws, he has a duty to report if he believes his patient poses an imminent physical threat to members of the community, including you.

I had a very uncomfortable encounter with Reisman at his apartment last night. I felt personally threatened. Reisman does not seem to have a healthy understanding of personal boundaries, nor can he perceive how his words and actions make others feel unsafe.

My sense is he doesn't intend to harm people, but his behavior may not always be in accord with his intentions. I believe him when he says he cares about a person. He just doesn't know how to express it. I see him as a tragic figure, Edward Scissorhands without the charm.

Sorry this didn't work out, Roscoe, but I don't believe Reisman is your thief. I doubt he has any kind of vendetta against you, or even any ill will. If his behavior has led you to believe that, it was likely unintentional.

My final recommendation, if you insist on getting rid of him, is to ask him to submit to an independent psychological exam with a doctor of your choosing. If the doctor concludes he is truly a danger to you or your employees, or if he is psychologically unfit to carry out his duties, you have grounds to let him go. The safety of the workplace comes first.

Keep in mind also that it's your company. You can fire him at will. I don't think you need to fear any retaliation from him. I don't believe the man is capable of violence.

I put down my pen and wondered what Lehmann would do with my report. It didn't matter. It was Lehmann's problem now. I wanted to get rid of the notebook and the photos and move on.

I called Lehmann. The phone rang eight times, and then what sounded like a computer-generated woman's voice gave a generic message. "The party you are trying to reach is not available." The line went dead.

How could that be? I just talked to Lehmann last night on this very number.

I called again. Same message.

Okay, I thought, I'll drop off the notebook at his house, and that will be the end of it.

I picked up my keys and headed for the door.

10

I called one last time as I approached the Beltway on River Road. Same result. The party was unavailable and there was no option to leave a message.

On the overpass, I noticed a police cruiser in the rearview. I checked the speedometer. Three miles over the limit. Most cops won't pull you over for that, not on that stretch of River Road, but I slowed down anyway.

He was still behind me after we'd crossed the Beltway. I slowed to eight miles under the limit, thinking he'd move into the left lane and pass, but he didn't.

At Seven Locks Road, traffic on the left was zooming past us. The road narrowed to a single lane ahead, and if he didn't pass soon, he wouldn't get another chance until the road widened out again at Potomac Village, a mile or so further up.

My experience with Lincoln a year and half earlier had left me sensitive to anyone following me, even if it was a cop. Any car lurking in the rearview for too long triggered my anxiety. I watched the cop and wondered with annoyance, *Is he just going to sit on my ass all the way up this road?*

Apparently, he was. He followed close behind for the next mile.

Finally, he put his flashers on as we approached the shopping center. I heard his siren bloop once and then cut off.

I turned into the lot on my right and pulled into one of the diagonal spaces. He pulled up behind, blocking me in.

I reached for my bag, found my license and registration, and rolled down the window to a blast of humid summer air. I could see him coming in the sideview. Tall, thin, hair cropped close. Dark blue Montgomery County uniform.

He palmed the rear of the car as he approached. A cop's trick to leave evidence proving he'd been in contact with me.

In a second, he was at my window.

"Was I going too fast?" I handed him the documents.

"Claire Chastain?"

He said my name without even looking at the license.

"Yes?"

Now he checked my ID.

"You mind coming with me?"

"For speeding?"

"No ma'am. Just want to ask you some questions."

"About what?"

"Jacob Reisman."

"Is there a problem with Jake?"

"Jake doesn't have any problems anymore." He handed my license and registration through the open window. "Can I trust you to follow me? Walk into the station of your own accord? Looks better than being led in in cuffs."

"I... I'm sorry, what?" Nothing he said made sense.

"Will you follow me to the station? Makes it easier on everyone. You can call your lawyer on the way. If you feel you need one."

I stared at him speechless for a couple of seconds. All I could say in the end was, "Okay."

11

Between the entrance to the Derwood station and the offices in back, I saw a familiar face. Reisman's next door neighbor, the busybody I'd seen two nights in a row. What was her name? Ms. Jasenko.

She wasn't wearing her apron this time. She seemed to have dressed up for the occasion, whatever this occasion was, in her best polyesters from TJ Maxx. She gave me a dirty look.

"In here." The patrolman who had pulled me over guided me into the office of a waiting detective. "You want some water? Coffee?"

"Water, please."

The patrolman left.

Detective Dennis Kowalczyk, reclining in a swivel chair behind his desk with his hands behind his head, sized me up. I did the same to him. He looked to be about fifty, barrel-chested, average height, with grey hair and dark flashing eyes that showed an active mind.

I was wearing black slacks and a short-sleeve white top. I know I come off to others as intelligent and competent. But whatever registered in his mind when he looked at me, I couldn't guess. His face showed he was thinking but gave no hint of *what* he was thinking.

To my surprise, he stood to greet me. The suddenness of his motion startled me. He shook my hand, motioned politely toward a chair. "Have a seat, Ms. Chastain."

I sat. "What happened to Jake?"

Kowalczyk eyed me quietly, suspiciously it seemed. For a second, I thought he would say, "I was hoping you could tell me."

Instead, he was blunt and to the point. "Jake was the victim of a very brutal murder. Someone took a hammer to his head." His kept his eyes fixed on my face, watching my reaction. If he saw anything more than the blank expression of a woman receiving news she could not comprehend, it was the projection of his own cynical mind.

My mind flashed back to the neighbor, Jasenko, and the dirty look she'd just given me.

"In his apartment?"

Kowalczyk leaned back and nodded.

In my mind, I saw the hammer I had picked up from Reisman's desk. The one I'd dropped inside his door on my way out.

"Was this a robbery?" I asked.

Kowalczyk shook his head. "Whoever did it entered peacefully and didn't take anything. New laptop, new phone on the table. His wallet was still in his pocket."

I thought about the people Reisman knew and trusted. Lehmann, Carl Graves. Maybe the neighbor. Maybe someone from the building staff coming to look at that hole he'd knocked in the wall. Who else? Who else would he have let into his apartment?

"You were in his apartment last night?" Kowalczyk had a way of staring that made me feel accused and convicted.

"Yes."

"May I ask what your interest in Jabob Reisman was?"

I hesitated. There was a clause in my contract with Lehmann saying the investigation would be confidential until he decided to release information about it. That was part of the standard agreement I'd drawn up.

But a criminal investigation would override our contract's confidentiality clause. The state had a right to evidence in a case like this. I was in a quandary. However little I cared for Lehmann, I didn't want to violate my own contract on my first-ever case. Trust goes a long way in a line of work where people invite you to dig into sensitive personal and business matters. I really didn't know what to do.

"I think I have to consult a lawyer on that."

Kowalczyk didn't like that answer. To him, it must have smacked of guilt. He leaned toward me, eyes boring in. "You want a lawyer now?"

I don't know if he intended it, but I heard menace in his tone.

"Do I need one? Now?"

"I think it would be in your interest."

I stared at him, unbelieving, trying not to get angry. His insinuating tone and his burning stare—like a predator trying to intimidate its prey—roused my anger and my instinct to fight. I don't like people making insinuations about me, especially not to my face, and I don't like being pushed into a corner by anyone. Try it and you'll have a fight on your hands.

He could see the anger in my eyes, even though I controlled it, even though I didn't lash out, and I could see him count that anger against me. There was almost a subtle nod, as if he were ticking off an item on his checklist, confirming to himself that I had a quality of defiance he'd expect in a criminal. He was so smug about it, so sure of himself, if he wasn't a cop, I might have smacked him.

"You honestly think I killed Jake Reisman?"

"I'm a homicide investigator. I investigate. You recognize the woman out there?" He pointed to the waiting area, where smug Miss Busybody sat puffed with righteousness. Or maybe she was just bloated and had irritable bowels.

"I saw her last night."

"And the night before," Kowalczyk said. "You were looking at an apartment. But you never contacted the property manager to say you were interested. You walked past the front desk more than once, but you never stopped to ask about available apartments or the cost of rent. You also have six months left on your current lease in DC."

How did he know that?

"I can explain what I was doing."

"After you consult with your attorney?"

"Right."

"When did you first meet Reisman?"

"Two days ago."

"Let me tell you what troubles me about this case." Kowalczyk put his elbows on the desk and clasped his hands together. "Reisman let someone he knew into his apartment. There was no forced entry. Let's say it was you—because I think it was. Let's say Reisman, who by all reports was a little off, let's say he makes a pass at you."

"He didn't."

"You might want to keep your mouth shut until your lawyer arrives. Let's say he makes a pass, and you don't like it. You push him away. He tries to force it. Doesn't sound like Reisman from what I've heard, but let's say that's what happened. You panic. You whack him with the hammer. He's stunned. You run out of the apartment and tell the neighbor, or the front desk, or you call 911, tell them you just bashed a guy with a hammer. Your adrenaline's flowing and your nerves are on edge. People in the building try to calm you.

"These things happen sometimes when a woman is stuck in an apartment with a guy she barely knows.

"What does *not* happen is she bashes his skull in with repeated blows. What does *not* happen is she keeps hitting him when he's down on the floor and probably no longer moving. What does *not* happen is she leaves the apartment covered in blood, runs to her car and peels out of the lot and never tells anyone anything. That's not self-defense. Show me your hands, Claire."

"What?"

He grabbed my wrists and pulled them toward him.

"Let go of me!"

"In a struggle where self-defense is warranted—" He examined the scratches and bruises on my knuckles, the red gouge on my wrist I hadn't even noticed. "—we see cuts and bruises on the knuckles, breaks in the fingernails. How'd you get these bruises? This scrape?"

"Cleaning the ice out of my freezer."

"Uh huh."

He let go of my wrists. "Why don't you call your attorney? From here on out, anything you say can and will be used against you in a court of law."

My stomach started to churn and I felt nauseous.

"You want me to step outside?" Kowalczyk asked. "A little privacy while you make the call?"

"Yes. Please."

Kowalczyk left. I stood, took out my phone and paced.

Maybe a normal person would have frozen at this point. Maybe they'd be so lost they wouldn't know what to do.

That's not me. I mean, I *was* scared. But when I'm scared, I act. I do something, *anything*, so long as I control the action. So long as some part of me has some control of *something...*

Panic is pointless. Act!

I didn't know any criminal defense attorneys or even where to find one. But—Noreen Williamson, my professor at American University, Foundations of Criminal Justice Systems—was a retired prosecutor.

I called her office line. No answer. Not surprising that a university professor would be away in July. I called the department, begged for Williamson's cell number, pleaded emergency.

They gave me her number and my next call went through.

"Professor? This is Claire. Chastain, from—"

"I remember. What's up Claire?"

"I need a lawyer. Criminal defense."

"For a friend?"

"For me."

"Really? You didn't strike me as the type. Would this be white collar? Embezzlement?"

"Homicide."

"Oh, Claire! Come on!"

"No, seriously. It's a mistake, but I'm not going to get myself in trouble during an interrogation. I need someone who knows the system to guide me."

"Where are you?"

"Montgomery County."

"I know just the guy."

"Is he good?"

"You'll know how good he is when you see the hatred in the cops' eyes when he walks in."

I took the number, made the call.

Anton Durant seemed pleased to hear I was in trouble.

"What's the rap?"

"Murder. It's completely bogus. A mistake on the cops' part, but understandable. I just need to get this sorted so I can go home."

"Sure, sure. How much have you told them?"

"Nothing."

"Ah, you told them something. You probably just don't know it. You're nervous, huh?"

"How soon can you get here?"

"Where are you?"

"Derwood station."

"Mmm. Give me a couple hours. You have ten thousand bucks?"

"I can pay you. Don't worry about that."

"All right, I'll see you soon. Keep your mouth shut till I get there."

12

I don't like to show fear, or even acknowledge it to myself, but you can tell just how scared you are by how much time has slowed. The hours between that call and Anton's arrival were two of the longest of my life.

While I waited, two female officers put me in a lineup with three other women who didn't look much like me. One of them, I thought, worked at the station as a clerk. I had seen her on my way in. Another woman, about the same height as me, with the same hair color, had rotting teeth and scabs all over her face, probably from picking at herself while high on meth. The third woman, a Latina who had to be instructed in Spanish, was at least ten years older than me and thirty pounds heavier.

I knew the busybody neighbor would identify me, but the process took longer than I expected. Maybe they had more than one witness looking at us.

They did.

When I left the lineup, I heard Kowalczyk say to another cop, "Three for three put her at the scene. Plus, Graves from the warehouse. We're batting a thousand."

He meant for me to hear that. It was an intimidation tactic.

Graves and the busybody had identified me. Okay, but who were the other two? The concierge in the lobby never looked up. The building had security cameras. I would surely show up on the videos. But who else would they have brought in to identify me? Lehmann? He couldn't have placed me at the scene.

I was booked on suspicion of second-degree murder. They took my fingerprints, photographed the cuts and bruises on my hands, swabbed the inside of my cheek for DNA, and shut me in a holding cell to wait for Anton Durant. By then it felt like six hours had passed.

They took my phone, my wallet and keys, my shoulder bag that had the notebook I was supposed to deliver to Lehmann. They asked me to sign the inventory. All of this was by the book, exactly as described in the opening chapters of the textbook on the criminal justice process. Seeing how the system worked from the inside was a good experience. It wasn't just words on a page anymore. Now it was real. I was in it, and I understood the sense of bewilderment, of having no friendly face to turn to, of being less than human in the eyes of the people processing you. I was being swallowed by an indifferent machine.

I kept asking myself what I could do, what action I could take right now to fix this mess. My mind could not accept the fact that I could do nothing, that all of this was beyond my control. I couldn't stand being locked in a room, unable to act on my own behalf, unable to guide my own fate. I was shaking with energy that had nowhere to go while the criminal justice system pressed forward in its effort to wrong me, to destroy my future.

My mind and stomach churned as I paced the holding cell. I felt a new sympathy for the animals in the zoo and for everyone who has ever been locked up, guilty or not. The sense of physical entrapment, of abject helplessness, of being wronged, of not being listened to—all of it was dehumanizing.

I tried to think through the panic and the anger and the fear to get a clear sense of what they were accusing me of. Second degree murder is a crime of passion. It's not premeditated. They weren't saying I went there with an intent to kill. They were saying something happened, emotions got out of hand. I snapped and killed him.

Well, someone killed him. It just wasn't me.

This was a mistake, a horrible, nightmarish mistake that needed to be fixed. And I was a caged tiger trying desperately to hold on to her sanity.

13

After what seemed like several more hours, a uniformed woman took me from the holding cell to a windowless room where I met Anton Durant. Six feet tall, well fed, dark hair, dark eyes, he wore a two-thousand-dollar salesman's suit and his expression said he was delighted to meet me. Too delighted.

He had the face of a showman, someone who liked trouble because it gave him a chance to be in the spotlight. I pictured him in court, pacing before a jury, twisting a story in ways that would enrage a prosecutor and pull at the hearts of jurors who should be looking at facts instead of theater.

"Claire!" He shook my hand vigorously. His smile was too broad, like he'd practiced to make it visible to nearsighted jurors in the back row. Everything about his manner told me he loved his job.

"Mr. Durant."

"Anton," he corrected. "So..." He smiled again. This was fun for him. "You killed someone! Should I keep my distance? Do you have a temper?"

"This isn't funny."

"I know. But a little levity doesn't hurt."

"Please don't joke."

"You understand the charge?"

"Second degree murder."

"They say you went in to talk with this guy Reisman, got into some kind of dispute and then you bashed his head in with a hammer."

"Damn." I bit my nail—a habit I had broken myself of at age twelve, through a massively determined effort.

"What?"

"I picked up that hammer. I had it in my hand."

"Did you wipe the prints off?"

"No! Why would I?"

"When you're a homicide suspect, it helps if your prints aren't on the murder weapon. Why were you talking to Reisman?"

"His employer hired me to investigate him."

"You're an investigator?"

"Trying to be."

"You have a license?"

"Not yet."

Durant clicked his tongue. "Okay. We'll have to work on that part of the story. Why'd you go to his apartment? What part of the investigation warranted that?"

"His employer thought he was stealing. One thing I wanted to know was whether Riesman was living beyond his means."

"Was he?" Durant turned his back and walked toward the far wall.

"The rent alone was beyond his means." *I hate talking to a man's backside. To anyone's backside. Goddammit, look at me when I talk!* "All the furniture in the apartment was new. And expensive."

Durant turned, paced back toward me, rapped his knuckles absentmindedly on the table. "So, you think he was stealing?"

His casual air was infuriating.

"No," I said, struggling to contain myself. "I don't think he was capable of it. He's too anxious. He can't make a simple decision without agonizing deliberation, and then when he does, he checks everything three times to make sure he's done it right."

"Past tense, Claire. The guy's gone, remember?"

I'm going to fucking strangle you if you don't start taking this seriously. But at least I'm still alive. Poor Jake. Poor Jake is...

I shook my head. "It's sad. He had his problems, but he was a decent person."

Why are we talking about him? I don't want to talk about him. I'm the one in trouble here. Can we both acknowledge that?

"Sure, sure. So, if he wasn't stealing, how do you think he paid for the furniture?"

"No idea."

"Because maybe he got into debt and owed someone money. Maybe that someone came by to collect and the situation got out of hand."

"I can't see a guy like Jake taking any kind of risk or getting involved in anything shady. Just buying a phone was nerve racking enough."

"Well, you never know. When you're looking at a prison sentence, it pays to turn over every stone, because you didn't do it, did you, Claire?" He eyed me closely. "Did you?"

"Of course I didn't do it."

His face broke into that showman's smile again. I could see why Professor Williamson said the cops hated him.

"That's what I like to hear." He patted my shoulder.

Uninvited touch from a man I'd just met would have set me off a year ago, even six months ago. I would have put him in his place. But I reminded myself that this man was on my side. If he didn't yet understand my boundaries, I could educate him on the matter later. Right now, I needed an ally.

"Okay, next up," he said with a cheerful clap, "is the county jail. Not a nice place, but not as scary as you might think. Unless they put you in with someone bad, but I'll have a word with them about that. They have 72 hours to arraign you. I can push to get it done by end of day tomorrow."

"How?"

"They don't like me," he said with delight. "I pester them until the arraignment, then I'm out of their face. They know the drill. If you want to make this easy, give me access to your bank account so I can get cash for bail or at least a bond."

"You don't think they'll release me on my own recognizance? I've never been in trouble before."

"Like I said, they don't like me. And this was a violent crime. I expect them to make this difficult, regardless of your clean record."

I signed the papers to formally hire Durant as my attorney and to allow him access to my accounts. I hand-wrote an addendum to the contract stating that access to my accounts was for the purpose of posting bail or bond only, and that his fees and expenses would be provided for separately, only after I had reviewed and explicitly approved them.

"You don't have to write that," Anton said. "It's implied."

"Nothing should be implied in a contract," I said. "The whole point of a contract is to be explicit. Now it is. Initial that."

I gave him the pen and saw that he did it. He chuckled, like he was amused at the idea of a client forcing him to initial terms in his own contract.

All I could think was, *Don't laugh too hard, Anton. This will stop being funny the minute you screw up.*

I told him where to find the title to my car and how to get in touch with my investment advisor, who could release additional funds from my accounts.

"Now we're going to have another chat with Kowalczyk," Anton said. "I'm interested to hear what he asks. It'll give us some insight into the case. You'll say nothing, except to confirm your name and some personal details. Kowalczyk is a smart guy, but he's blinded by his paranoid cop mentality. In his mind, everyone is guilty until proven innocent. And then they're still guilty. They just beat the system. Guy hates me and I don't blame him. You ready?"

"As ready as I'll ever be."

"All right then, let's do it."

14

After twenty fruitless minutes with Kowalczyk, during which I confirmed only my name, address, and date of birth, I was transported to the county detention center in a patrol car. Durant told me not to worry, but I worried.

"Most of the people in there are as scared as you. Some are angry. Some are resigned. Some are just trying to get through withdrawal. Keep your eyes open and your mouth shut."

At intake, they strip-searched me. They took my clothes and gave me a jumpsuit. Then they put me in a cell with three other women. The woman with the bad teeth and scabbed face—the meth addict who'd been in the lineup with me earlier—sat in a corner hugging her knees, looking lethargic and dazed. A short Latina woman paced the aisle between the bunks and spoke in rapid Spanish I couldn't understand. A black woman, fiftyish and rail thin, sat on a lower bunk watching her pace. She seemed to be half listening to the woman's rant.

For a while, none of them showed much interest in me.

Finally, the black woman asked, "What you doin' here?" Her tone and eyes were guarded, but not unfriendly. She was feeling me out.

"I got in trouble."

The woman smiled. "Mmm-hmm. Scariest thing about a white person in jail is they actually did it. Berta here," she pointed to the pacing woman who was still talking, "cut her husband. That one," she pointed to the woman in the corner, "she got a monkey on her back. Me, all I gotta do is show my face. They always fuckin' with me. Bet you got a good lawyer."

"I hope so."

"I ain't payin' for no lawyer. The state want to fuck with me, let them pay the bills. Cops, jail, food, prosecutor, defender, and judge. Whole damn system set up to keep me in check. I keep hoping someday they'll sit down and do the math. Figure out they done spent a hundred thousand dollars harassin' my ass. Say to themselves, Why don't we just leave her the fuck alone and save some money? Put that hundred thousand into a new school. I ain't ever done nothin' worth gettin' locked up for.

"You musta done somethin' bad. They don't go lockin' up white ladies for a trace of cocaine. You musta stabbed the judge. This one here," she pointed to the pacing woman, who was now muttering her story to herself, "they gone send her back to El Salvador. Her husband a landscaper. Makes okay money, but MS-13 come in every week and take a cut. Come to their house at dinner time to collect."

"How do you know that?"

"That's what she been sayin'."

"You understand Spanish?"

"Enough that when she say if fifty times, I get it. She ask her husband why he don't put his foot down, stand up to those boys, stop givin' 'em money. He get drunk and hit her. So she cut him up good. Guess she had enough. Only so much a woman can take from a man."

The black woman's name was Yvonne. She told me how MS-13 extorted families in Maryland by threatening to kill their relatives back in El Salvador.

"They got boys up here, they got boys back there. They say they gonna do somethin' three thousand miles away, they gone do it. All these people, they bust they ass to get into this country, tryin' to get away from that mess back home, but the mess follow 'em here. Same gang ruinin' they life down there ruinin' it up here too. Cops can't do nothin' about it. It's like they trapped. She start tellin' me this stuff, I say welcome to America. You the wrong color for this country's dream. Least you came of your own free will. Some of us got dragged into this mess. I wish I had a damn cigarette."

Before dinner, Yvonne warned me the food would be bland. I didn't feel like eating anyway.

I spent a long, sleepless night looking at the bottom of the bunk above me and listening to the other white woman in the cell, the meth addict, grunt and peep like a dog having fitful dreams.

At breakfast I had only water. At lunch, water and a bread roll.

At two p.m., they let me put my clothes back on. They took me out to a patrol car. I arrived at the courthouse in Rockville a little after three.

Anton Durant was waiting in the hallway inside. "Take the cuffs off her," he barked. "She's not an animal."

The cops ignored his showmanship. They left the cuffs on.

15

When my hearing came up, a female officer escorted me into the courtroom. Durant told me to stay quiet while he, the prosecutor, and the judge worked out the next steps of my case.

Again, I tell you, I cannot be passive while others decide how I'll be treated and what will become of me. My fate is mine and mine alone. I don't care what credentials any man has, he has no right to judge me, to tell me who I am, or to speculate about what I've done. He has no right to slander me before judge or jury, and he has no say in what my life will be.

This I believe to the bottom of my soul, and it took every ounce of strength and will to suppress my own nature, to not speak out for what I knew was right and true, while these three men who didn't even know me talked about what was to be done with me.

The prosecutor, a blond-haired man not much older than me, laid out the charges. Murder in the second degree. His version of the story was that I had gone to Reisman's apartment, we had a dispute, and then I brutally murdered the victim with repeated hammer blows to the head.

The judge explained the charges and asked for my plea.

"Not guilty."

Durant had instructed me to say, "Not guilty, your honor." But in the moment, I felt no honor for the man who was presiding over this charade.

Durant asked that I be released on my own recognizance.

The prosecutor argued that given the brutality of the crime, I was a danger to the community. Given my relative wealth and ability to travel, I was a flight risk. He asked that bail be set at one million dollars.

"Your honor," Durant began, "counsel for the state should not be allowed to express its frustration against counsel for the defense by penalizing the defendant. Claire Chastain is not violent, has no criminal record, and has been a fully employed, contributing member of society for many years. I ask again that she be released on her own recognizance."

The judge's opinion of Anton Durant didn't seem to be any higher than the prosecutor's. He set bail at five-hundred-thousand dollars and ordered me to surrender my passport.

Anton told me he would transfer fifty thousand dollars from my accounts to his bail bondsman and I'd walk free that day.

I told him, no. "Skip the bondsman. I'll put up the whole five hundred thousand."

He looked for a second like he was going to lecture me. Like he was going to explain to a little girl what was in her best interest.

"Do you know how the bond system works?" has asked in a patronizing tone.

"I know how it works."

"You only need to put up ten percent. Fifty thousand."

"I just told you I know how it works. My problem is that even if I win my case, the bondsman keeps the fifty thousand. If I put up the money myself, I get it all back when I'm acquitted."

"Let's not talk about acquittal until we know the facts."

"I know the facts, and I'm not going to forfeit fifty thousand dollars on a case I'm going to win, a case that should never have been brought."

I could tell by the way he was looking at me, he was trying to decide how far to argue his point. Finally, he said, "Do you even have that kind of money?"

I had close to three hundred thousand dollars in equity, savings, and investments. The line of work I'd been in back in New York had taught me where and how to invest.

As for the remaining two hundred thousand, I was the trustee of the account into which I'd put the money from the sale of my grandmother's house. That money was supposed to pay for her long-term dementia care. Dipping into it would not be ethical. It would be a breach of fiduciary duty.

But I was angry. I felt wronged, deeply wronged, and I really didn't want the system that had screwed me this far to screw me out of fifty-thousand dollars after I forced them to admit they were wrong.

Anton tried to talk me out of it, but I reminded him that I was paying him and I was in charge.

He printed out some papers there in the courthouse, and I authorized the release of funds. The financial details would take another day to work out. Until then, I had to go back to jail.

The first night, I'd been too scared and upset to sleep. Now, on the second night, I was too angry.

At five the following afternoon, they sent me to the same room where I'd been forced to surrender my clothes two days earlier. I put them back on and Anton met me outside the booking room.

My first questions to him were, "Where's my car? And why didn't I get my phone back?"

"What? No 'Thank you?'" He smiled. "No 'Nice to see you, Anton?'"

I suppose a man has to find some way of coping in the dreary business of criminal defense, but his levity pissed me off. These were serious matters.

He opened the door for me, and we walked into the hot afternoon sun.

"They're evidence, Claire. Your car is in an impound lot with forensics examiners crawling through it like lice. Your phone is in the hands of a detective who can copy its contents to a computer for thorough examination. Why'd you ask? Do you think they'd treat you differently than any other criminal?"

"I'm not a criminal."

"You don't get to say who you are anymore. Not till this is over."

He walked me to a black Mercedes S 560, a car I knew cost over a hundred-thousand dollars. He opened the passenger door and ushered me in. It was the kind of ingratiating behavior you'd expect from a man whose livelihood depended on convincing jurors that his clients were not assholes. He walked around to the other door, settled into the driver's seat and started the engine.

"You're studying criminal justice I hear?" His voice was smooth and easy.

"I am."

"I'm all for book learning, but you can't get a real sense of the system until you're in it." He pulled the car to the edge of the lot and waited for an opening in traffic. "Consider this your apprenticeship."

He hit the gas and the car accelerated, strong and quick, into a narrow space between two trucks that I wouldn't have had the nerve to try to enter.

"We're going to have a little talk in my office, and then I'll drive you home. Unless you want to eat first."

16

Durant's office in Bethesda looked out over Wisconsin Avenue near East West Highway. The sharp lines of the modern decor looked like a photo spread from Architectural Digest: black rug atop a white carpet, white leather sofa and chairs, black wood end tables.

This was no ordinary criminal defense attorney. Those guys just scrape by, defending people who can barely pay. Durant was apparently smart enough to find clients whose pockets were as deep as their legal troubles. He was a showman, and his office was a set piece designed to impress.

The lines of the furniture led the eye to the centerpiece of the exhibit, the floor-to-ceiling windows that looked across the street into the offices of respected corporations and investment firms. The view lent an air of legitimacy to a practice that would otherwise be associated with criminals.

Durant's massive black desk had a computer panel in the middle and stacks of folders at either end. The stacks were so perfectly even in height, I figured he must have arranged them just for show. Between the folders and the monitor, the desk was empty, a spotless no man's land except for the keyboard and mouse. The point, I gathered, was to give the impression of a man with a lot going on who made the space he needed to get things done.

"Have a seat." He motioned to one of the white upholstered chairs.

"I'll stand if you don't mind."

"I don't mind. What do you like to drink?"

"Water."

"Only water I have has tea in it. You want an iced tea?"

"Sure."

He pulled two bottles from the mini fridge beneath a shelf of law books.

"Lemon or peach?" He held the bottles out for me to see.

"Lemon."

Durant twisted the cap off with a pop and handed it to me. I wished he'd given me the cap as well.

He opened his bottle and walked to the window, sipping his tea along the way. He said, with his back to me, "You're in trouble, Claire."

"No shit."

I set my bottle down on a coaster atop the black end table. I hadn't even tasted it.

"You want me to lay it out for you?"

"Please."

"All right." He paced in front of the windows and began without looking at me. "You were seen with Jacob Reisman at his work and other places. The cops have statements from Carl Graves and another man who saw you in the warehouse talking to Jake. You agree with all this so far?"

I nodded. "Go on."

"You lied about who you were. Said you were working for an insurance company."

"I can explain that."

Durant held his hand up like a cop ordering traffic to stop. "We'll get there. Let me continue. You were seen entering Reisman's building twice, on two consecutive days."

"By whom?"

"Security cameras. Also, his neighbor. She saw you go into his apartment."

"She didn't actually see that. She saw me outside his door and assumed I was going in."

"Doesn't matter. You went in, right?"

"Yes."

"Okay. Reisman was murdered sometime after you entered. Sometime before ten-thirty p.m. The neighbor heard noises but didn't try to check in with him until a few minutes later. Ten thirty-six. There was a smudge of blood outside the door. She knocked, got no answer, called the police. How's this look to you so far?"

"Not good."

"It gets worse. The cops find Reisman on the floor with his head bashed in. Killed with his own hammer. I believe you said you touched the hammer?"

"I did."

"But you wiped it down?"

"No."

"Someone did. It was all a smear of blood with no recoverable prints. Now there was no sign of forced entry to the apartment. Whoever was in there, Reisman let them in. He trusted his killer. May I ask what you were wearing when you visited him?"

"Slacks like these, but they stopped just short of the ankles."

"Mmm hmm. And a light blue blouse? Short sleeves?"

I nodded.

"And you left by the service entrance? Around 10:28 pm?"

"I left through the lobby. Before nine."

"Right. But you returned just before ten."

"No, I didn't."

"That's not what the cameras say. You came back around 10 and left again around 10:28. From the service entrance in back."

"I didn't."

"Two witnesses say you did. With blood on your hands and blouse. Light blue blouse, navy ankle-length slacks. Security cameras say the same thing, but they're black and white."

"That's impossible."

Durant sat against the edge of his desk frowning and shaking his head. "Inadmissible at best, and I'm not even sure I can swing that. Prosecutors love video evidence. Cameras don't lie."

"They're wrong."

"They don't look wrong to me, and they won't look wrong to a jury either. You want to tell me what you were doing with Reisman in the first place?"

"I told you before. His employer asked me to investigate him. He thought Reisman was stealing."

Durant shook his head gravely. "That's not gonna fly, Claire."

"Why not?"

"I talked to Roscoe Lehmann this morning. He said he's never heard of you."

"What? That's impossible! I met him at his house. We spoke for twenty minutes. We signed a contract!"

Durant stared at me, trying to size me up. "I can't figure you out, Claire Chastain. You want to get off this rap, you're going to have to come up with a better story than that."

"Lehmann hired me. I have the contract."

"Lehmann told me no one was stealing from him."

"I had a feeling from the beginning this case was about something else. Lehmann wanted to get rid of Reisman, dig up some dirt, fire him for cause without risking a lawsuit."

"When were you at Lehmann's house?"

"Five days ago."

Again, Durant shook his head.

"What?" I asked.

"Lehmann was in Los Angeles five days ago. He got back last night."

"I was at his house!"

"You sure it was his house?"

"I..." I put my head in my hands. "Oh my God. I don't know."

"It gets worse, Claire. The cops found a notebook in your car. You were following Reisman."

"For Lehmann."

"But Lehmann said he didn't hire you. So, the notebook looks like a ruse. And your phone was full of photos of the guy. At work, at some storage facility, at Best Buy. Looks like you were stalking him. Tell me what happened inside his apartment. Did he touch you?"

"He didn't touch me. He made me uncomfortable. The man has psychological problems."

"Had, Claire. Is that when you picked up the hammer? When you felt threatened?"

"Yes."

"Were you going to hit him with it?"

"I wanted to make sure he couldn't hit *me* with it."

"Okay, this is something we can work with. The jury sees a mentally unstable man. They think danger. He makes a move on you."

"It wasn't quite like that."

"We're talking to the jury here. He makes a move and won't take no for an answer. You're alone. You have to defend yourself."

"That's not how it happened. Nothing like that happened. He was a decent person."

"In a jury's eyes, a woman has every right to defend herself. And you're a very pretty woman."

"What fucking difference does that make? Does anyone *not* have the right to defend themselves?" My color was rising now. My face was burning hot. "How does my appearance factor into anything?"

"It's a factor in the jury's mind. You take off that scowl and put on a dress, they'll see a pretty young victim—"

"I'm not a victim."

"You need to be if you want to beat this rap."

"Jake was the victim."

"Okay, we have another problem, Claire. You were involved in a drug case six months ago."

Apparently, Anton had done quite a bit of research during the two days I was locked up.

"Not as a criminal," I said.

"No, but in the police report, it says you tasered a man repeatedly. You knocked him down and fractured his skull."

"Do you know what he did to me? Do you know how hard he worked to earn what I did to him?"

"You're going down the wrong road here, Claire. The prosecutor's going to drive it down the jury's throat that you attacked a dangerous man. That shows aggression. You tasered him repeatedly. That shows cruelty."

"Do you know what he did to me?"

"It doesn't matter. You're the one on trial. The fact that you fractured his skull—"

"*He* fractured it! He fractured it when he fell."

"After you tasered him. The fact that you fractured his skull and then Jake Reisman dies with multiple head wounds, multiple *skull* fractures—the prosecutor's going to be all over that."

"Anton, I didn't do this!"

"How do you explain the fingerprints in his apartment? How do you refute the witnesses? The security footage?"

"There's an explanation somewhere."

"I don't see it, Claire. You have a photo of the murder weapon on your freakin' phone! And your demeanor doesn't help. You looked like you were going to hit me a minute ago."

"I have a temper, and you are sorely trying it."

"Don't let the jury know that. Look, I busted my ass to keep your mug shot out of the news. At least for now. You're going to be the subject of a lot of attention, and how you appear is going to be more important now than at any time in your life. You want my advice, get rid of that scowl. Put on a dress and your best nice-girl face. *You* have to be the victim here. Not him."

By now, I was shaking with rage. Durant looked wary of my clenched fists.

"I'm just telling you what you need to do to survive," he said. "You're in a different world now, Claire. This is the criminal justice system, and no part of it was designed to make you feel comfortable. Until we sort this out, I want to see a smiling girl in a sundress. I want to see a pretty little sweetheart that no jury in the world would want to send to prison."

"You have no idea how angry you're making me."

"Yes I do. It shows on your face, plain as day. Now wipe off that scowl and remember that if you don't like this, you're not going to like prison at all."

Durant pushed himself off the desk. "Come on. We'll get something to eat, or I'll drive you home. You can practice controlling your emotions when you sit next to me in the car. Christ, you look like you're ready to kill someone."

17

Anton told me he had his own investigator to look into my case.

"Who?" I asked. "And what has he found?"

"*She*," he emphasized the word, "hasn't found anything yet. Let's give her some time. The main guy I'll get on the job, Freddy Ferguson, is wrapping up a case for another client out of town. He hasn't found anything because he hasn't started yet."

"Well, that doesn't help me."

"He'll be back in a couple of days."

"Well, I'm a detective, and I'm here now."

I already knew he looked at my case like a chess match. If you can't checkmate your opponent, force a draw.

For me, the case was my reputation, my future, and my life. I wasn't going to accept a draw in a case I clearly deserved to win. I wasn't going to compromise on anything.

Too angry to go home after my conversation with Durant, I made him drive me to Enterprise to rent a car. I could have gotten a cheap Chevy, but they had a new BMW 228i. I don't know if you've ever been in one of those, but they're a hell of a lot nicer than jail. I splurged.

Then I went to Best Buy in Tenleytown and bought a phone. I spent twenty minutes arguing with Verizon to get my number ported to the new device. Part of me wanted to erase the old phone out of spite for Kowalczyk and the Montgomery County Police department. I could do it remotely, leave them with a useless brick, but that would have destroyed evidence, which was itself a crime.

I drove back to my apartment and—I don't know why it didn't occur to me that the police would have searched the place. I was expecting to walk into a sanctuary of privacy after two nights in jail. I was looking forward to a place of quiet order, a door I could lock against the world, fresh clean clothes, a shower, and a cup of tea.

Why?

Why did they have to leave the place like this? I understand that when you're looking for blood-stained evidence, you need to examine all my clothes, but is it really that hard to put things back? Did you have to leave my underwear all over the floor? Did you have to leave your boot print on my favorite satin blouse?

What were you looking for in my pantry? Did you spit in my cereal? Put your hands in my bread? Could you not be bothered to put those last few items back in the freezer?

I wanted to throw out everything they had touched, those bastards!

The bread and cereal and the thawed Trader Joe's Indian food went into a bag that I hauled to the alley. I separated my clothes into whites, colors, delicates, and dry cleaning. All of it in bags for tomorrow, or whenever I could get around to washing it.

I spent thirty minutes in the shower, washing the smell of jail from my hair, then put on a pair of sweats, trying not to imagine who might have touched them. Then I made a pot of tea and tried to calm myself.

I can tolerate just about every feeling other than injustice and helplessness. I will not let anyone put me in a position of victimhood, a position where I cannot act on my own behalf. I had enough of that in childhood, and I swear there will be no more.

I tried to moderate my outrage with meditation, but the mantra that was supposed to soothe me turned into a violent stream of obscenities.

I told myself there was nothing I could do until the next morning, that it was pointless to stew in anger, and still I stewed all night.

* * *

At 8:15 the next morning, fifteen minutes before they opened, someone finally answered the phone at Lehmann's showroom near Montgomery Mall. The manager confirmed Lehmann had an office there, and that he'd be in by 9:30.

Before I left my apartment, I synched up the new phone with my photos, contacts, messages, and settings. On the drive to Lehmann's showroom, I found Noreen Williamson's number in my call history and tapped the Call button.

Professor Williamson answered on the second ring.

"This Claire again?"

"It's Claire."

"What's up?"

"Why did you recommend me to Roscoe Lehmann?"

"Who?" she asked. "What did I recommend you for?"

"You didn't speak with him? About an investigation into one of his employees?"

"No. I've never even heard of him."

"Damn it!"

"You sound disappointed, Claire? Should I know him?"

I let out a sigh. "No. Sorry to bother you, professor."

"Are you all right, Claire?"

"Check the news. Or just Google my name and see what comes up. That'll give you an idea of how I'm doing."

The story of Reisman's murder was already in the Post and other local news sites; though, this being DC, it didn't warrant more than a couple of paragraphs.

Police Investigating Rockville Homicide. Victim was Loner.

Where do they get off saying things like that? The victim was a human being. A troubled person trying to make his way in the world like the rest of us, only he didn't quite have all the tools.

Suspect in Custody. It was nice of them to print my name, but it's Claire, not Clare.

Lehmann's showroom, fronted by plate glass windows, was immaculate and well lit. Row upon row of washers, dryers, dishwashers, refrigerators, ranges, microwaves, and air conditioners. A shrine to the automation of our comfort and daily chores.

I was three steps past the door when a chirpy young sales rep tried to inflict her cheerfulness on me.

"Anything I can help you find?"

"Roscoe Lehmann."

"Mr. Lehmann should be here any minute. Do you have an appointment?" She wore the Lehmann uniform: tan chinos and a white button-down shirt with the green Lehmann logo.

"No. Is that his office back there?" I pointed to a door in the rear.

"I'm sorry, if you'd like to set up an appointment—"

"I would." I walked past her. "Tell him I'm waiting in his office."

I marched through a line of ranges and dishwashers to the door in back. It was unlocked. I let myself in.

The woman at the desk inside looked to be about sixty. In front of her sat a keyboard and monitor, a name plate, and a tin of cookies with a red satin bow. Mrs. Janice Stewart (according to the nameplate) glanced up from her computer over the top of her half-glasses with vague indifference.

"Here to see Roscoe?"

"Yes."

"In there." She pointed toward the back office. "He'll be here in a few. There's a water cooler by the door if you're thirsty."

"Thank you."

I passed the cooler without a glance and went into the back office.

It was a humble, functional space, not like Durant's showy stage piece. A path worn into the light grey carpet split in two at Lehmann's desk. One branch led to the old wood and leather chair behind, the other stopped in front, where Lehmann's secretary probably stood to brief him or ask for signatures.

The desk was a heavy wooden relic, the kind you'd see at the front of a public-school classroom in the 1950s. The old Dell monitor was scuffed in back and the putty-colored keyboard, leftover from the nineties, had a coiled wire like an old landline telephone. The whole setup was on the right side of the desk, leaving the center clear so Lehmann could see who was going in and out.

I imagined the occupant of this office was a heads-down worker, too focused on the business at hand to care about his environment. The furniture in his home showed that he liked the finer things, but maybe he thought showing too much finery at work would encourage his employees to ask for raises. In my consultant days, I had found that mindset in a number of owners who had built their businesses from the ground up. Look scrappy and work hard.

The wall on the right side of the office had a built-in bookcase, the shelves full of outdated product catalogs, maintenance manuals, a volume on accounting and one on the tax code. The dust told me they hadn't been touched in years.

There was a framed photo of older man standing beside a younger one who looked enough like him to be his son. I don't know why I didn't put it together right away, that the older man was the real Roscoe Lehmann.

Beside the first photo was a second. The older man was handing an Employee of the Year award to Carl Graves. The year on the plaque was 2015, five years ago.

Beside that stood one last photo, dated a year ago. The older man was receiving an industry award for "Best Service, Consumer Retail Appliance." The most remarkable thing about the pictures was how much the man had aged—more than a decade, it seemed—in the space of four years.

Something must have happened in that time. Cancer treatment, some tragedy or crushing illness. It wasn't just age that changed the face. It was sorrow. Grief had set its mark on the man.

A high window behind the desk, six feet wide and one foot tall, let in daylight without allowing anyone to see in or out. I was just turning to get a look at the rest of the room when the man himself walked in.

He didn't notice me at first. He was carrying the tin of cookies with the red satin bow, reading the fine print on the side as he walked.

"He knows I can't eat this," he sighed. "Janice, please write up a card thanking Mr. Mathers for this—"

He stopped short, startled at the sight of me.

Somehow, I was expecting to see the man who had hired me, even though I knew by now that man had been an imposter.

The person who stood before me appeared to be in his late sixties, perhaps seventy. His face wore a look of shock. He must have heard the news of his employee's murder. Maybe he tried to look up details on the internet. I wondered if some site I had missed had actually posted a photo of me. He looked that scared.

"Mr. Lehmann?" I said. "Roscoe Lehmann? I've just come to talk. If you're more comfortable talking in the showroom, we can talk out there."

If he was worried about getting his head bashed in, it might reassure him to move our encounter into a public space full of witnesses.

But the fearful look passed. He set the cookies on the shelf to his right, stepped forward and shook my hand.

"You are?"

He let the question hang. Apparently, he hadn't seen a photo, or he would have known who I was.

"Claire Chastain."

This man looked more like what I would have expected after my first glance at the shaggy lawn and leaf-filled pool behind his house. His dark wool pants, expensive and neglected, were wearing at the knees. His yellow silk tie looked new, but the white shirt beneath it hadn't been properly pressed. His thinning grey hair had been blown out of place behind an open car window.

"Yes, I know." His handshake was firm and vigorous. "I've been following the news."

"Oh—" For a moment, my confidence faltered. "I'm sorry, Mr. Lehmann, I know this is awkward. You lost an employee. I'm sorry for your loss. If you read the news, you think I killed him, but I didn't."

A series of questions flashed through my mind. Was I supposed to stay away from people involved in the case? They didn't say that at my arraignment. Maybe it was in written instructions they gave to Anton. Reisman's family—of which there was none—would be off-limits for sure, but his employer? What if Lehmann were asked at some point to be a witness? Could the prosecution claim witness tampering if they knew I came here and talked to him?

I should have thought of this beforehand, but all I could think of was clearing my name.

Too late now, I thought. Might as well get on with it.

"I don't want you to feel threatened, Mr. Lehmann. Would you like to talk outside? In the showroom?"

He just kept staring at me. I couldn't tell if his eyes were wide with fear or something else.

"We'll talk here," he said at last. He turned and closed the door. "You may have a seat if you'd like."

"Thanks. I'd rather stand. I've been a little anxious these past few days."

"So I imagine."

"I didn't kill Jake Reisman."

"I'm sure you didn't."

I couldn't tell if he was saying that just to placate me or if he really believed it. How can anyone be sure of anything? His acquiescence seemed too easy, so I thought he was just being polite. But his face told me he really had decided. The fear he had shown a few seconds earlier was gone. It wouldn't have left him if he thought I was a murderer.

He continued to stare at me. I think he knew it too. He knew he was staring, but he couldn't stop himself.

"Can I ask you, Mr. Lehmann, why you hired Jacob Reisman?"

My question seemed to break the spell.

"I felt sorry for him."

"How did he find you?"

Lehmann ignored my question. "Why did you tell your lawyer I hired you?"

I forgot Anton had called him to check my story.

"Because *someone* hired me."

"What made you think it was me?" He walked around the back of the desk, rolling his knuckles on the surface with each thoughtful step.

"He told me his name was Roscoe Lehmann. And I met him at your house."

"Hmm." His tone and expression were indifferent, as if this was just a matter of intellectual curiosity. "What did he look like?"

I described the man and watched as Lehmann tried in vain to match the description to someone he knew.

"Can you tell me the address of the house where you two met?"

I gave him the address, and I told him what the house looked like inside.

"That's my house all right. You said this man hired you to investigate Jacob Reisman?"

"He thought Reisman was stealing."

"Jake couldn't steal gum from the supermarket. He's too nervous. You're an investigator?"

"I'm trying."

"This is your first case?"

"My first paid case, yes."

"Hmm." Lehmann sat, put his hands on the armrests of the old swivel chair and leaned back. "But you were involved in another case, no?"

I knew what he meant, but I didn't want to go into the whole story of Gavin Corley and PharmaCore and the Friday Cage.

"Your lawyer told me it was a drug case. Seems trouble has a way of finding you."

"It seems that way."

"You know, I've never actually hired an investigator. I've always believed that if you want something done right, you have to do it yourself."

"We think the same way."

"I've also believed that people are never more motivated than when they have a personal stake in the outcome of their work. A little skin in the game." He gave me a pointed glance. "Avoiding prison is strong motivation. Very strong. Isn't it, Claire?"

"What are you getting at?"

"I want to hire you."

"For what?"

"To investigate the murder of Jacob Reisman."

"Excuse me?"

"He was a troubled and innocent young man. There's something very compelling to me about a person who struggles so mightily with the basics of life, the things the rest of us take for granted. He certainly didn't deserve to be murdered."

"You want to hire me?" I repeated. I really wasn't sure I had heard him correctly.

"He was an innocent. In the wrong place at the wrong time, and he ran into the wrong person."

"You understand I'm the chief suspect?" I reminded him. "You know I've already been booked for his murder?"

"Then no one will be more motivated than you to solve the case."

I shook my head. "This is like the Twilight Zone. I don't even know where to start."

"Let me ask you something, Claire. When you met this man at my home, was he alone? Or was there a woman in the house?"

My look of surprise told him all he needed to know. "I suggest you start there," he said.

18

Sitting in my car outside the showroom, the AC blasting against the morning humidity, I swiped backwards through my photos until I found the one of the SUV parked in Lehmann's drive. I typed the Florida plate number into a free license lookup site, only to learn that Florida doesn't permit civilians to look up license plate info. Only law enforcement can do that.

I looked again at the photo. The frame around the plate said SIXT. What was that?

A rental agency, according to Google. Their website showed they specialized in high-end vehicles, luxury SUVs, and sportscars. Their only location in the area was at Dulles Airport, forty-five minutes away. If the fake Lehmann who hired me had picked up the Yukon there, maybe someone would remember him. He would have had to show his license. He would have paid with a credit card that had his name on it. I put the car in gear and headed for Virginia.

The Dulles Access Road, flanked on both sides by tech giants and defense contractors, ended at the sprawling airport complex. A quarter way around the pond, I turned right onto Ariane Way. The agency I was looking for was the last in the long row of rental companies. Past Avis, Alamo, Budget and the rest was a lot full of high-end cars.

When I turned in, a man in black slacks and white polo shirt asked if I was returning.

"I need to speak to someone in the office."

He waved me into a spot near the building, where I sat for a while in the cool air behind the wheel, watching the employees come and go.

The man who had waved me in was helping a new arrival out of a Porsche Cayenne. He was slim, Latino, maybe in his late twenties, with a friendly face. I took a moment to size him up: cheerful greeting, shirt neatly tucked, crisp and efficient in his motions as he pointed his customer to the office. He scanned her paperwork, ducked into the driver's seat to get the mileage, popped the rear gate and removed her suitcases.

Not him, I thought.

Inside the glass door, the middle-aged woman behind the counter stood with her eyes glued to her computer monitor. Too stiff, I thought. Too business-like. Get you in, process you, get you out. Not the kind who'd be willing to grant a favor.

In the rearview, I caught a glimpse of another man. As he rounded the car toward the office, I could hear the scuff of his feet above the air conditioning. White guy. Overdue for a shave and a haircut. Couldn't tuck his shirt in right, or couldn't be bothered to try.

The attendant rolling the big suitcases from the SUV called to him before he reached the office door.

"Yo, Frankie!"

Frankie turned, looking irritable. I knew the type. Annoyed at having to do the job they pay him to do.

"Take this in."

The friendly attendant pulled the electronic scanner from his belt and handed it to Frankie, who didn't look too pleased to receive it. He turned without a word, and when he stepped toward the door, I saw the laces flying around his untied hiking boots.

That's why his heels scuff when he walks. And that's my man.

I cut the engine, got out and followed him in, hoping to catch him before he disappeared in back.

SUV woman stood at the counter in front of efficient middle-aged woman, neither looking at the other as they went through the standard questions.

"Any damage to the car?"

"No."

"You fill the tank before you brought it back?"

"I filled it ten minutes ago."

Frankie was rounding the far end of the counter. I picked up my pace. He was headed to the door behind efficient woman, to a back office where he'd be out of reach. He slid the hand-held scanner onto the counter and kept walking. I made it to the customer side of the counter just in time, leaned across and tapped his shoulder as he passed.

He turned in surprise. I waved him silently toward the far end of the counter, away from the other women. He pointed to himself and gave me that questioning look that asks, "Who? Me?"

I nodded and he followed me to the end of the counter. Up close, he looked hung over. I guessed he was in his late thirties.

I leaned in and whispered, "I need a favor."

He lit right up. I'm not sure what kind of favor he thought I was asking for, but he sure seemed happy I asked.

He glanced down the counter at efficient women, then whispered back, "You mean, like an upgrade?"

I shook my head and smiled. "I need you to tell me who was the last person to rent a GMC Yukon before July thirteenth. I can give you the license number."

He eyed me for a second, unsure. "Who are you?" he asked in a low voice.

"Someone who's about to give you a hundred dollars."

His face broke into a broad grin. "Maybe this day ain't shapin' up too bad after all. Step over here."

He went to the computer terminal. I pulled up the license plate photo on my phone and handed it to him with a hundred underneath. Frankie looked down the counter, saw his coworker was at the printer with her back turned, checked the bill and slid it into his pocket.

He typed in the license number, drummed his fingers, typed again and clicked. "You said July thirteenth?"

"Whoever last rented it on or before the thirteenth."

"It went out on the twelfth. Came back on the fourteenth."

"Was it a woman or a man?"

"I'm gonna go out on a limb here and say Buzz DiNardo was a man. Hold on. I can print a copy of the rental agreement with his license number, address, and all that."

Five minutes later, I left the lot with DiNardo's paperwork.

19

Back in my apartment, I brewed a pot of coffee, put Stan Getz on Spotify and dug in to the first and best clue I'd found so far. Buzz DiNardo's license said he was sixty-two years old and lived in Evanston, Illinois.

If I had to guess what he did for living after meeting him that one time, I would say he's a salesman. He was constantly reading my reactions, trying to say things he thought I wanted to hear.

Salesman or con man. He was one of the two.

I checked LinkedIn. He wasn't listed. No listing on Facebook either. He had to be a con man. No active salesman in a legitimate business would refuse the free and easy networking opportunities of social media.

I checked Instagram. If he was a con man, he might want to project an image of wealth and power. Photos of himself at resorts with Ferraris. It's a lot easier to gain people's confidence when you look like you've got it made.

No Instagram. At least, not under his own name.

I did a Google search. Nothing.

Hmm. What if he had once had an internet presence and then gone back and wiped it out?

I checked the Internet Archive. They would have captured his past presence.

Nothing there either.

I looked again at the info Frankie had given me. Buzz DiNardo, sixty-two, lived at 1451 Chicago Avenue in Evanston, Illinois. According to Google Maps, that's right between the First Presbyterian Church and a florist called Bloom 3, directly across from Nichols Concert Hall.

There's no building there. It's a public park.

So much for my first clue. All I knew at this point was that whoever I had spoken to at Lehmann's house that first day had rented a car at Dulles Airport and had returned it to the same location. He probably flew in just before he got the car and flew out after he returned it.

If he lived outside the DC area, I might have to travel to find him.

I closed the laptop and called Anton Durant.

"Claire!" The joy and enthusiasm in his voice sounded like he was greeting a long-lost friend. "You find any nice dresses yet?"

"Shut up, Anton."

"You better not be scowling. Work on that resting bitch face, will you?"

"I have a question."

"Make it quick. I have to be back in a deposition in five."

"What did the judge say about traveling at my arraignment? My nerves were shot, and I can't remember."

"Stay in the country."

"Well, I know *that*. They have my passport. What about domestic travel?"

"Stay in the DC area. If you need to go somewhere, tell me. I'll let the prosecutor know. If you fly around without telling them, they can revoke your bail and you'll be back in county detention. Let's try to stay on their good side."

"What about your detective?"

"Ferguson?"

"What's he done? Has he talked to anyone in Reisman's building?"

"No, I have someone else on that. Ferguson is still in LA."

"He hasn't started yet? What the hell, Anton?"

"I have a lot of work is what the hell. So does he. Do you know how long a criminal trial takes? Just to schedule? Months, Claire. Months. Don't get impatient."

"Put someone else on the case."

"I have my second-best investigator on it now."

"Second best?"

"Yeah. She's connected to some good sources."

"I don't want my fate in the hands of anyone who's second best."

"Well, she's the first best right now. We'll pick up Freddy when he's available. Understand now, he's not my employee. Works for an agency in DC. But I got dibs on him. As soon as he wraps up his current case, he's ours."

"You understand what you're telling me, right?"

"I understand what you're hearing. What you're hearing is you have to take matters into your own hands, do it all yourself. What I'm telling you is something different. This is a long game, Claire. We can't force the outcome by rushing the first play. Wait for Freddy."

"Screw Freddy."

"Smile, Claire! Pretty dress and happy face!"

"Fuck off, Anton."

I could hear him laughing as I hung up.

I wasn't going to sit around like some damsel in distress waiting to be rescued. I already had my next move planned: The Cortona Center.

While re-examining the photos I'd taken inside Reisman's apartment, I zoomed in on the mess of documents on the table. Beneath the murder weapon were Reisman's discharge papers from the psychiatric facility near Germantown. He had spent several weeks there before Lehmann hired him. Given the length of his stay and the recency of his discharge, they would have to remember him.

Patient confidentiality laws would prohibit anyone working at the center from telling me the details of Jacob Reisman's case, but I might be able to learn something about his life outside of treatment.

How did he choose Cortona of all places? Did he have friends? Visitors? A careless talker, one who didn't flat out refuse to speak, might give me more information than they intended.

20

The Cortona Center was a four-story building of modern brick and glass at the end of a long, wooded parkway. Approaching the building from the side, I could see a lawn in back, metal picnic tables on a stone patio, and a mother duck leading a line of chicks across a quiet pond.

Reisman hadn't been employed before moving cross country. He couldn't have had top-flight health insurance. How could he have afforded an extended stay in an expensive private facility like this?

I thought back to the furniture in his apartment. All new, and not cheap. Where did his money come from? As I pulled into the lot, I made a note to look into his storage facility sooner rather than later.

The visitor's lot just past the building entrance had two rows of spaces, enough for thirty cars. Most of it was empty. I parked and checked the time. 4:33. The peak of the summer heat.

The cicadas buzzed in the canopy of oaks and sycamores as I walked to the building. Above the entrance, a mockingbird perched atop the steel awning poured its heart out in song.

If I ever go nuts—and there's a good chance I might—this is where I want to be. This little pond-side haven tucked into the woods.

I opened the glass door to a blast of air conditioning. I had expected to see something like a hospital waiting room—dull neutral-toned carpet, rows of chairs, a table stacked with magazines. Instead, I found a slate floor, walls of paneled cherrywood, two black leather couches, several tall potted ficus trees, two elevators, and a medical reception desk behind a sliding glass window.

A young black man in light blue scrubs was on his way out with a woman dressed in a tan business skirt and blouse.

He was looking back toward the desk as he walked. "You can have my break when I get back."

"Don't be late," said the man at the desk.

"If I am, I'll make it up to you."

He hooked his arm through the woman's as he turned and almost walked right into me.

"Sh—" He stopped himself before his startled curse came out.

"Excuse me," I said politely.

He scowled at me, then turned and said to the man at the desk, "Yo, Squints, you can deal with this one."

On his way out the door, I heard him say under his breath, "'Cause I sure as hell ain't gonna."

Did I really look that unpleasant? I heard Anton's voice again. *Work on that resting bitch face, will you?*

Sometimes I think random encounters like this happen for a reason. I was there to get information, but I was still tense and worried. It must have shown. Maybe it made me look sour. This man reminded me to put on a nice face, and he'd done it just in time to save me from potentially putting off a person who could give me the information I was after.

That's what I told myself anyway.

As I approached the desk, I understood how Squints got his nickname. The way he squeezed his eyes together, he'd have crow's feet by the end of the month if he didn't have them already. I put on the same warm smile that had worked on Frankie earlier that day, but I had the feeling this guy couldn't see it.

He looked to be in his late twenties, chunky, with short dark hair and a broad face. I had the impression he might have been an athlete in high school and then gave up exercise in favor of eating.

"Can I help you?" he asked. His obnoxious tone told me he didn't want to help anyone.

"I was wondering if you could give me some information about a patient."

"Probably not."

He picked up a pair of glasses from the counter, put them on and opened his eyes normally. He did have crow's feet. His eyes bugged out for a second, and he put the glasses back on the counter.

"Something wrong?" I asked.

"Those aren't my glasses."

"You had a patient here a while back named Jacob Riesman."

"Of course we did." His tone had a strange mocking edge, like he was trying to antagonize me.

Had I done something to offend him? Or was he just naturally rude?

My instinct is to respond in kind to how I'm treated. Kindness begets kindness. Rudeness begets anger. I had to check that instinct, collect myself and try to be polite because he had information I wanted—at least, I hoped he did—and I had no leverage in this situation.

"I was wondering what brought him here," I said as politely as I could. I tried to sound concerned.

"The guy was nuts. Why else would anyone come here?"

"No, I mean, why here of all places. He lived in California."

"Well I guess this is where he broke down."

Squints didn't seem very bright. Legally, he had no right to tell me anything about the facility's patients. In practice, there might be some leeway to share information with friends and family. For them, he might acknowledge a patient's presence, but he hadn't even asked me who I was. As long as he was talking, I wanted to press forward.

"Did you know him?"

"I don't feel like playing games today," he snapped. He picked up his phone, opened a game, squinted in annoyance and then laid the phone face-down on the counter.

His rudeness was so inexplicable, I began to wonder if he was a patient himself. You know that old saying about the inmates running the asylum.

I put aside my annoyance and frustration, and said politely, earnestly, "This is important."

"I'm sure it is," he said with smug sarcasm.

"Have you read the news lately?"

Squints leaned back and clasped his hands behind his head. "I don't read news," he said proudly. "The news is full of horror stories. You read that stuff every day, you'll go nuts. Wind up like Jake in room three-oh-eight."

"So you did know him?"

"Of course I did."

Squints rocked in the chair with his hands behind his head in a motion that struck me as inadvertently obscene. I don't think he was aware of how he looked.

"My name is Claire Chastain, I'm—"

"Oh, Claire, is it? Nice to meet you..." He paused for a second for dramatic effect, then stretched out my name. "Claaaaaire." His sarcastic tone was even ruder than before.

I gave him a dirty look, but he probably couldn't see it.

"Are you a patient here?" I asked. "Or an orderly?"

Squints tugged at his scrubs. "Check the outfit, Claaaaaire." He pulled his shirt forward again and looked at it as if to make sure he was wearing what he thought he was wearing.

"What's the matter with you?" I was really starting to lose it. This guy was like an obnoxious twelve-year-old.

"I don't like you," he said flatly.

"Well, that's apparent. Are you going to help me or not?"

"I doubt it."

Deep breath, Claire. Keep your cool and press on.

"Look," I said. "Jake was a sensitive, anxious person. I'm trying to find out what would make someone like that drive across the country. Because that's a big undertaking even for a healthy person."

"Why do you think?" His tone was snippy.

"Excuse me?"

He started rocking again. "He came in clutching that report and he carried it with him everywhere he went."

"What report?"

"What report?" Squints mimicked in a snotty tone. "The one he printed off the internet. Like you don't know. Stop wasting my time."

He leaned forward and slid the glass panel shut with a violent flourish, slamming his fingers in the process.

I left to the soundtrack of his infuriated cursing, wondering what in the world had just happened. Nothing in this bewildering encounter made sense.

21

In the lot outside Cortona, I sat behind the wheel with the AC on low and the windows down. The mockingbird had taken a break from its song, but the cicadas were still going strong.

I swiped back though the photos of the previous week until I landed on Reisman's keys. He had only four: one for his truck, one for his apartment, one for the door of his storage unit, and the last, a small padlock key, must have been for the storage bay door.

I reinstalled one of the key-copying apps that I'd put on the phone the cops confiscated. The app asked for my location, then showed a map of nearby stores that printed keys. I chose one on Rockville Pike south of Shady Grove. I would pass it on the way home.

I skipped the truck key and the padlock key and selected photos of the two that looked like they fit door locks. When I got to the store half an hour later, they were ready.

I wouldn't try to enter Reisman's storage space in daylight. My current situation looked bad enough, with eyewitness identifications, security footage, and all the photos the cops had found on my phone. I didn't need to be seen entering the victim's storage space with a stolen key. I would have to do that under cover of night.

When I got back to my apartment, I called Anton Durant.

"I have some questions for you."

"Shoot," he said.

"Have you seen the security videos from Reisman's building?"

"I saw them the other day and I got my own copies today."

"How do they look?"

"Grainy. Bad. But like you. We have footage from the parking lot cameras as well. They show you parking by the service entrance in back just before the murder, getting out, entering the building. You're practically running when you come back out. Your car leaves the lot in a hurry."

"My car?"

"BMW 3 series, right?"

"Can you read the tags?"

"Not from those cameras."

"Then how do you know it's mine?"

"Claire, I can work on the evidence at trial, hammer home all those doubts and make the jury so confused they'll forget what they're there to decide. *If* you want this to go to trial. But with all the other evidence, all the witnesses, the photos on your phone... Let me put it this way, even if I remove one piece of the jigsaw puzzle, the jury still sees the big picture."

Anton and I were too far apart on this matter to have a productive discussion, so I changed the subject.

"Lehmann hired me."

"You already told me that."

"No, the real Lehmann. He wants to know who killed Reisman."

"Claire?" This was the first time I'd heard Anton confused.

"I have another question," I said.

"Are you in your right mind?"

"What would it take to get the cops to look into the possibility that someone else did this?"

"Won't happen," Anton said flatly. "When they have a case as solid as this, they want to seal it. They have no interest in exonerating you."

"What is your so-called second-best investigator doing for me right now?"

"My so-called second-best investigator is a person well-placed who I do not want to expose. She feeds me good information. She can also pull some strings inside the system."

"Is she available to work with me? To help me figure out what happened here? I could really use some help, and, Anton, if you knew me, you'd know what a big thing it is for me to ask."

"Claire?"

"What?"

"I understand this is a traumatic event. It's natural for the mind to try to deny what happened. You feel trapped and you want to squirm out."

"I'm not denying what happened. I'm saying it didn't happen the way you or Kowalczyk say it happened. I have to get out of this. I have to!"

"Claire, we're going to have another meeting, you and I, and I'll lay out our case more fully. As I said, you have every right to defend yourself against a psychologically unstable man in a dangerous situation."

"You're not listening, Anton. I didn't kill the man."

"Juries understand self-defense. It's just the fact that you fled and never reported it. That looks bad. It's going to work against you. And the fact that you said nothing about self-defense to the cops when you could have. Like I said, it's reasonable and it's allowed under the law."

"Someone murdered a man who didn't deserve to be murdered."

"You need to sleep on this, Claire. Maybe see a doctor. Maybe get some anxiety meds."

"And that person is running free."

"Okay, good luck telling *that* story. Do you understand what a trial is? It's our story against the prosecutor's story. Whoever tells the most compelling story wins. A woman trapped in an apartment with a crazy man, with no one and nothing to defend her, that's a compelling story. A woman denying what she did—even if she had every right to do it—doesn't look good. It doesn't breed sympathy in the minds of her peers."

"But it's not what happened."

"Okay. So tell me what happened then. Tell me a story better than the one the prosecutor is going to tell."

I sat quietly biting my nails.

"If you can't convince *me*, you'll never convince a jury."

I hung up with a sense of defeat. I had planned on walking down 18th Street for Ethiopian food, but now I felt too depressed to make the effort. My appetite was gone.

I watched two episodes of *Orange is the New Black* and decided I wouldn't fare well in prison. At dark I picked up Chinese food and brought it back to the apartment.

I browsed aimlessly through half the internet, looking for clues on Buzz DiNardo, hoping something new might have magically appeared since this afternoon.

No luck.

Then I looked up Roscoe Lehmann. I already knew he had no online presence because I had looked him up before I met him. Before I met his imposter, that is. Lehmann's name appeared on his company website, but there was no photo. His name showed up in a few other places, mainly in connection with his business.

On the third page of search results, he was mentioned in his son's obituary. George Lehmann, victim of a boating accident in the Chesapeake Bay four years ago, was survived by his father Roscoe and sister Mary.

I thought back to the photos in Lehmann's office. Five years ago, he looked happy and energetic. Then he had aged dramatically, his face lined with sorrow.

I wondered if he had wanted his son to take over the business.

I could ask him directly.

Or I could ask someone else.

22

During my days in the corporate world, when buyers sent me in for due diligence, I learned to trust my gut. There was always someone in the organization I was investigating who had some special knowledge, and I could usually find them and dig it out.

Today, my gut told me to talk to Carl Graves. When we toured the warehouse together, he was open and forthright. A plain-spoken man who got to the point.

But there was one thing he said obliquely and then dismissed.

Roscoe's good people. I got to know him on a professional level. We think alike. 'Bout business, anyway. The family stuff, I stay out of.

Graves had been with Lehmann eleven years. He was the one employee of the year whose photo Lehmann kept in his office. If he respected Lehmann and they thought alike, why would he want to stay out of Lehmann's family business?

I didn't want to talk to him at work. Detective Kowalczyk mentioned that Graves had identified me as the woman who came to inspect the warehouse. That meant he was officially a witness. Any contact I had with him could be construed as witness tampering by a malicious prosecutor, and all prosecutors are malicious when they think you're guilty.

I called Lehmann's showroom and got the number for the Derwood warehouse. I wondered if Graves would even want to talk to me after what had happened to Jake. He did seem to care for the guy. He did stick up for him.

I dialed and a man picked up on the fourth ring.

"Warehouse."

"Is Carl Graves in today?"

"He's here. Want me to get him?"

"Please."

"Can I tell him who's calling?"

"Claire."

"Hang tight, Claire."

Graves picked up a few seconds later, his voice crisp and clear.

"This is Carl."

"Carl?"

"Claire..." He left my name hanging. I didn't know what to make of that.

"I understand you may not want to talk to me after all that's happened recently—"

"Where you at?"

"Home. DC."

"You know this coffee shop, Java Nation?"

"No."

"Down Rockville Pike. Way south of here. North of you. I got a break coming up in an hour. Meet me there?"

"Sure."

Graves spoke as if he'd been expecting my call. The fact that he wanted to meet me far from the warehouse made me hopeful that he had something to say.

* * *

I was finishing my second cup of coffee when he walked in. I stood to greet him. He met me with a nervous smile and a sweaty handshake.

"You want some coffee?" I asked.

He shook his head. "I got five minutes max, and I'll still be late getting back. Not that I have to explain myself to a supervisor." He pulled out a chair and sat. "I *am* the supervisor. Which means I'm the example. If my boys see me slacking, they'll start slacking. What's up?"

"I wanted to ask you about George Lehmann."

Graves sucked in air through his teeth, shook his head uneasily. "I was wondering when this was coming."

"He died four years ago."

Graves nodded.

"And Roscoe looks like he's gone downhill since then."

"It hit him hard."

"Was he grooming George to take over the company?"

Graves nodded. The rising tension in his body, and the fact that he responded without words told me I was getting close to something uncomfortable.

"Do you know what happened?"

"Got killed in a boating accident."

"You know anything about it?"

Graves shook his head, rubbed his palms on his pants.

"Why did you say you were wondering when this was coming?"

"Roscoe said if you contact me, I should talk."

"But you're not really talking."

Graves was quiet for a long moment. I could see beads of sweat along his brow. At last he said in carefully measured words, "Look, I don't like being put in this position. Roscoe's been good to me. I'm loyal to the man. I think he knows what I think. I think he believes what I believe. He just can't say it, so he's trying to get me to say it. But I'm not going to say it." He shook his head. "No ma'am. Uh-uh."

He stood and pushed his chair in.

"If Roscoe asks, tell him I talked to you, just like he asked. I'm sorry for the position you're in, but I got a family to look out for. I think what I think, and I keep my mouth shut, and that's how the world holds together. You have a good day, Claire."

I chased him through the door.

"Wait. You have to tell me something. Why did you say you stay out of Lehmann's family business?"

"Because I do."

"What happened to George?"

"Whatever the news said." He turned and walked to his car. "Tell Roscoe I met you. Tell him I talked. I did what he asked."

23

Only two accounts of George Lehmann's death remained online, a single paragraph in the Washington Post, and two paragraphs from The Annapolis Capital Gazette. All I could glean from them was that the accident happened around dusk on a warm July evening while George Lehmann was waterskiing on the Chesapeake Bay. A police boat brought his body into the marina at Deale two hours after his sister called 911.

The wealthy keep their tragedies out of the news as much as possible, while the tragedies of the poor are overlooked. Death is so mundane, it only earns attention when it taints a politician or celebrity, or when the details are lurid enough to horrify the public in the way the public loves to be horrified.

If any details of this particular death remained, they wouldn't be found in the electronic bits of the internet, but in the mortal memory of a living witness.

The drive from Rockville to the Chesapeake took an hour and twenty minutes. When I arrived, a cool wind was picking up off the water as dark thunderheads steamed up from the south.

The marina office doubled as a store, selling drinks, snacks, sunscreen, fishing tackle—all the things that might slip a boater's mind before a trip.

The young woman behind the counter looked like a college student on summer break in her white Phillips Seafood t-shirt. She was sipping a milkshake and looking at her phone. The sun had bronzed her skin and bleached the hairs of her arms to a pale gold.

"Can I help you?" She raised her eyes from the phone and smiled, the straw still in her mouth.

"I want to talk to someone about an accident."

Her eyes widened. "You crash your boat?"

"No. This is about something that happened four years ago."

"Oh, phew." She smiled again. "That was before my time."

"You know anyone who might have been around then?"

She leaned back and looked out the side window toward the slips.

"Follow me." We went out the front door. "You see the Bristol down near the end?" She pointed with the straw of her shake.

"Which one?"

"The forty-five-footer with the dark blue hull. Red cooler aft."

"Okay."

"That's Rook. He's been here twenty years. Twenty summers," she corrected. "He spends the winters in the Keys."

"Summer works," I said. "Summer is all I need. Thank you."

"Mmm hmm." She spun on her heel, straw in mouth, and returned to the shop. A blast of cool wind slammed the door behind her, and the first fat drops of what promised to be a drenching rain splatted onto the dock.

I watched a man emerge from the cockpit as I walked toward the Bristol. Skinny legs, pot belly, white beard, Bermuda shorts, striped polo shirt, no shoes or socks. He pulled a bottle from the open cooler, slapped the top down, and ducked back below deck.

The drops began to fall more thickly. To the south, grey sheets of rain raked the bay. As the wind kicked up, the water slapped against the hulls, thumping boats against the dock. I ran as the clouds began to unload. By the time I ducked into the Bristol's cabin, my hair and shoulders were wet, and the noise of the rain had risen to a roar.

The dark cabin smelled of salt spume and stale laundry.

"I been prayin' ten years for a woman to fall into my lap, and it looks like the Lord finally heard me! Hallelujah!"

The leather-skinned old man at the table had a playful smile.

"I'm just kiddin' now. What can I do you for? You come to visit old Rook, or you just trying to get out of the rain? 'Cause no one's been in that much of a hurry to see me since I was paymaster back in my crabbing days."

I shook the rain off my hands. "I was looking for someone who might have been here four years ago when there was a boating accident."

"And you are?"

"Claire Chastain. Investigator."

"A cop?"

"No. Private."

"Want a beer?" He raised his bottle to show me what he was drinking. Rolling Rock.

"No, but thank you."

"Have a seat."

I took the seat across the table.

"You got a specific accident in mind?"

"A guy named George Lehmann. He was waterskiing."

"Sure, sure. Lehmann's been coming here for years. Longer than I been coming. You know them?"

"I know Roscoe."

He chuckled. "How is Roscoe?"

I thought about that for a moment. "I'm not sure."

"He ain't been the same since George died."

I looked at him curiously, trying to place his accent. "You from here?"

"Nope." He took a swig of his beer. "Calvert County."

"That's five minutes south of here."

"Yup. This is Anne Arundel, and I ain't from here. Sure you don't want a beer?"

"No, but thanks again."

"Joint?"

"I don't smoke."

"Got some edibles."

"Okay, just as a general principle, I don't like anything that makes my mind feel disorganized and out of control."

"What do you do for fun?"

"That's a good question. I don't actually know."

Now that my eyes were better adjusted to the dark, I took a look around. This was the kitchen, and it looked like Rook did a pretty good job of keeping it clean. I could see a sliver of the next room. Piled with clothing and junk, it looked like the sorting room at Goodwill, only the garbage and the good stuff hadn't been separated yet.

"Were you here in the summer of 2016, when George Lehmann died?"

"I was here when they brought his body in." He took a swig of beer. "That was a sad sight. A sad, sad sight. His dad was on the dock. They told him to stay away, but he wouldn't. There's a difference between knowing someone's dead and actually seeing it."

"You know what happened?"

"He was out waterskiing. Taking turns with his sister. He'd drive while she skied, she'd drive while he skied."

"And George took a spill?"

Rook shrugged. "Everyone falls."

"Was the weather bad?"

"Naw. Just hot. But it was gettin' dark. See, there's the problem." He tipped his bottle toward me as if offering a toast to his own insight. "The girl could handle a boat. You watch her come in, she'd cut the engine forty yards out, bring her in on a drift and kiss the dock every time. But your skills don't matter if it's too dark to see."

"Was it dusk? Or night?"

"Twilight. He fell, she went round to pick him up and ran right over him. She called in on her phone and two boats went out to help. George didn't wear a vest when he skied. They had trouble finding the body in the dark. Police boat picked him up a while later, after they sent the girl back to shore. She wasn't no help. Imagine you kill your own brother. You're in no state of mind to aid a search. They brought her back here. I think Roscoe knew the outcome as soon as he saw her. They used to have a house up there."

Rook tipped his bottle vaguely toward the shore.

"Roscoe took her up there, then he came back. Don't know if it was the right thing to leave her alone just then. They ain't been close since. Not that they was before. But a thing like that..."

Rook shook his head and drained off the last of his beer. "That's the kind of thing that can break up a family. Grief. You know, everyone deals differently."

"What about the mom?"

"Mary Margaret?"

"Was that her name?"

"She died when the kids were young. Roscoe was flying solo with those two. And trying to run a business."

"Was there an investigation? Into George's death?"

Rook shrugged. "Cops wrote it up, I guess. Why all the interest?"

"I'm not sure yet."

"You close to Roscoe?"

"I'm doing some work for him."

"He still selling appliances?"

"Still is."

"Well, you see him, you tell him to come out and have a beer with old Rook."

"I'll tell him," I said. The heavy drone of rain on the deck above had thinned to a gentle patter. "Thank you for your help."

"You're most welcome, ma'am."

As I left the cabin, I heard him mutter, "Ah yes. The Lord giveth and the Lord taketh away. How 'bout the next one stays a while? She ain't gotta be as pretty as that. A homebody'll do just fine."

24

I waited till after midnight to approach Reisman's storage space. I drove through two residential neighborhoods on the way, circling darkened blocks of houses and checking my mirrors to see if anyone was following. The last thing I needed was Kowalczyk or the prosecutor seeing what I was up to.

I parked a block from the facility so my car wouldn't appear on security cameras. A steady rain soaked through my canvas shoes. An extra-large poncho hid the shape of my body, and every strand of hair was tucked beneath my hood. If I showed up on surveillance cameras, they wouldn't know if I was a man or a woman, fat or thin. They wouldn't know my hair color. I would be just a wet blob in the dark.

I kept my head down to avoid showing my face. The liquid reflection of the blue-white lights splashed up from the pavement as I made my way to Reisman's door.

I tried the first of the two keys I had printed. It turned, and I stepped into the dark. I closed the door behind me and stood dead still listening for sounds of movement. What if the police had sent someone here to wait for me? I waited ten seconds, then twenty. The only sound in the dark stuffy room, besides my soft breathing, was the drip of rainwater from my poncho onto the concrete floor.

The room was stiflingly hot and smelled of cat urine.

I felt for a switch on the wall beside the door. The overhead light came on, dimmer than I had expected, but bright enough to light the place. It took a moment to make sense of what I was looking at.

A stained white sofa—a two-seater—stood atop a dingy, threadbare Persian rug. Before it sat a television on a cheap black stand that might have come from Walmart. The particleboard was warped. The plug from the television lay on the concrete floor, attached to nothing.

To the right was a small dresser, scuffed and scratched. On top of that, a round swivel mirror on a pedestal. Against the far wall, a twin bed neatly made, a nightstand with an old-fashioned ceramic lamp, and a travel chest.

It looked like Reisman had packed his old life into his truck, driven it across country, and reassembled it here. I felt like I was standing in a diorama of the apartment he had left behind in San Luis Obispo. The old worn rug that might have anchored the living room in which Jake and his mother once watched television was covered with fur. The rug and couch smelled of cat urine.

There was no litter box. I didn't think he kept a cat here. It seemed like the cat hair had survived the move, like he kept it on purpose to make the place a more faithful recreation of the only home he had ever known. There was something horribly sad about that. I felt a pang of grief and pity for him. Why on earth would anyone kill such a man?

As far as I could tell, the bed hadn't been slept in. The chest at its foot was filled with clothing: jeans and sweat pants, t-shirts, sweatshirts, socks. Shapeless, oversized comfort clothes you wear when you're not planning on leaving the house. I couldn't tell if they belonged to Reisman or his mother.

The top drawer of the dresser was filled with papers. The remaining drawers were full of clothes. These definitely belonged to a woman. They hadn't been washed. Why would Jake hang onto these? To keep his mother's scent? The thought gave me a shiver.

I reopened the top drawer and sifted through the papers. Utility bills. Gas, electric, and water, all for an address in San Luis Obispo, all carefully ordered by a compulsive and conscientious mind. They followed a pattern. Three months of bills, each with the payment stub still attached. Then a warning that the utilities would be shut off for non-payment. Then a month of bills with no stubs. Those had been paid. Then the cycle started again.

The bills went back several years. Why would Reisman hang on to them? Maybe to show that for all his troubles, he always did come through in the end? To show the world that he was ultimately dependable? Or maybe he just wanted to reassure himself that, as dark as things looked, they always somehow worked out in the end.

I dumped the contents of an overstuffed manila envelope onto the dresser top. Receipts and owner's manuals for items Reisman or his mother had bought for the apartment. A microwave. A popcorn popper. A stereo with a CD player. Reisman had underlined sections of the microwave manual: warnings about trying to heat metal, suggestions for how to clean the turntable.

Do not run hot glass tray under cold water. That got two underlines. Perhaps Jake had had a word with his mentally ill mother about this.

I slid the manuals and receipts back into the envelope and dug further into the drawer. Warnings from the health department about a sewage odor. A letter from the landlord explaining that Brinley Reisman would be responsible for the plumber's bill. A letter from the court telling Brinley when to appear for her shoplifting hearing.

Beneath the bills and letters that described the outlines of a chronically troubled life, one last manila envelope lay flattened against the bottom of the drawer. It was thin, empty perhaps. It had no markings on either side.

I removed it from the drawer, opened the clasp and found a single page inside. It was too soft and worn to slide out on its own. I had to pull it. The first thing I saw as it emerged, there on the bottom, was the URL of the website from which it had been printed. A genetics testing site.

The paper had been handled so much, it had the feel of limp cloth. I remembered what Squints had told me at Cortona. *He came in clutching that report and he carried it with him everywhere.*

The type on the ragged paper had faded beneath Reisman's obsessive touch. I had to hold it under the bare overhead light to read it.

What would lead a troubled, anxious man to drive across the country? A mama's boy who'd lost his mama?

There it was on the page. The sole human being to whom the genetic test could match this lonely man.

Jacob Reisman had a sister.

25

"Okay, let's walk through this." Anton Durant was pacing the carpet behind the couch on which I sat. On his desk by the window, his laptop stood open. Beside it, a notebook and an open folder of papers.

I was tired from being out late at Reisman's storage space the night before.

"You walked into Reisman's apartment at what time?"

"I don't know. Eight thirty? Nine?" I covered a yawn with both hands.

"According to the neighbor it was eight forty-seven."

"How does she know what minute it was?"

"She's nosy, Claire. Keeps a notebook for all we know. But that's her statement, so we'll go with it. You walked in at eight forty-seven. When the prosecutor asks if that's when you entered, you say yes. That's if I put you on the stand. If!"

My shoulders went up and I sighed loudly. The thought of the prosecutor dictating my story made me angry. He wasn't even there. He didn't and couldn't know what happened, but he was going to make up a story about it, a story constructed on purpose to ruin my life, and he would tell it to a jury right in front of me while I was supposed to nod in agreement.

"Don't do that in the courtroom," Anton commanded. I assumed he meant my tensed shoulders, my angry expression.

"Don't lecture me. Do you have any idea how much this whole situation pisses me off?"

"You need to work on your reactions."

"I *am* working on them. I've been working very hard on myself these last few months."

"Testiness doesn't show well in court."

"You should have seen me a year ago. I swear, I'm a sweetheart compared to that. I promise you I've been working hard."

"Well you're not there yet. Tell me why you picked up the hammer in Reisman's apartment."

"I told you. I felt threatened."

"Like he was going to assault you?"

"Like he wasn't totally in control of his feelings, and possibly not his actions either. He wasn't behaving like an emotionally healthy person, and I wasn't going to take any chances."

"What were you doing in his apartment in the first place?"

"Jesus, Anton! We've been through this!"

"I'm the prosecutor. We haven't been through this. You have to answer in a way that is both factually true and sympathetic to a jury."

He paced past me, and I twisted now to face him. "I got a name and an address."

"What? For who?"

"The guy who pretended to be Lehmann."

"You really want to chase this story?"

"I want one of your investigators to look into it."

"Claire..."

When I stood, he saw my fury. "I'm paying you, goddammit. Investigate!"

"All right, Claire."

"And don't tell me to calm down." My eyes narrowed. "Because I know you were about to."

Anton walked to his desk and picked up a pen. "What's the name?"

"Buzz DiNardo."

He leaned with one hand on the desk and wrote. "Where's he live?"

"Evanston, Illinois. But not really."

"What's that supposed to mean?"

"It means he doesn't exist. It's a fake identity."

Anton looked annoyed. "Well then how does that help us?"

"If he rented a car under that name, he may have flown under it too."

"Flown?"

"He rented a car at Dulles and he returned it to Dulles."

"How do you know that?"

"I went out there and asked. And I also did some research on your investigator, Freddy Ferguson. He was involved in that airline case a few years back. That flight that left gate seventy-six in San Francisco and never made it to Hawaii."

Durant stared like he didn't know what to make of me.

"He was working for the airline on that case," I said. "Right?"

"Yeah."

"Does he have an in with them or with TSA? Would he be able to find out where a guy named Buzz DiNardo flew in from? Where he flew back to?"

Durant looked at me in amazement. "This is what you do when I'm not around?"

"This is what I do, Anton."

"All right." He straightened up and dropped the pen. "I can ask Freddy to look into it. Now let's finish our walk-through. We're going to go through this a dozen times in the coming weeks—"

"Uh-uh," I said flatly.

"No?"

"This is a waste of time and it's just going to piss me off." I picked up my shoulder bag and stood to leave.

"I can't help you if you don't cooperate."

"Buzz DiNardo," I called on my way out. "Buzz DiNardo can help."

26

I left Durant's office at noon, ate a quick lunch at the Woodmont Grill then called the Cortona Center and asked if Squints was working that day.

The woman laughed.

"Jerry? He's here. You want to talk to him?"

"Not really," I said, remembering our last encounter. "How late is he working?"

"He'll be here till six."

I got to Cortona before two. A woman sat behind the sliding reception window, her head resting on her hand as she read. She looked up as I approached, frowned, and pushed her papers aside.

Bitch face, I reminded myself. Soften. Look friendly.

I put on a smile, but it didn't work. The woman flung the window open and asked rudely, "What?"

"Hello." It took some effort to muster a polite tone, and I could tell she didn't want to hear it. "I called a little while ago."

I waited for her to take the hint, but she just looked annoyed, like I was an unwanted interruption in already bad day.

"About Squints," I said.

"Oh? You want me to call him down?" Her snotty tone was like acid on the thin veneer of my patience.

"Why are you so rude?"

"Why don't you ask yourself the same question?" She rattled the glass shut with a bang and picked up the phone.

I could hear her through the glass. "Jerry, your girlfriend's here."

Everyone in that place seemed to have an attitude problem. I changed my mind about wanting to be locked up there if I ever went nuts.

She hung up and pointed over my shoulder.

I turned to look, expecting to see Squints, but there was no one there. Just the two black leather couches and the plants.

"What?" I asked.

"Have a seat."

I would have sat if she hadn't commanded so rudely.

I stood by the building entrance with my arms crossed, looking out through the glass doors at the parking lot and the trees.

After a few minutes, the elevator slid open and Squints came out squinting. He had a loping walk, arms swinging loosely at his side. He didn't seem to see me until I unfolded my arms and took a step forward.

"Over here," I said.

"Oh, you again." He couldn't have been less pleased to see me.

"Let's talk outside," I said. I couldn't take the vibe of the receptionist glaring at us on top of Squints' childish surliness.

"Sure." Squints loped past without stopping. He didn't hold the door for me.

He continued along the concrete walk around the side of the building, saying nothing. He never turned to see if I was following.

At the patio around back, he took a seat at one of the shaded tables. I walked around to the other side and pulled out a chair.

"You know why I'm here?" I asked.

"Do I care?"

"You told me Jake came in here clutching a paper he'd printed off the internet."

"And?"

"He had a sister."

"Oh! My! Gawd!" he said in mock surprise.

"What's the matter with everyone here?"

"What's the matter with *you*?"

I took a deep breath to calm myself and tried to reframe my expectations. Be patient, I thought. Whatever his problem is, it's his problem, not mine. If he wants to act like a twelve-year-old, I'm going to talk to him like a twelve-year-old.

"Jacob Reisman," I said slowly, "had a sister named Maggie Smith."

Squints rolled his eyes and groaned.

"There are hundreds of Maggie Smiths in the US. There are dozens in the DC area. I'm trying to discover if Reisman's sister lived anywhere around here."

"And you're asking me?" He sounded incredulous, almost offended.

"I'm asking you," I said patiently. "Did Jake ever speak of her while he was here? Do you know if he ever contacted her?"

Squints tapped his fingers on the metal tabletop and glared angrily at me. He squinted to see if his angry look was getting through, but I don't think he could see my face well enough to tell. He gave up squinting and looked confused.

"Do you know if *she* ever contacted *him*?" I asked.

"Why do you waste my time?"

"Visitors have to sign in, don't they?"

"You know they do."

I leaned in and asked in a low voice, slowly and clearly, "Did Maggie Smith ever sign in here?"

Squints frowned angrily.

"Did she?" I repeated.

"You're a bitch and a nasty one too. Stop playing games."

"Answer the question."

"You can't mess with my head the way you messed with his, because I'm not crazy."

"What are you talking about?"

Squints stood abruptly, pointing angrily at me as his chair fell over behind him.

"You're Maggie Smith."

He turned and left.

27

After leaving Cortona, I stopped at an ATM and picked up two hundred dollars cash. I called ahead to make sure Frankie was working at the Dulles rental agency. The clock on the dash told me it was almost three. Traffic on the Outer Loop of the Beltway was backed up from the Dulles Access Road in Virginia to River Road in Maryland. The Waze app showed a solid red line of bumper-to-bumper traffic.

The air conditioning struggled to cool the car in sweltering fumes beneath the hazy afternoon sun. The motorists around me were frustrated and angry, honking at cars that had nowhere to go. When I could, I nestled in the shade of a tractor-trailer.

Anton Durant called as I crawled across the American Legion Bridge into Virginia.

"I got something for you."

"What's that?"

"My investigator, Freddy, says Buzz DiNardo flew from Las Vegas to Chicago to Dulles on July 12th. He never returned though. It was a one-way ticket. Ferguson got that from his contact at the airline. You want to tell me more about this meeting you had with fake Lehmann?"

"Later. I'm onto something else at the moment."

"Something jury-worthy? Better than the prosecutor's story?"

"Not yet."

I reached the Dulles toll road at 4:25. By the time I rolled into the rental lot, it was past five.

Frankie was scuffing along beside a Jaguar SUV, wiping beaded water off the windows with a rag. I parked near the office and walked across the hot asphalt.

"Let the drops dry on the glass," he said as I approached, "and they leave spots." His face was bright red, whether from sunburn or the ninety-nine-degree heat, I couldn't tell.

He balled up the rag and dried the side mirror. "Days like this, I like to work inside."

I reminded myself of Durant's advice for charming juries. Smile. Look pleasant. It still doesn't come naturally when my mind is on business.

"I have something for you to do inside."

"Wait till my manager leaves."

"When's that?"

"Five minutes."

I followed him to the rear of the Jaguar and watched him wipe down the back window.

"Last time I was here," I said, "the guy asked me if I was returning when I drove in."

"Tico?"

"Is that his name?"

"Far as I know."

"Do you rent BMWs here? Because most places don't."

He pointed to a white 5-series in the corner of the lot. "We rent the high end. People want a Kia, they go to Avis. They want a Mercedes, a Jaguar convertible, they come here."

He gave me a pointed look then nodded toward the office door. I turned to see the manager, Ms. Efficient, on her way to her car.

Frankie moved to the passenger side. "Wait till she drives out." He wiped down the windows, the door handles and the mirror. When his manager's car left, he said, "Come on."

Inside, he logged on to the computer at the end of the counter furthest from the office door.

"Whatcha want this time?"

"I want to know if you rented a blue BMW 3 series on July twelfth or thirteenth."

"Hold on." He pecked at the keyboard with his index fingers and said under his breath, "Joo… lye… thirteen."

He clicked, and I watched him scroll the mouse wheel.

"July thirteenth we rented a 5 series hybrid."

"What about the twelfth?" I picked up a brochure from the counter rack and slid five twenties into it as Frankie pecked at the keys.

"Joo... lye... the twelfth."

I laid the brochure beside the keyboard. Frankie slid it into his pocket, squinted, and scrolled.

"Nope. But hang on. July fourteenth, we rented a blue 330i. 2019 model."

"To Maggie Smith?"

His eyes scanned the page. "To Anna Graham."

"Did you happen to see her?"

He shook his head. "I don't remember the Bimmer or the woman. Coulda been on break when she came in."

"Can you print that out for me?"

"Sure thing." He scrolled up and clicked, then walked to the whirring printer at the far end of the counter.

I followed him, staying on the customer side.

"Do you clean all the cars when they come back?"

"I do some. Tico does some. If it's not my shift, it could be a couple other people."

He pulled the first two sheets off the printer and waited for the rest.

"Do you write up damage? Stains? That sort of thing?"

"If it's bad, it comes out of the customer deposit."

"You clean the inside?"

"Damn, you got a lot of questions."

"I need to know. Do you clean the interior?"

"Yeah. Before we send it back out."

He pulled the last two sheets from the printer and handed the stack to me.

"That'll do ya?"

"That'll do. Thank you, Frankie."

"Thank *you*," he said. "Anything else you want to know, I'm here Monday through Friday till six."

I read the printouts in the car, Buzz's SUV rental and her BMW. The BMW was the same model and color as mine, but a year newer. Black interior. If it came back with a drop or two of blood, no one would have noticed.

Ms. Graham picked it up on the morning of Tuesday the fourteenth, fifteen minutes after Buzz DiNardo returned the SUV. She had reserved it for a week, but returned it early morning on Thursday the sixteenth, the day after Reisman's murder.

I called Anton Durant.

"Can I get your guy Freddy to check something else for me? You have a pen?"

"How come you never say hello?"

"Write this down. Anna Graham, Fort Collins, Colorado."

"What about her?"

"See if she was on the same flight as DiNardo. Also, if he can, get the names of all the female passengers who were on both flights with DiNardo. Vegas to Chicago to Dulles on the twelfth."

I had a feeling that if DiNardo wasn't travelling under his real name, neither was the woman who accompanied him. The woman whose scent I had smelled on the stairs in Lehmann's house.

I laid the papers on the passenger seat and headed back to Maryland.

28

On the drive to Potomac, I considered calling ahead to make sure Lehmann was home, but I decided against it. I didn't want to give him a chance to say no, or to put me off with some excuse about how this wasn't a good time.

I had a pretty good idea now what was happening. It bothered me that he had withheld information that could have saved me a lot of time and angst.

If I could confirm what I was thinking, we could move forward. If not, I'd be back to square one, and my mind would race all night trying to make sense of where the case now stood.

When I got to Lehmann's house, the swollen red sun was sinking in the western haze, though it wouldn't dip below the horizon for another hour. There were two cars in the drive: one white, one black. The black one, a Dodge Charger, looked like an unmarked police car.

I pulled in behind it. As soon as I cut the engine, the door of the Charger flew open. A uniformed Montgomery County officer stepped out, wiping his hands on his pants while he chewed a bulging mouthful of God knows what.

He loomed over me when I opened the door, blocking my exit. My first thought was that Detective Kowalczyk had sent him to intercept me, but how could Kowalczyk have known I'd be here?

"You have an appointment?" His name tag said Gutierrez.

"I'm here to see Roscoe Lehmann."

"That's not what I asked."

"I don't have an appointment. I work for him."

He didn't seem to believe me. He looked at me like he was trying to match my face to a description. "What's your name?"

"Claire Chastain."

"You sure?"

"I think I know my own name."

"You have ID?"

A voice called from the house. "Let her in, Mike."

Gutierrez turned. "You sure? She says she's—"

"I know who she is," Lehman said from the door. His white shirt was unbuttoned at the collar and his tie was gone. He started toward us.

"You want me inside?" Gutierrez asked. "You know she's on bail."

"I know." Lehmann was on the drive now. "Claire, come in."

"Call if you need me," Gutierrez said.

When we got inside, I asked Lehmann if the county had stationed Gutierrez out front or if Lehmann had hired him.

"I hired him."

"You have something to fear?"

I was pretty sure by this point he did.

"Old age is full of fears. Why did you come?"

"I want to look at something."

"Be my guest."

We walked down the hall toward the kitchen, stopping at the stairs. Lehmann stood beside me. I looked at the discolored space on the wall where two heavy wall anchors once supported a painting.

"You collect art?"

Lehmann shook his head. "It's beyond my means. Since Home Depot and Lowes got into the game, I'm barely holding on."

"Where is this painting?" I pointed toward the space.

"In the basement. I can't bear to look at it."

"You mind if I do?"

"Down the stairs," he said. "Past the pool table. There's a door in the panel wall. It's not obvious, but if you look for it, you'll find it."

Lehmann looked tired, resigned.

"I'll be in my office," he sighed. "Take your time."

The stairs led to a large, open rec room with a bar and pool table. The orange evening sun shone in through sliding glass doors that led out to the pool deck. The pool table was full-size with red felt and leather mesh pockets. The cues on the wall were neatly arranged in the rack, but most of them had no tips. To the left, near the patio doors, tiny holes in the paneling surrounded a dart board. In my mind's eye, I could see the parties the Lehmann kids must have thrown here in high school.

I saw the narrow gap in the panels that indicated a door. It had no handle, so I pushed. Nothing happened. I pushed the other edge. The door clicked and opened outward with a rush of warm musty air.

Deflated rafts and pool rings covered the floor inside. On top of those, goggles, swim fins, a snorkel and mask. Little torpedoes for divers to retrieve. An old book of word puzzles, the kind you find at the supermarket checkout, lay moldering on top of it all.

And to the right, propped against the wall, a painting in a carved gilt frame. When I moved it away from the wall, the puzzle book fell onto the rec room carpet. I dragged the painting out and leaned it against the side of the pool table. The heavy gold frame blazed with life in the glow of the orange sun.

There was Roscoe Lehmann in happier days, wearing a tennis sweater and dark slacks. His face showed the proud smile of a man who had gotten all he wanted from life, and the satisfaction of knowing he had worked for it.

The young man to his right, a younger version of himself, intelligent and gentle looking, must have been George.

To his left, daughter Mary could have been mistaken for me at first glance. Same dark hair, same facial structure, same eye color. She stood shoulder-height beside her father, the same as me. Her lips were thinner than mine and her eyes less friendly. I know how I come off to others. All business, right to the point, don't waste my time. Not exactly friendly, but not this. Not what I saw here. This woman's eyes were calculating. Look into them for a second or two, you might wonder what she's thinking. Keep looking, and you might decide you'd rather not know.

Now the reactions made sense. The way Buzz DiNardo stared at me when I first came into this house, Lehmann's look of surprise at our initial meeting in his office. He couldn't take his eyes off me. And the inexplicable rudeness of the myopic Squints. *You're a bitch, and a nasty one too.*

Jake Reisman had a sister, Lehmann's daughter, and she had visited Jake at Cortona. What had she said to him there? Something unpleasant.

You can't mess with my head the way you messed with his, Squints said, *because I'm not crazy.*

What did she say to mess with Jake's head?

In his apartment, Reisman asked me, seemingly out of the blue, *Do I look like the kind of person you would hate?*

Had his sister told him she hated him?

And those photos in the manila envelope. The ones I thought looked like me. They were all versions of her.

Our exchange in Jake's apartment:

Jake, you're scaring me.

I don't mean to, but this is what happens... you back away. Would you say mean things about me to my face? Would you hate me?

I left the painting where it was and went to shut the panel door. On the way, I picked up the puzzle book and flipped through the pages. Crosswords, anagrams, cryptograms, and word searches. They'd all been completed in a girl's looping hand. I flipped to the first page inside the cover. She had written her name. M. M. Lehmann.

Upstairs, I found Roscoe Lehmann reclining in the Aeron chair behind his desk, a wet washcloth over his eyes.

"Any chance your daughter Mary's middle name is Margaret?"

"I'd say there's a hundred percent chance." Lehmann's voice sounded small and distant. He didn't move or adjust the cloth.

My phone rang. I didn't recognize the number so I let it go to voicemail.

"Is she married?" I asked.

"Divorced."

"From a man named Smith?"

"Robert Smith."

"And she goes by Maggie?"

"Since her mother died."

"Is that why the cop's in the driveway? Are you that scared of your own daughter?"

Lehmann sighed, removed the washcloth, and rubbed his tired eyes. "I don't know that fear is the right word. It feels more like dread. Like the dread of something inevitable."

"We need to talk."

"We certainly do."

My phone rang again. Same number.

"Hold on, Roscoe. Let me get rid of whoever this is."

29

I went to the kitchen to take the call. It was Anton's detective, Freddy Ferguson.

"I have something for you."

"A name?"

"There were four women on the Vegas to Chicago flight who were also on Chicago to Dulles. I think the one you want is the one who sat next to Buzz DiNardo on both flights."

"What's her name?"

"Angela M. Ginhem, that's G-I-N-H-E-M. Spokane, Washington. I can give you her full address, but it won't be worth anything. The building's been unoccupied for ten years according to the city's motion to condemn the property."

"Thank you," I said. "That's very helpful."

"I'll give you another bit of information."

"What's that?"

"If these two, DiNardo and Ginhem, had fake IDs good enough to get past TSA, they're not amateurs. The people you're looking for are organized."

"That's good to know."

"You think? I actually think it's bad."

"No, I mean it's good to be aware of the fact."

"Anton says you're a spark plug."

"Does he? I always thought of spark plugs as short and fat, but I'll give Anton the benefit of the doubt. I read about your work on that airline case. Gate 76. Someday, I want to pick your brain."

"Well that might be someday soon. I'm wrapping up a case in LA."

"Listen, I have to go. Thanks again."

30

When I returned to the office, I found Lehmann looking more alert. Looking like he wanted to talk and get a few things off his chest. He motioned me to sit, but I had too many things on my mind.

"Why didn't you tell me about your daughter when you hired me?"

"You have a better understanding of the situation when you have to piece it together yourself. Besides, I have only hunches and suspicions. Those don't hold up in court. Evidence does, and that's what I hired you to gather. Tell me what you've learned."

"Reisman was your son."

"Yes."

"You paid for him to stay at Cortona. You must have. He couldn't have afforded it on his own."

"He should have stayed longer, but he desperately wanted a normal life. He wanted to prove that he could do what everyone else could do. Hold a job, pay his bills, live independently. At bottom, I think, he was looking for respect. Just a fundamental sense of confidence and self-respect."

"You paid for his apartment?"

Lehmann nodded.

"And all that furniture? You bought that for him?"

"I gave him a credit card. He bought it. He wanted to do it himself."

"When I walked into your office—"

"I knew what had happened the minute I laid eyes on you."

"You were staring. I didn't know why."

"You know now."

"But you didn't want to tell me then what you suspected? That your own daughter killed your son? That she hired me to follow him, to go to his apartment, to be in the wrong place at the wrong time so all the witnesses would think they saw *me* covered in blood, would identify *me* to the police?"

"Claire." He tented his fingertips together as he leaned back in his chair and raised his moistening eyes toward the ceiling. For a moment, I wasn't sure he'd be able to hold himself together.

"Claire, I have suspected a number of things over the years—"

"You suspected she killed George? Hit him with the boat on purpose?"

"I've never said that."

"But you thought it?"

"Some suspicions are too terrible to bear, and even more terrible to speak. Especially if they're wrong. What do you do with such thoughts? You wither under them. They lodge in your heart and slowly they kill you."

"This is the topic that you and Carl Graves don't speak about? The boating accident?"

"This is the one."

"Couldn't Carl assuage your fears? If Carl thought better of your daughter? If he thought she didn't have it in her to kill, wouldn't he have said so? To comfort you?"

"If Carl thought... Oh, God, Claire. Let's not get into this."

"No, Roscoe." I sat in one of the green upholstered chairs in front of the desk. "We're going to walk though this from the beginning. Tell me about your daughter and George and that evening on the bay."

I could see how much it pained him to start. When he was confident and strong and in his element, nothing in him would have told me he was related to Jake Reisman. Now, in his moment of weakness, oppressed by grief and anxiety, I saw the resemblance for the first time. It was faint, but it was there in the pale blue eyes that hesitated to meet mine.

"Take your time, Roscoe."

After a long while, he began.

"Everyone processes grief differently. Some people rage. Some collapse. Some ice over. When George died, I collapsed. I didn't go to work. I could barely leave the house for months. I stayed here and Maggie took care of me, as much as she's capable of taking care of anyone."

"What do you mean? As much as she's capable?"

"Only two things matter in Maggie's world. Maggie and money. She tolerates others insofar as they serve her, and she resents them insofar as they make claims on her. For years, I thought her coldness was the result of losing her mother so young, of not knowing how to process those emotions. A person can get stuck in loss, especially if it happens when they're young and they don't have the tools to work through the grief. I blame myself for that. For not getting her more help."

"How old was she when she lost her mom?"

"Five." Lehmann reflected sadly. "A tender age."

He seemed lost in thought for a moment, perhaps remembering his wife, perhaps picturing his daughter at five. I could see a feeling coming over him. Grief? Fear? I couldn't tell, but he cut off whatever train of thought had led him to it and went on speaking in a controlled voice.

"Over time I started to wonder whether there wasn't something organically wrong with her. We're all wired differently at birth. We have different temperaments, different innate levels of conscience and empathy that experience will sometimes nurture and sometimes destroy. Conscience and empathy were never her strong suits. Nature didn't have much to work with in her case."

"That's a hard thing for a man to say about his own child."

"Is it? I'm going to make a drink. Would you like one?"

"No, but thank you."

"Well, I need one. If you'll excuse me for a moment."

He went to the kitchen and returned with a glass of what I guessed was scotch on ice. He held the glass up to the window and moved it in little circles, peering through the golden liquor into the red of the setting sun.

"The months after George's death are a blur to me," he said slowly. "Looking back, I can't distinguish one day from the next. But I do remember my feelings of frustration and helplessness at Maggie's lack of emotion. To lose a sibling is bad enough. To be the one who killed him, whether or not it was intentional—"

"Do you think she killed him on purpose?" I wanted him to say it out loud, at least for his own sake. I wanted to see if he could give me a clear yes or no.

"I could never bring myself to say that. Never in a million years."

"But you think it."

Lehmann sipped his drink, then walked to the desk and put it down on the bare wood.

"I have reconstructed the scene a million times in my mind. She could handle the Nautique as well as anyone."

"The ski boat?"

Lehmann nodded. "And her eyes are sharp as eagle's. The accident happened at twilight. It wasn't yet completely dark. George knew to call when she was getting near. He knew to wave. But it wasn't those details that led me to think... to think what I cannot say. It was the way she behaved afterward. She showed no emotion. All she talked about was her husband and their money troubles. Why fixate on that? Did she need to displace one painful thought with a less painful one? An irreparable loss with a fixable one? Was that her way of coping?

"When I tried to talk with her about the accident, she refused. I was seeing a grief counsellor at the time. He told me if Maggie wouldn't talk about it, it was probably because she couldn't. I should drop the subject until she brought it up. And by the way, she never went to counselling. She refused to go with me. An event like that, it helps to process as a family. But she wasn't interested.

"After a few weeks, she went back to Las Vegas, back to the husband she was always complaining about. I don't know what their lives were like, except that when they weren't rolling in money, they were broke. There was no in-between. She married a gambler, you know.

"They say girls marry their fathers. Well, Maggie didn't. I never liked or respected the man. I was always careful with money. This man was reckless. I like stability. It's been the guiding principle in how I run my business and my life. Maggie didn't respect stability or anyone who strove for it, or any element of society that embraced it.

"You—" He pointed at me. "She would hate you. Anyone who plays by the rules. Anyone willing to work within the system...

"Her choice of husband was a thorough repudiation of everything I stood for, and the worst part of it is, I'm sure the marriage made her miserable. Though she's as reckless as he is, she hates being without money. Sometimes I wonder if she stayed in that life so long just to spite me. You know, allowing herself to be unhappy because she thought it would make me more unhappy."

"You said they're divorced? Who left whom?" I wanted Lehmann to clarify, just so I had it straight.

"She divorced him. He was a savage man. And she was his equal. They're criminals. Both of them."

"That's a harsh thing to say about your own daughter."

"Is it harsh to speak the truth? How about hiring a police guard to sit in the driveway twenty-four-seven? Isn't that more harsh? Actions speak louder than words, don't they?"

Lehmann described the period after George's death. Maggie stayed with him for eight weeks. She wasn't getting along with her husband at the time. He was out of money. Otherwise, Lehmann said, she would have gone back to him immediately.

"My doctor gave me anti-anxiety medicine, tranquilizers and sleeping pills. He prescribed the same pills to Maggie, but she never took them. She gave them to me. She was double dosing me, turning me into a zombie. She'd take me out in public, around friends, and point out what a weak mental state I was in. How I could barely put my words together. It was part of an organized campaign. She paraded me in front of friends and associates to demonstrate that I wasn't mentally competent, so she could get power of attorney."

"To do what?"

"To make all decisions for my health, my personal property and my business."

"Full power of attorney?"

"Yes. She wanted my money. The house. My lawyer put a stop to that. Never underestimate the value of a good attorney. They're your best ally in times of trouble. Eight weeks after George died, Maggie went back to Vegas, to that horrid man. A year later, she left him. Put him in jail, actually."

"For what?"

"Abuse. He was a savage man, and the worst kind. A smooth-talking con artist with a heart of stone. But as I said, she was his equal. She wasn't taken in by him. Maggie uses, she doesn't let others use her. They were partners in crime."

"What kind of crime?"

"Anything to get money. As I said, he was a gambler. They had *that* to feed. I know that twice, in two different states, Maggie was accused of identity fraud, taking out loans and lines of credit under other people's names. She'd show up with a fake license, forged documents saying she was someone else, an actual woman whom she had researched, who owned property and could secure a loan. She would show the ID, all the documents, and take out a second mortgage against some poor unsuspecting woman's property. Once she walked off with a hundred and fifty thousand dollars. Another time it was over two hundred thousand. And those are just the ones I know about."

"Was she ever convicted?"

Lehmann shook his head. "Neither case went to trial. I don't know why."

"When's the last time you saw your daughter?"

"When she left after George's death. Four years ago."

"You ever talk to her?"

"She calls once or twice a year asking for money. She blew through a trust fund of one and half million dollars. Or her husband did. Gambled it all away. I don't ask what she's up to or where she is."

"Did you ever think of going to the police? About George's death?"

"With what evidence? It's hard enough to suspect a thing like that, but to bring in the police? To accuse your own family, after it's already been torn apart? That's like pouring gasoline into an open wound. And what evidence could they find? It was just the two of them out in the water without any other witnesses."

Lehmann went back to the window and looked over the yard to where the sun had set.

"Suspicion is toxic," he reflected. "What do you do with a belief that you fear in your gut is true, that you can never prove, that you don't ever want to be true? It becomes a bomb you sit on for the rest of your life. You watch your actions and your words because you don't want to set it off. You engineer your life *around* it, hoping to avoid it, and in doing so, you make it the center of your existence. The very thing you want to avoid."

As much as I felt pity for the man, I also felt he wasn't telling me the whole story. Except in cases of mental illness, it's rare for a single member of a healthy family to go so far astray, to show such psychopathology. In most cases, the whole family is a mess. While the supposedly healthy ones uphold the front of normalcy, the black sheep acts out the symptoms for the rest of them.

I had some pointed questions for Lehmann. His responses and the way he delivered them would tell me a lot.

"You said Maggie blew through a trust fund of a million and half dollars."

"Yes. With her husband."

"Did George also have a trust fund?"

His body stiffened at the question, which told me he knew where I was going.

"Of course."

"Had he tapped into it?"

Lehmann shook his head.

"What happened to his trust when he died?"

"It would have gone to his children, if he had any. Or to his spouse, if he had been married."

"But he wasn't. So, who got the money?"

"Maggie." He said her name almost reluctantly, as if conceding a point he didn't want to concede.

"How much?"

"Over a million."

How long would the legal process take to transfer a trust from one child to another, I wondered. If it was properly structured, eight weeks might be a reasonable amount of time to get the ball rolling, make sure all the paperwork was headed in the right direction. Eight weeks, and then Maggie goes back to her husband, the gambler, with a huge load of cash.

"Roscoe, when one person kills another and the killer inherits a million dollars from the deceased, the police look into that. The coroner too has to make a ruling. Accident or homicide. And where there's a motive, a million-dollar motive..."

He stood with his back to me, silently staring into the twilight.

"Roscoe?"

He sighed but said nothing.

"You said you didn't want to drag an already broken family into a police investigation. You said you like stability, the guiding principle in how you run your business and your life."

I left the rest unsaid. If Maggie had been the beneficiary of a million-dollar insurance policy, the insurer would not have let the case go without a full investigation. But Lehmann didn't want his family's dirty laundry dragged into the news. The police would understand a cursory investigation was best for everyone. If the family wasn't going to complain about it, why bother with an expensive investigation? It was less work for the cops to close the books on an accident.

Lehmann was willing to deny a crime he should have addressed. The toll it had taken on him was visible in the photos he kept in his showroom office. Ten years of aging in four years' time.

What would make a woman choose a husband who was such a thorough repudiation of her father? Was it the moral cowardice she perceived in him? Her disappointment in a man not worthy of the trust and respect she had invested in him?

These things must have shown before the accident, years before, to have primed Maggie to respond to the reckless, savage man who was her equal.

I wondered how much more there was to this story, and how much I could rely on Lehmann's version of it. We hadn't even gotten to Jake Reisman yet.

31

The sky was dark now. Lehmann came back from the kitchen with a second drink. He turned on the lamp on his desk and settled into his chair.

"You're sure Jake Reisman was your son?"

"Oh yes. I believe the test. The day he arrived here, he logged in to the generics site and walked me through the results. The tests showed he and Maggie had the same father. And I remember his mother."

Lehmann recounted the story. Sixteen months after he'd lost his wife, he left his son and daughter with the nanny and flew to California on business. He met Brinley Reisman in a bar near his hotel after a long day of meetings. A chance encounter.

"She must have been twenty-five. I was thirty-eight. There was something about her. In the eyes. That flashing spirit of the creative mind. Like the artist, or the mentally ill, as I now know, she didn't quite inhabit the same world as the rest of us. I hadn't touched a woman in wee—"

He cut short and corrected himself. "In over a year. We spent a night in the hotel, and that was it. I don't think there was any expectation on either side of anything more."

"You hadn't touched a woman in weeks? Or over a year?"

The question seemed to fluster him. He put his drink to his lips. Not from thirst, but more, it seemed, so he wouldn't have to respond.

"Which is it?" I asked.

"Oh, it doesn't matter."

"It might," I said. "Were you with other women before your wife died?"

"That's outside the bounds of this investigation."

His knee-jerk reaction told me how comfortable he was with that topic. One thing that might turn a girl against her father, I thought, is ill treatment of her mother. Betrayal. Infidelity. He didn't seem to want to go into that part of the family past, so I went back to Brinley Reisman.

"Didn't you use protection? When you were with Jake's mother in the hotel?"

"It broke. I did worry about that, but she didn't seem to care. When Jake showed me photos of his mother, I was shocked to see what had become of her. She was unkempt, haggard, like she'd been living on the streets. But I did remember her. The bar, the hotel room, the whole night. Funny how vividly you can recall something you hadn't thought about in decades. I wonder if some memories are pristine precisely because we haven't touched them."

"Did Jake say how he found you?"

"His mother told him his father's name was Lehmann. After his mother's death, when he learned he had a sister, Jake called hundreds of Maggie Smiths across the country, asking if their maiden name was Lehmann. Can you imagine? Maggie said yes, and then they got into an argument. She could be very abusive. He traced Mary Margaret Lehmann to this address, where she'd grown up.

"If I had taken that genetic test, I would have shown up as his father. He could have found me that much more easily. But it was Mary he wanted. He was clingy with women. He wanted a mommy who could love him. One who wasn't insane. He didn't contact me before coming here. I think, after his call with Maggie, he was worried I'd reject him.

"He packed his truck and trailer and showed up in the driveway carrying everything he owned. He had gambled everything on this trip. Or maybe it's more accurate to say he had nothing to leave behind, no life to go back to after his mother died.

"He was in bad shape. Fragile, physically and emotionally exhausted. I couldn't turn him out. This is my flesh and blood. And after seeing what had become of his mother, I feared for him. I asked if he wanted to go to a hospital to rest. Cortona was the nicest place around. It did him good. When he got out, I gave him a job I thought he could handle. The warehouse needed a conscientious worker.

"He asked me often about Maggie. Why was she mad at him? What had he done wrong? Could she love him? I can tell you why she was mad, though I didn't say it to him. She's been waiting for me to die ever since she left home. All she wants out of me is her inheritance. She knows my business has been struggling, my assets dwindling. She's hoping I'll kick off while there's still something left to bequeath.

"Now a sibling comes along to split what little money remains. She'd take that personally. That's how she thinks, because she's the center of her world. From anger to rage is a very short step for her, no matter how cool she appears on the surface. Let her stew five minutes about a man who appears from nowhere to claim half her fortune, and she'll want to bash his head in. She'll convince herself she's justified in doing so.

"I said nothing of this to Jake. He was fragile enough as it was. I asked him what made him think she was angry with him. He said people don't talk that way to each other unless they're mad.

"I asked when he'd spoken with her. On the phone before he came here, he said. And then at Cortona. Twice. She'd flown across the country to see him. She wasn't going to let this slide, this threat to her inheritance.

"She toyed with him, sweet-talked him and threatened him. One of the orderlies overheard it. Not the words, but the tone. Sweet and then harsh, kind and then cruel, like she was driving a wedge into his broken mind. She wanted him to go away. She thought she could scare him off.

"But I don't think her words had the intended effect. Her behavior might even have felt familiar to him. The sweet-talking, the 'I love you, welcome to the family' juxtaposed with, 'I hate you. Get out of my life, you horrid lunatic.'

"How far off was that from the kind of treatment Jake might have received from an unstable, mentally ill mother? That was what he understood of love. And now it was coming from a younger woman, a woman nearer his own age, from whom he might have wanted affection. He was compulsive to begin with, and I think he became obsessed with her. On the day I picked him up, he was sitting at a table on the patio behind the building, cutting out photos of catalog models who looked like her. Same hair and build and coloring. It gave me a chill. That was when I realized she'd visited him."

"You need to talk to the police about this," I said.

"I will. But for now, all I have are suspicions, that bomb I've been sitting on all these years. If you don't have the courage to detonate the bomb after one year, you won't after four. You're welded to it, paralyzed. I need someone else to come in and hit the detonator. And there must be real evidence. Not just suspicion and accusations. Evidence to vindicate me, to show my thinking isn't crazy. That's why you're here, Claire."

That was a funny way of putting it, I thought. Making this about himself, about vindicating *his* suspicions. What about justice for his son? Both his sons?

He stood and picked up his scotch. "I'm going to dump this out. It doesn't seem to help the way it once did. Would you like something from the kitchen?"

"Ice water. Do you mind if I come with you?"

The atmosphere in the darkened study had grown too somber. We walked to the kitchen, with its bright, clean, open space.

Lehmann stood at the freezer and filled two glasses with ice.

"There's another thing," he said. "I hadn't told my attorney about Jake."

"That's a problem," I said. "If the estate is the motive for his murder, and your attorney can't confirm there was another heir..."

Lehmann handed me a glass of water and I took a long drink.

"I was to meet with him next week to revise my estate plan, and I think Maggie knew somehow. I mean, look at the timing. Jake dies a week *before* I revise my will. And how did Maggie know I'd be away? How did she know she could use my house to set up that meeting between you and... whoever that was?"

I leaned against the counter, swirling the ice in my glass and reflecting on my meeting with DiNardo.

A simple case, I had told myself, despite the red flags. *Just tail a guy and find out if he's stealing. It'll give you some practice. A perfect starter case for the first-time detective.*

It wasn't funny, but still I had to laugh.

"A penny for your thoughts," Lehmann said.

"Why didn't you just cut Maggie out of your will? If she had nothing to gain by your death, you wouldn't have to live in fear. You wouldn't have to pay a cop to sit in your driveway."

"But what if I'm wrong?" he asked. "What if she didn't kill George? What if it was an accident. I feel bad enough about what I did to her..."

"What did you do to her?"

"I mean, about her losing her mother. I mean, maybe I didn't get her the right support after that. A girl... A girl's mother, after all... If Maggie's not emotionally normal, well, it isn't her fault. Not entirely. And if she is innocent and I cut her off..."

Roscoe Lehmann was a confused and conflicted man. His inability to stick to one opinion made me think yet again that there was some key fact he wasn't telling me. He struck me as a man in denial. How did Maggie's loss of her mother become something he "did to her?" And why would he have to "get her the right support?" Why not *give* her support? Isn't that what a father is for?

When I was a girl, I used to dream of having a father, of having someone whose eyes lit up when I entered the room, someone to take me to soccer games and ice cream shops. Someone who listened and cared and counseled.

If Lehmann had been my father, I might have dreamed of being an orphan, just to relieve myself of the burden of being related to an avoidant, indecisive man who couldn't connect emotionally. Just to reassure myself that my genetic makeup didn't condemn me to being like him, that I could grow up to be strong, direct, decisive. And if he couldn't connect with me, I'm sure I would have resented the strength of his bond with his son, the bond that was so clear to see in the photo in Lehmann's workplace.

I'm sure I would have felt slighted as the lesser child. And as for not having a mother to confide in, not having the comfort of maternal love that seems the birthright of every person in the world, I already knew what that felt like. You fill that hole whatever way you can. Through drink, drug, food, sex. Whatever gives you the illusion of comfort or control. For me, it was always work.

The one lesson my hard-hearted grandmother drove home to me was that no one would ever give me anything. She wanted to toughen me up, and she did. Her version of tough love was not to love at all. It was cruelty. And I learned early on that if no one was going to give me love, they weren't going to give me respect either.

Unless I made them.

And I did.

For all her callousness, my grandmother was a model of self-reliance. She did teach me to take care of myself, to not rely on others, and she did it in the harshest of ways, by denying love and comfort and even basic sympathy. I became too self-reliant, too untrusting, too isolated.

But what if I hadn't had the strength she modeled? What if my model had been someone like Lehmann? Weak and indecisive? Someone who seemed fundamentally dishonest with himself, who lived in fear of some dark secret he would have been better off facing?

Would I have given into to the sense of resentment and victimhood that used to well up in me in my teens? Would I continue to obsess over the object of my resentment, as I did when I was young?

The more I saw of Lehmann, the less I respected him. This case was not about an inheritance. Not entirely, anyway. If it was, Jake Reisman would have died a simpler death. Shot at night, or run over, something a professional could have taken care of.

This case was about Maggie Smith hating her daddy. She wanted him to feel the blows, every one of them, to know who did it and why. It was their little secret. And some part of Lehmann seemed to acknowledge that she had reason to hate him. Otherwise, why not come clean? Why sit with such uncomfortable suspicions all these years? Why not open up the past and investigate? Lay it all to rest? Unless there was something beneath it all he didn't want to find. Or didn't want others to find.

I knew it was pointless to ask more about his family, so I asked about someone who might actually have some information on the case at hand.

"You said Maggie's husband's name was Robert?"

"Yes."

"Smith? Great. Another impossible name to trace. Do you know where he lives?"

"In the state prison at Ely, Nevada. Or if he's out now, he's probably back in Las Vegas."

When I got back to my apartment that night, I found that the State of Nevada publishes a monthly list of parole board actions. The latest was from July first, three weeks ago. There he was, on page fourteen.

Offender Name: Smith, Robert.
Action: Grant Parole.

32

At seven the next morning, I called Lehmann to get a fuller description of Robert Smith. When he told me that Smith was a gambler, I had pictured a stubble-faced drinker sleazing around the low-end casinos in jeans and a stained t-shirt.

Smith's mug shot showed something different: a handsome man exuding confidence, a charmer who smiled into the camera after being arrested on a battery charge. The description Lehmann gave of him was closer to the photo than to my initial image.

"He can come off very well when he wants to. If you met him in an airport or a coffeeshop, knowing nothing of him, you'd think he was the head of sales at a successful company. He can hold a conversation—for as long as he wants to. After a while, you see it's just a front. A con man's polished veneer. When it slips, what's underneath is ugly."

Smith was a high-stakes gambler. He didn't waste time on slots or five-dollar blackjack.

"He always played big," Lehmann said. "I think that's part of what drew Maggie to him. She thought the same way. Big risks for big payoffs."

I asked Lehmann if Smith was approachable.

"He'll talk to anyone he thinks he can con. He'll size you up right away to see how much you're worth. If he thinks he can get something from you, he'll engage. If you do talk to him, keep in mind that he's playing you. He's not chatting for fun. He wants to extract something from you."

"Sorry, Roscoe, the word 'extract' makes me think of a pickpocket."

"Then you're thinking along the right lines."

I tried to push him again to talk to the police, to help me out of this bind by letting them know that he suspected his daughter in Jake's murder, but he went back to his old refrain: suspicions weren't enough, he needed me to gather evidence. The thought of the police terrified him. He couldn't stand his private business being dragged into public view.

I had to bite my tongue to keep from telling him what I thought of his cowardly hesitation. For four years he'd sat on his suspicions, and for four years he'd done nothing. Until this new trauma had shocked him into action.

And then he takes this half-measure of hiring me. What would I be able to find that the police could not? They could uncover more evidence than I could. They had the power to compel people to turn over information. They could dig up the whole truth, or at least as much of it as time hadn't destroyed.

But Roscoe Lehmann didn't want that. He feared that.

Why?

It couldn't be because of his sons. They were already gone. It wasn't to protect his daughter. He was scared enough of her to hire a round-the-clock guard.

So, what then? What was there to be frightened of?

I knew not to push him.

At 8:30, I called the contracting firm that had placed me in the Securities and Exchange Commission. Though I didn't have an active placement at the moment, they were still technically my employer.

"Janet?"

"Claire?"

"I need you to do me a favor."

"You're ready to come back? I don't think I can place you when you're under indictment for—"

"I need to you to write up a document saying you're sending me to Las Vegas on assignment."

"Huh?"

"Write a document that says I need to go to Vegas for work."

"I'm not sending you there. We have no business there. And you're not on assignment now anyway."

"I know that. I just need you to write the document and sign it. You don't have to send me anywhere."

"Okay, back up and explain. This makes no sense."

I explained to her that under the terms of my bail, I couldn't leave the DC area, except with the approval of the judge, and the only travel he'd approve would be for work or to care for a sick family member.

"You're asking me to lie for you?"

"It's not technically a lie. I *am* going to Vegas. And it *is* for work. Just not for... Yes, I want you to lie."

It took a while to convince her, but she finally agreed.

My next call was to Anton. I told him what I was doing. He didn't like it.

"Do you remember what you said to me, Anton? That I had to come up with a case more compelling than the prosecutor's? Well, I'm working on that. None of this happens without work."

"I think you're being rash here. You're being stupid. Break bail and you lose half a million dollars."

"That's why I'm getting the letter from my employer. Now you've been putting me off for days, dragging your feet on my case, which is my *life*, while you defend some other crook and give me excuses that your investigator is busy."

"He's available now. He's in LA and he can get to Vegas faster than you."

"I know the case, Anton. He doesn't."

Without going into the details of the boating accident, I explained to him what I had learned from Lehmann the night before. That Jake was his son, that there was an inheritance involved. That Lehmann suspected his daughter of one killing already and was scared enough of her to hire off-duty cops to guard his house. For the first time since I'd met him, Anton listed in complete silence.

"And there's a physical resemblance, Anton. Between her and me. A strong one. It was no accident I was in Jake's apartment the night of the murder. I was paid to be there."

When I was done, he let out a long whistle.

"You dug all that up on your own?"

"Like I said, Anton, it's just a question of putting in the work. Now I want you to do some work and get the judge to approve my travel."

"When are you going?"

"Tomorrow."

"Kind of short notice."

"The letter will say this trip was planned weeks ago. What'll you tell the judge?"

"That my client, who has never been in trouble before, needs to maintain gainful employment to be a contributing member of society. Hey, listen, you have to get this guy Lehmann to talk to the cops."

"I'll do that, Anton. He's reluctant right now. He's had a problem on his hands for years and he hasn't been able to admit it, like an addict in denial. The first step is to admit the problem to yourself, which I think he did when he hired me. But he's not ready to go public yet. Opening up his world to a police investigation is a big, scary step, especially when it means uncovering something he spent so many years hiding.

"He's a reluctant witness in this case," I said. "But he gave me a lead on Maggie's husband in Las Vegas. You remember your guy Freddy traced Buzz DiNardo's Dulles flight back to Vegas? And the woman who sat next to him. Vegas. They both flew out of there under fake names. Maggie's ex-husband, Robert Smith, might have something to tell me."

I told him what Lehmann had told me about Maggie's marriage.

"I don't like the idea of you talking to a convicted felon on your own."

"You don't think I can handle myself?"

"He was locked up for battering a woman."

"His wife. I think it was personal. I haven't done anything to offend him."

"Yeah, but you look like her. Could be a trigger. I'm going to have my guy Freddy meet you, so you'll have some backup if things go wrong."

"All right, Anton. I'm interested to meet him."

"Where are you meeting Smith?"

"I don't know. I haven't got in touch with him yet."

"You know where to find him?"

"I'll know soon enough."

"How do you know he'll talk to you?"

"I'm not going to give him a choice."

"You're pretty sure of yourself."

"I'm angry, and I'm not going to rest until I've fixed this."

Anton sighed. "Okay, Claire. Send me the letter."

At noon, I was talking to the Nevada State Parole Board. Within a few minutes, I had Smith's parole officer on the line. I told him I was an investigator from Washington, DC. I believed Smith's wife was involved in identity theft and credit fraud. That was plausible enough, given what her father had told me.

"Ex-wife," he said. "She divorced him after he beat her up."

"Right, ex-wife. I want to ask him some questions about her."

Smith was living in a halfway house, working as a dishwasher. I got his phone number.

He didn't answer the first time I called, so I left a message. I didn't tell him my full name. If he Googled me, he'd see the news story and know why I wanted to talk with him.

I was willing to bet he didn't have much affection left for the woman who had sent him to prison. All I said in my message was that "my firm" was looking into some credit fraud.

He must have listened to the message, because when I called back an hour later, from the same number, he recognized it and greeted me by name.

"Hello, Claire."

I kept in mind what Lehmann had said about Smith the con man, Smith wanting to extract something. It would help if I let him think he could get something from me. After three years of prison food, I thought he might appreciate a nice meal.

"How'd you like to have lunch tomorrow at Top of the World?"

"I'd like it a lot, if the Strat would let me in. How about Pasta Mia?"

"Around one-thirty?"

"Sounds good. I'll tell you all about my lovely wife. And you can tell me what kind of crap she's buying on those stolen cards. Actually, I bet I can tell you. I used to have to pay those bills myself."

I booked a 6:30 AM flight to Vegas, arriving at 11:00. That would give me just enough time to make it to the restaurant. I'd fly out at 6:00 pm and be home again after midnight.

I called Anton and told him where his guy Freddy should meet me.

33

I met Freddy Ferguson at a coffeeshop in McCarran Airport. He was a big guy, and I could tell he'd been a fighter. His nose looked like it had been broken more than once. He had a small but deep scar above his right eye. One of his pinkies was crooked, probably broken on another man's face.

He was not the person to talk to Smith. If Smith really did look at people the way Lehmann had said, sizing them up for a con, he'd see right away that this was not a man he could exploit. Freddy came off as sharp, observant, streetwise and wary. He didn't have to tell me he'd grown up having to look out for himself. One look at his face told me that.

We made a plan: Separate Ubers to West Flamingo Road. He'd be in the restaurant before Smith or I arrived. He'd watch the conversation.

"Don't leave with him," he said.

"Why would I?"

"If he's like what your friend Lehmann says, he'll want cash for information. How much you have?"

"Two hundred."

"If he does have info for you, that might not be enough. He'll make you go to an ATM."

"And what? Jump me?"

"No. He's on parole, remember?"

"Then what are you worried about?"

"I'm worried about him seeing me if I have to follow you both out. I'm gonna follow the guy no matter what. I just don't want him to know I'm with you. You get me?"

"Okay."

"Go to the cash machine and get another three hundred."

"You think I'll need that much?"

"Guy's fresh out of prison, washing dishes. He'll sell anything he can for as much as he can get."

I did as he said, while he went on ahead to the restaurant.

34

Robert Smith was waiting inside the door when I arrived. He wore a dark blue suit that I assume had been packed away during his prison days. I'm sure he didn't wear that in the kitchen where he worked. The fact that he had dug it out just for me made me nervous.

That, and his face. He looked like an aged magazine model. A well-structured face lined with years of hard living. Gambling, late nights, prison. He was in his early forties but looked older. His pale grey eyes scanned the room like a lion surveying a herd of gazelle.

The way he startled when he saw me told me just how much I looked like his ex-wife. He covered his reaction quickly with a bright, white-toothed smile that was disturbingly at odds with the measuring predatory eyes. That smile might have fluttered hearts when he was young, before time had thinned his oily hair and etched the outlines of an unprincipled character onto his aging face.

"Claire!" He made a little bow with his head. There was that veneer of civility Lehmann had mentioned.

It didn't last long. He started unloading on his ex-wife before our drinks arrived. To hear him tell it, she was the nastiest woman who ever lived, self-centered and mercurial, coldly indifferent one minute, eyes hot with rage the next.

He couldn't shut himself up, and initially, I thought that boded well for me. In the course of unleashing his feelings, he'd tell me anything I wanted to know. But the fact that he had so much resentment toward her, and that I looked like her, made me uneasy. I didn't want him transferring his hatred to me. I was glad Freddy was there.

After several minutes of listening to him tear the woman down, I finally asked why he married her.

"What do you mean, why'd I marry her? Why do you think I married her? You ever heard of spousal privilege?"

"You didn't want her testify against you?"

"Prosecutors have this trick. They turn people against each other. Compel them to testify. It's nice to have a business partner who can't be compelled. You understand?"

"What kind of business were you in?"

"Doesn't matter. Water under the bridge, as they say. But if I had it to do over again, I would not have married her. You ever heard that expression, Sleeping with the devil? Well, I was literally sleeping with the devil. She's got a nasty streak a mile wide and you never know when it's coming."

Smith told me over appetizers that his primary occupation was high stakes poker.

"I needed a sponsor, you know? You need money to make money, right? I mean, that's true in business. It's true in gambling. The second I met her, I could read her. I knew exactly what she wanted. More. More of everything.

"She had money. A trust from her dad. I told her, watch this. You front me ten grand, I'll turn it into forty by the end of the week. And I did. Actually, fifty. But I told her forty and pocketed the rest.

"We were partners. We played the game for a long time. I'd be flush and we were in a penthouse, then I'd go bust and we'd tap the trust fund. But, you know, for all I lost, it wasn't me who put us under. It was her. She had to have everything top of the line. The Mercedes—you know, the Maybach. Why? What's she trying to say with that? Hey, look at me, I spent two hundred grand on a fucking car. Does that impress you? To me it says you're stupid. A midline Mercedes will get you where you're going just as fast, and it's easier to turn back into cash. That's the key because cash is king. You gonna eat that shrimp?"

I pushed my plate toward him. "Take it."

He held the plate up to his mouth and shoveled the shrimp in as if someone might snatch it from him if he didn't hurry. I reminded myself he'd only been out of prison a few weeks.

"How long were you two together?"

"On and off, six years." He wiped his mouth with the linen napkin. "Like I said, we had our ups and downs. She just rolled with it, though she hated being broke. Hated it. When we were down, I never heard the end of it. You know, her tastes, the designer brands, it was like an addiction. I have a theory about that. You see these beautiful women in the fashion ads and you think they're on top of the world and their lives are golden and they must command all this respect. That's what Maggie was trying to buy. Like if she put on the right clothes and drove the Maybach then she would be all that. Her world would magically transform into the perfect world of the ads. She'd be the glamourous one everyone looked up to, the one they all envied and wanted to be.

"But she was never that. Not in her own mind. In her own mind—I don't know. She had a skewed sense of self-worth. Like she secretly hated herself. And I'll tell you where that comes out. Not in public. In public she wants respect, puts up a big front. In the bedroom, she wants to be treated how she really feels about herself.

"And why? I don't know. She didn't come up as hard as me. She had it easy. Cush house in Maryland, rich dad, swimming pool. She even had a second house on the Chesapeake Bay. So what's wrong with her? How come, no matter how much designer crap she buys, how come she's still not happy? There's something down deep that's broken. She lost her mom when she was sixteen, you know. Maybe that's part of it. And she hated her dad. That's never a good sign in a woman. Especially if you marry her. That means I got a shit-ton to manage."

"She lost her mom when she was five," I said. That's what Lehmann had told me two nights before.

Smith shook his head. "Sixteen. Her mom went into the home when Maggie was five."

"What home?"

"Nursing home. She was an invalid. Like, in her thirties, but an invalid. Maybe that messed Maggie up. I don't know. She didn't talk a lot about her past. All the things that bothered her, she kept to herself. I was always wary when she got quiet. That meant she was mad and she was planning something. And the only things she ever planned were how to get more money and how to get back at someone, because in her mind, she was always a victim.

"She kept a running score of every insult, every slight. This person did this to me. This person did that. She'd get quiet and you could see her mind working. That always put me on edge 'cause, you know, I had to wonder who she was pissed off at this time. Was it me? A lot of the time, it was. You live with someone, you share a bed, you're gonna piss them off sometimes, just cause you're always around.

"And me, playing poker, my job is to read people. What cards is the guy across the table holding? How confident is he in that hand? You get good at reading people after a while. That's how you win. But her, when she got quiet..." He shook his head. "The best I could do was find out *who* she was mad at. As long as it wasn't me, I was Okay. If she wouldn't tell me who she was stewing over, I had to assume it was me. Get out for a few days. Let her cool off. That's part of the bargain. Part of the devil's bargain. You gotta look out for yourself at all times."

"When did you two split up?"

"I don't know. A few years ago."

"What finally did it?"

"She was running out of money, for one. That trust fund. She blew through it, and we started getting in fights. I told her to sell some of her damn jewelry. I need cash to work with. She didn't like that.

"And then... She went back East for a while. Her brother died. She came back with a lot of cash, and we lost it. All of it.

"We weren't getting along and things were ready to blow. Then I made a mistake."

He wiped his mouth and picked up a bread roll from the basket.

"You gotta understand, when I say we weren't getting along, we weren't getting along as civilized human beings. But we had a way of working through our frustrations."

He buttered the roll, stuffed half of it in his mouth and continued talking as he chewed.

"I mean, on an animal level, we got along fine. Remember what I said about her in the bedroom?

"There was a thing we liked to do, a little thing, and I made a mistake and I let my guard down. It's uh..."

He trailed off, tugged at his ear and I could see in his eyes that he was processing a memory that was still vivid. He put the other half of the roll down.

"The thing with her is, no matter how well you know her, you never know when she's gonna blow. Most women, their temper builds and then they let it fly. Her, she tucks it away, nurses that sense of victimhood, and watches coolly for an opportunity. I still don't know what I did to set her off. All I can say is I didn't see it coming. If I had, I would never have let my guard down like that.

"But it was a thing. It was a thing we used to do. And I didn't have any reason to believe that it would be different this time. I mean, out of all the times..."

I noticed his hands were clenched and he rubbed his thumbs tightly across the knuckles of his index fingers.

"I don't like to talk about what goes on behind closed doors, because I'm a gentleman. I am. See, if you got to know me better, you'd see that. But that bitch tried to kill me, so fuck her, I don't care about her damn secrets."

"Maggie tried to kill you?"

"And she tried to pass it off like nothing happened. Like, you know, we've done that stuff before. It just got out of hand."

"What stuff?"

"You know, like..." He looked at me trying to gauge whether I understood. He didn't seem to want to say it.

"Like what?" I asked.

"Like, you ever, uh... Well, maybe you haven't, but maybe you've seen a video. I mean, I'm not saying you watch porn or anything, but maybe you do. Do you?"

"No."

"Well, it's... You know if you get strangled when you're about to have an orgasm, it's very intense. It's a very intense experience. The French, they call orgasm The Little Death. Try getting choked when you're having one. That's like the big death. It magnifies the experience."

He leaned in, put his hand on my thigh and asked with a smile, "You ever try that?"

"No." I gently brushed his hand away.

"You might want to think about it. But you gotta be careful, because if you're in a volatile relationship, you might really want to kill the person. Or they might want to kill you. And they might not even be aware of it. I mean, you have this underlying hostility, and it just bubbles up. Or, I don't know, maybe she planned it all along. You can't tell with her."

"She choked you?"

"She choked me out so hard I didn't wake up for I don't know how long. An hour maybe. I don't know. It was dark. My brain was foggy and I was like, what the hell happened? My ears were ringing, my head ached, and my throat hurt like hell. I swear she just about crushed my windpipe.

"It took me a while to put the pieces together. She was on top and she strangled me with both hands and she pressed her thumbs into my windpipe. Hard."

He put his hands around his throat, pressing his thumbs to demonstrate.

"That's not how you're supposed to do it. All you need to do is cut off the blood flow for a few seconds. You don't crush someone's windpipe.

"I got up, and I'm like, where is that bitch? But I'm unsteady on my feet. The choking messed up my balance. I'm thinking maybe she did some permanent damage. I have to sit down for a few, put my thoughts together, make sure I have full control of my arms and legs, because I didn't at first, and I didn't even know it until I tried to stand.

"In a few minutes, I get up again. I smell coffee. I think, who makes coffee in the middle of the night? What's she gotta stay awake for that she needs to make a pot of coffee?

"I see this glow in the living room. She's on the couch with the lights off and she's looking at her iPad. I walk up behind her. She knows I'm there, but she doesn't turn or look or say anything. Just sips her coffee and looks at the iPad.

"I'm like, what the hell is she looking at? Turns out, it's my bank account. The one she didn't know I had. She spent us broke, and I put some money that she didn't know about in a place where she couldn't touch it. How'd she find it? How'd she get the password for the account? I never did figure that out.

"I'm standing there, and she knows I'm there, and she knows I see her looking at my money, but she doesn't acknowledge me. Finally, after like thirty, forty seconds, she says, 'How you feeling, Bob?'

"Like, she just fucking strangled me and now she's in my bank account and she asks how I'm feeling. She's messing with me, playing mind games. Like, if she acts like nothing happened, then I'll start to doubt myself, start to question whether this is really happening. Well, she misjudged me. Like I said, things had been ready to blow for a long time, and that was the last straw. There's a line you do not cross, and she was about a mile past it. I let her know what the score was, and I told her in a way she understood.

"If I had it to do over again, I wouldn't have hit her so many times in the face. Or maybe I would have killed her, I don't know. But that swollen face, she took that straight to the cops and got me on domestic violence. Battery. That was my first time going to jail.

"While I was in there, I started thinking about that trip she'd taken back to Maryland. She goes out boating with her brother and he dies. Not that I hadn't thought of it before. We just didn't talk about it. Like I said, she kept the family stuff to herself. But in jail, I'm thinking, she crossed a line with me. Why not with her brother too? She's got a lot of anger, and she waits till her mind is nice and cool to let it out. That's the most dangerous kind of person there is. That's the kind you learn to stay the fuck away from in prison. A hothead makes mistakes. The cool, calculated kind—they outthink you before the attack even begins."

"Did she ever say anything about her brother?"

"Just that he was her father's favorite. She had her gripes against her brother, just like she did about everyone, but nothing serious. If she hated anyone, it was her fucking dad. God knows why. I met the guy. He wasn't worth hating. He was a nothing. A great big nothing. What's this got to do with credit cards anyway? You told me on the phone this was some credit fraud thing."

"I'm trying to find her."

"Why? You like poking at rattlesnakes? Just cancel the cards and forget about whatever she did. You're the second person today to ask me where she is. I don't know where she is. You look like her, you know that? I mean, at first glance."

"Who else asked about her?"

"Guess."

"A cop?"

"Of course it was a cop. Who the hell else would want to find her? I told him I had no information. If I did know where she was, the first thing I'd do is make sure I'm at least a hundred miles away. That bitch is fucking psycho."

"Did he say what she'd done? Why he was looking for her?"

Smith shrugged. "Same kinda shit you're talking about. She goes into a bank with a fake ID, tries to take out a loan."

"Do you know if she's friends with an older man?"

"She's not friends with anyone. She's got a screw loose."

"A man in his sixties. About six feet tall, with deep tan lines on his face?"

Smith scrunched up his face. "Dice?"

"Who?"

"The guy have a beard?"

I remembered the razor burn on the face of Lehmann's impersonator, how the bottoms of his cheeks, his chin and neck were lighter than the surrounding skin, like they'd been shielded from the sun by recently shaved whiskers.

"Maybe," I said. "Ever heard the name DiNardo?"

Smith shook his head.

"Buzz?"

"Buzz?" Smith's face lit up. "He have a deep voice?"

"Somewhat deep, yeah."

"Smooth talker? Sounds educated, like he comes from money? Weak handshake? Hands always clammy?"

"Yes. All those things."

"Shit, that's Dice. Is Maggie with *him*?" His tone was laced with contempt.

"I don't think so," I lied. "But he may be able to give me a lead."

Smith shook his head with a knowing smirk. "See, Dice—me and him have a difference in philosophy. I don't go to hookers and I don't bet on craps. He'll bet on anything. Horses and dogs. He gets a rush watching them run in circles 'cause it gives him two minutes of suspense where he thinks he might win. And then he's broke again. Fucking dumbass. That's like the crack addict's version of gambling.

"I hope for his sake he's not with her. Dice knows he can't play Maggie. She's too smart. He thinks if he's nice to her, she'll screw him. She'll screw him alright, just not the way he wants. If he's smart, he'll stick to his whores. They do what you pay them to do, and then they go away."

"What's Dice's real name?"

"That's what you want, huh?"

I watched him size me up to figure out how much I'd be willing to pay. He checked my hands for jewelry, my wrist for a watch. I wore neither, but my suit was new, and I could tell by his own choice of suit that he recognized quality.

"You have a thousand bucks?"

"For a name?"

"You need the name. I need some juice to get back on track. Can't gamble with nothing."

"A thousand dollars is a lot for information that might not be correct. How do I know I'm getting the right name?"

"You think I'm gonna scam you?" Smith put on a hurt expression. "Have I held anything back? This whole time we've been talking? I think I've been more than decent, especially considering I don't even know you."

"You already told me you're a con man."

"When did I say that?"

"Every word out of your mouth told me that."

"All right, well now I have something you want, so let's cut the crap. This is a straight-up transaction. I get what I want, you get what you want."

"That's what I want to be sure of. That I get what I want. How do I know I'm getting the right name?"

Freddy sat two tables away. He'd been reading on his phone, but I could tell the sharp tone of our exchange had his attention.

"I'll show you," Smith said.

He typed something into his phone, scrolled, and clicked.

He covered the bottom third of the screen with his hand and showed me the photo.

"That him?"

"That's him," I said.

Smith slid the phone into his pocket. "Thousand bucks."

I let out a sigh of annoyance. "You're a real gentleman, Mr. Smith."

"I know, right?" He smiled. "There's an ATM in The Palms next door."

Freddy must have asked for his check when he heard Smith name his price. He paid and was out the door before us. He knew I'd have to go to the ATM.

Smith insisted on holding my arm as we left the restaurant. To an observer, it might have looked like a cop escorting a prisoner, a tight grasp above the elbow to prevent the accused from attempting an escape. It felt like something different to me. A fondling grasp, gently squeezing the muscle to test its firmness, hand inching upward, fingers "accidentally" brushing against my breast.

I kept my mind on two things: getting that name and figuring out where Freddy was. I was surprised that a guy as big as him managed keep an eye on us without me noticing. For a while I thought he'd lost us.

In The Palms, I stood at the ATM with Smith looking over my shoulder, his hand stroking the small of my back, inching slowly downward.

I gave him the money and he showed me the screen, a mug shot from the Clark County sheriff's office. Colson "Dice" Moran.

"Check Tahoe," Smith said with grin. "They don't let him in the Vegas casinos anymore."

He thanked me for doing business and said if I ever needed help again, he'd be happy to oblige.

He went straight to the counter and changed the whole thousand for a stack of chips.

Freddy Ferguson stood twenty feet behind him, tapping out a text. To me.

"Go home. I got this."

35

I looked up Colson "Dice" Moran's criminal history while I waited for my flight at McCarran. He had been convicted of four counts of document forgery and identity theft. The defendant's name in the case included six aliases. Apparently, he was making and selling bogus driver's licenses and other forms of ID. He served time in state prison, though I wasn't able to find out where. If he went in immediately after his conviction, that would have been around the same time Maggie's husband, Robert Smith, went in.

The department of corrections didn't seem to have corrected Dice Moran. He was now flying around as Buzz DiNardo, accompanied by Anna Graham, or Angela M. Ginhem, or whoever she chose to be.

I wondered about something Smith had said. If Buzz/Dice had been banned from the casinos in Vegas, why would the ones in Tahoe let him in? Weren't they owned by the same corporations? Wouldn't they share information?

My flight was boarding in fifteen minutes, so I wouldn't have time to look that up. I was about to text Freddy to ask him to look into it when he called.

"Claire?"

"Hey."

"Just a heads up. Smith called a guy named Dice a few minutes ago and asked how the tables were running down there. Told him some investigator had been asking about him."

"Why would he tell him that?"

"Courtesy call. I'm sure he'd want his buddy to do the same if someone was asking about him."

"Any mention of Maggie?"

"No. Listen, your guy Smith here is already up two thousand on the money you gave him. He's at a poker table with a bunch of guys who are out of their league. I already called his parole officer to try to get him locked up again."

"Why?"

"Because he's an asshole. I can't stand the look of the guy. Reminds me of the manager who ruined my boxing career. It's all I can do not to punch him in the face. Anyway, turns out there's no provision against gambling in his parole. That's a special condition in Nevada. This guy's got standard conditions plus no victim contact and domestic violence counseling.

"Go figure. They gave him a stiff sentence on the battery charge because they knew he'd gotten away with a lot of other crap in the past. If he's gonna commit another crime, it'll be to pay back debts he racks up at the table, and the state lets him walk right back into the casino. This place is fucked.

"Right now, he's cleaning up. If he keeps going like this, he'll move up to higher stakes. I want to keep an eye on him, if you don't mind. I want to see what he does when he has real money in his pocket. You mind?"

"Why would I mind?"

"You're paying Anton for my time."

"Go ahead."

"Best thing to happen would be he calls Maggie. That's victim contact and that puts him back in prison."

"I don't think he'd call her after the way he spoke about her at lunch."

"No, but he called Dice. Only way to tell is to watch him for a while."

"All right, Freddy."

I called Anton Durant from the jetway as I was boarding my flight back to DC and told him I got the name of the guy who pretended to be Lehmann.

"So what does that buy us?"

"I don't know yet, but it brings us a step closer to... something."

"You sound wound up."

"I am."

"You need to come home and relax."

"I can't sit around and do nothing, Anton. It's not in my nature."

I was on the plane now, looking for seat 26A. "Look how much I've accomplished on this trip. In one day, I have a name and... And, crap, all I have is a name. And a second testament to Maggie's character. One more person saying she's capable of what her father thinks she's done, though I'm not sure how reliable this person is. And what have you done since I've been gone? Because I'm sure you're charging me for something."

"Never fear, Claire!" There was Anton, the charismatic showman. "The wheels of the criminal justice system turn night and day, and if you have faith in your case, you'll let them turn."

"That's not an answer, Anton. If the system will exonerate me on its own, then I don't need you, do I? I'd just let the pieces fall into place and everything would turn out in my favor."

"If you're as innocent as you say, maybe. You asked me what I've done, I'll tell you what I've *not* done. I've *not* put your goddamn bail at risk. You did that. I have *not* lied to the judge about your reasons for traveling. You did that. I have *not* let my hot head run away with me on a quest for justice. I *have* put pressure on the department to expedite testing of forensic evidence so you could get a break before you self-destruct. I *have* pulled strings in the DNA testing lab to get you pushed to the front of the pack, and I *have* gotten results."

"What are you talking about, Anton? Hold on."

I was trying to get into my seat, but when a huge, bleary-eyed drunk stumbled out of the middle seat to let me in, he almost knocked me down. He stood hulking over me as I slipped into the row.

"Anton, what are you talking about?" I was seated now. "Explain."

"They picked up several hairs at the scene, including some that match yours. Two of the hairs had skin attached because they had been ripped out in the struggle. The DNA on that skin did not match the DNA in the swab they took from you. It did match the DNA of the skin they dug out from under Reisman's fingernails. The killer was a woman, but it wasn't you."

I breathed a huge sigh of relief.

"Why didn't you tell me this before?"

"Because I just found out five minutes ago."

"No, why didn't you tell me you were rushing this process?"

"I didn't know if it was going to work. It's a complicated operation to get the right incentives to the right people. If I had told you about it, you'd be pestering me every hour to push harder."

"So, this means they'll drop the charges?"

"Not so fast. They still don't know whose DNA it is, and Kowalczyk doesn't like to be emptyhanded after giving up a promising suspect. You need to get Lehmann to tell the cops what he told you. If you or I tell them, they won't believe us. You're the accused, so you have a motive to shift the blame. I'm Anton Durant, so everything out of my mouth is a lie. You have to work on Lehmann. The cops will listen to him."

"All right. I'll talk to him when I get back."

36

I got back to my apartment at 2:36 a.m. I was at Lehmann's house less than five hours later. The cop accosted me in the driveway again, only this time it wasn't Gutierrez.

The new cop called Lehmann and got him to let me in.

Lehmann led me into the kitchen, where he was about to eat breakfast. Two slices of dry white toast and a cup of weak-looking tea sat on the island beside a copy of the Washington Post that was open to the business section. He ate standing up.

"Would you like some tea, Claire? I'd offer you coffee, but I don't drink it."

"No, thank you."

"I have cereal. Granola. My stomach is too upset to eat it now, but you may have some."

"No thanks."

"You seem agitated."

I was. I had two things to talk to him about, and I had spent the drive debating which topic to raise first. I chose his wife. From there, I could ease into the second.

"Roscoe, you told me Maggie lost her mother when she was five."

"Yes." He took a delicate bite of bread. "It was hard on her."

"Maggie's ex-husband said her mother died when she was sixteen."

"That's correct."

He sipped his tea delicately, like an invalid. It annoyed me. "Well, which is it?"

"Lost and died are two different things." He set the teacup on the counter. "Maggie lost her mother at five. It was a terrible scene, and I'm sorry she had to witness it. Have you ever seen a person go into anaphylactic shock?"

"No."

"The way they gasp, it's terrifying. Especially if you're a child and she's your mother."

Lehmann explained that his wife had taken a medication she was allergic to. She was the only adult in the house that morning. Both children witnessed her reaction. George, who was seven at the time, called 911. By the time the ambulance arrived, she had been without oxygen for so long that her brain was irreversibly damaged.

"She spent the next eleven years in a nursing home. She neither moved nor spoke. There's some debate as to whether a person in her state has any consciousness at all. Can they hear what's going on around them? We never knew for sure. But Maggie thought so. She visited her almost every week."

"Okay, this is the sort of thing would have been good to know earlier. Why didn't you tell me about this when you were telling me about George's death?"

"I told you she lost her mother."

"This is different."

I pictured the girl sitting vigil at her mother's bedside for eleven years. Was she waiting for a miracle? An awakening? Did she have that much hope?

And then what her husband had told me, that she saw herself as a victim. That she was angry with the world.

"Roscoe, you have not been honest with me or with yourself. You need to start telling the truth. The whole truth. You told me you've been sitting on this bomb for years. It takes work to stay in that position. It doesn't just happen. You have to actively protect the lie, for instance by not telling me the whole truth of your family past. In fact, I don't think I'm even the person you need to be talking to right now. You need a therapist, and you need to talk to the police."

"I told you, I will go to the police when I have evidence."

"When you have evidence," I repeated. "So that you can tell yourself it wasn't ultimately your decision. So you can tell yourself you were forced into telling your story, because you just can't tell it on your own. You can't take responsibility for what you know and believe. Is that right? Is that what it is, Roscoe?"

He picked up his tea and took a sip. It seemed like a calculated gesture meant to show that none of this bothered him, that he was taking it all in stride. But his hands shook.

He put the cup down and said nothing, just stood there looking weak and resigned, and for a moment, I understood his daughter's anger. There's something very unlikable about a man who is weak when he doesn't need to be, who won't stand up for his own beliefs, who is less than truthful in the face of a situation that demands the truth, who asks sympathy of others instead of courage from himself.

He wasn't going to speak without a prod, so I drove the knife in deeper.

"We have evidence, Roscoe. The DNA under Jake's fingernails belonged to a woman, but not to me. Do you know what you need to do now?"

If he knew, he wouldn't say. Or he couldn't. This cowardly, infuriating man! He seemed to want me to tell him. He wanted someone else in charge of the situation.

"You need to go to the police and tell them your story, and you need to give them a DNA sample. That will be your evidence. Your DNA will show them you are the father of the assailant."

"And the victim," Lehmann added ruefully.

"And then you won't have to worry about them thinking you're a crazy old man whose suspicions come from unresolved grief. The physical evidence will tell the story. You need to do this, Roscoe. The truth will set you free. Unless you want to spend the rest of your life sitting on that bomb."

He stood with both hands on the counter to support him. His face was pale, his eyes filled with fear.

I wasn't sure what to do. Despite what he had told me about the pain of suspecting his daughter in the death of his son, the thought of seeing those suspicions confirmed—publicly, no less, in a police case—seemed to paralyze him with terror.

He was stuck, and my intuition said that if I tried to force him, he'd go back into his shell, into his life of denial.

On the other hand, if I didn't at least nudge him in the right direction, he might not do anything at all. He had managed to deny a murder for four years, why not four more? And the longer he held out, the longer I might be under this cloud of indictment, with the state of Maryland in virtual possession of everything I owned, the state telling me where I could and could not travel.

Looking at him there, frozen in indecision, I knew there was more to this case. When a person spends as much emotional energy as this to maintain a painful status quo, it can only be because there's a fear of something worse beneath the surface. But what?

He was already estranged from his daughter. They hadn't seen each other in four years. What else did he have to lose?

This was not the time to ask.

I touched his shoulder. "Roscoe, look at me."

His eyes showed he had withdrawn deep into himself, like a wounded dog that no amount of coaxing would draw out of its hiding place.

"I'm going to call Detective Kowalczyk. He's in charge of Jake's case. You have to meet with him in person. Do you understand?"

He nodded.

"Today."

"Later," he said weakly. "I need to rest."

"Okay, later today. I'll see if I can get him to come out here."

I helped Lehmann into the living room where he slumped on the couch and put his hands over his eyes.

I made a call from the deck behind the kitchen, so he wouldn't have to hear. I told Anton that Lehmann would talk.

"Might talk," I corrected. "But Kowalczyk has to come out here. Lehmann won't have the strength to go to the station."

"Kowalczyk won't go out there."

"Why not? It's his job to solve the case."

"We have a problem related to that trip you took yesterday. You need to meet me in an hour at the prosecutor's office in Rockville."

"Crap!"

"Yeah, crap is right. Let's talk in the parking lot before we go in, get our story straight."

Before I left, I checked in on Lehmann one last time. He had gotten up from the couch while I was outside, and then he had lain back down. I knew because he had a wet washcloth over his eyes.

"Roscoe?"

"Claire?" he whispered.

"What was the name of the nursing home your wife was in?"

"I don't remember."

"Yes you do. She was there for eleven years."

He took a deep breath, and then his breathing became slow and steady, like he was asleep. But his hand still held the washcloth.

"Roscoe?"

"Our Lady of Mercy. In Gaithersburg."

"And your wife's name was Mary?" Rook had told me that on the boat. Mary Margaret.

He didn't respond.

"What was your wife's name?"

I knew he was awake. I knew he could hear me.

"Roscoe? Your wife's name was Mary, correct? Mary Margaret?"

At last he spoke.

"Maggie. She went by Maggie."

37

I made good use of my time on the drive to Rockville, calling Our Lady of Mercy and talking to a helpful administrator. I asked who might have been working there between twenty-seven years ago, when Maggie's mother came in, and sixteen years ago, when she died.

Two employees fit the criteria. The one who was working that day was no help. She didn't remember enough about the patient to tell me anything meaningful. The other employee who'd been there with Mrs. Lehmann was on vacation.

The last woman I spoke to in the administrative office told me to talk to Vanessa Ridge, who had been a nurse on rounds when Mrs. Lehmann came in and the head nurse when she went out. Ridge was retired now, living in Glen Echo. The administrator gave me her phone number.

While scouting a parking spot near the prosecutor's office, I saw Anton Durant leaning against his black Mercedes. He was scowling, arms folded across his chest. He didn't look like he loved his job today.

After I parked, he said, "According to the letter your friend wrote, you were supposed to have to gone to an office in Vegas for a meeting. You didn't."

"I didn't have time."

We walked in the middle of the road toward the prosecutor's office.

"You should have made time. Kowalczyk had a local cop out there tail you. You had lunch and went into a casino with a convicted felon. What do you think Kowalczyk and the prosecutor will make of that?"

"I'll explain it to them. They have the DNA from the crime scene and they know it doesn't belong to me."

"Whoa, hold on. We have a problem here. Kowalczyk doesn't know yet that the DNA has been tested."

I stopped in my tracks. "How can he not know?"

"Forensics hasn't submitted the report yet."

"Then how can you know?"

"Claire, when you hire an attorney, you pay not just for *what* he knows, but also for *who* he knows." He nudged me along and we started walking again. "I know someone who knows someone who could move things along in the DNA lab. Official channels are always slower than back channels. Maybe Kowalczyk got the report this morning, maybe he'll get it this afternoon. Whatever the case, we can't go in there and say the DNA report exonerates you because the first thing they'll ask is how the hell we know that, and then I risk losing a well-placed contact who knows how to grease the wheels of justice.

"I can tell you what's going to happen in there. The prosecutor's going to threaten to revoke your bail and keep your money. That's half a million dollars. If you agree to make a plea, you save Kowalczyk a lengthy investigation and the prosecutor a costly trial. He'll pretend he didn't know about your trip, you paling around a convicted felon. You keep your bail in exchange for a plea."

"This is the time to set the record straight," I said. "The felon was Maggie's ex-husband—"

"Nope," said Anton, shaking his head. "No, no, no. We're not going to talk about that. I'll ask them to write up a plea deal—"

"Why?"

"To buy us time. We'll look it over and hopefully sometime today, maybe this afternoon, Kowalczyk gets the report showing someone else's DNA under Reisman's fingernails. Come on, we gotta get in there or we'll be late."

"I don't like this."

"You don't like anything that's not your way. This is the criminal justice system. You just have to bend over and take it—"

"I hate that image."

"—until you can turn the tables."

"And I will."

"Not if you don't slow down. You're too rash, Claire. Your emotions are caught up in this."

"How can they not be? It's my life."

38

We met in a conference room inside. The prosecutor stood by the whiteboard at the rear of the room. A thin bald man in a three-piece suit, he glared at us when we walked in—first at me, and then at Anton.

Anton broke into a huge smile and said, "Bill!" He lunged at him, hand thrust forward in greeting, as if they were old college pals about to head out to a bar.

I can't imagine any gesture from a defense attorney that could have pissed that dour man off more.

"Anton," he said dryly. He looked at Durant's hand but didn't shake it. "You know why we're here."

Kowalczyk sat near the prosecutor, peering glumly into his laptop. He put his head in his hands and let out an anguished sigh.

The prosecutor was about to say something, but I spoke first. I took a gamble that Kowalczyk was reading what I thought he was reading.

"You took a DNA sample from Reisman, didn't you?"

Anton didn't want me revealing what *he* had done, but there was nothing wrong with me saying what the cops had done, what any cops would have done as a routine part of a murder investigation.

"Me?" asked Kowalczyk. "No. I don't touch DNA."

"I mean your team. Your forensics team would have taken a post-mortem DNA sample from Reisman so that when they test physical evidence they can distinguish Reisman's DNA from his assailant's."

Kowalczyk shrugged. "So, what? You watched an episode of NCIS and now you're telling me how an investigation works?"

His defensive tone and slumping shoulders told me he had the test results. And he knew I knew. He could see it in my eyes. He quietly passed his laptop to the prosecutor.

"Did you notice anything about Reisman's DNA and the DNA you pulled from under his fingernails?" I asked.

Anton shot me an angry look. That was a slip—knowing there was DNA under Reisman's fingernails.

"Should I have?" Kowalczyk asked.

"The victim and the assailant were brother and sister."

"We don't test for family relationships," Kowalczyk said.

"You wouldn't have to. In the lab they look for gene sequences unique to each person. They would have noticed that many of the sequences in the two samples were the same. Don't tell me your team doesn't pick up on basic similarities. I can tell you that our team will."

I looked at Durant. He seemed willing to let me go on. He even looked a little pleased.

"The defense has a right to the evidence," I said, "including the DNA. How will it look at trial if our experts say the DNA under Reisman's fingernails belonged to his sister and your team says they didn't notice that?"

"Reisman didn't have a sister," Kowalczyk said.

"No? How far have you looked into this case, Detective?"

"Watch it, Claire." There was Durant with the lawyer's habitual caution.

"Why have I managed to get a better picture of what's going on than you?" I prodded. "This is your job."

"You need to shut her up," Kowalczyk said. "What kind of lawyer lets his client jabber on like this when she's facing a murder rap?"

"One who knows his client is innocent," Durant said. "One who knows the DNA at the scene doesn't match what you were hoping to find. Something's bothering you, Dennis, I can see it."

"Your smile is bothering me."

"Cops usually like it when suspects talk." Durant grinned. He just couldn't resist giving the knife a twist.

Kowalczyk didn't seem to like being wrong. About anything. "Reisman has no living relatives," he insisted.

The prosecutor, standing behind Kowalczyk with the laptop, had read the results by now as well. I could tell because his face was working hard to hide his disappointment.

"He has at least two," I said.

"And you know where they are?" Kowalczyk asked.

"I know where one of them is."

"This supposed sister?"

"No. His father. He'll submit a DNA sample that shows he's the father of both the murderer and victim."

Kowalczyk leaned back and cupped his hands behind his head. He stared at the ceiling, thinking. The prosecutor slid the laptop in front of him, then turned his back to us and put his hands in his pockets. Maybe he was one of those thinkers whose thoughts showed on his face and he didn't want us to see.

"Why would Reisman's sister want to kill him?" Kowalczyk asked.

"Inheritance," I said. Though I thought there was more to it, I had no evidence yet, so I left it at that.

The prosecutor turned around. Kowalczyk straightened up and gave me a long appraising look, like he was trying to see through a con artist's scam. I remembered what Durant had told me about him that first day. Everyone's guilty in his eyes.

"The father has money? Reisman's father?"

"And hers," I said. "Probably a few million between his house and his business."

Kowalczyk shook his head. "This isn't how it works."

"This isn't how what works?"

The prosecutor's stare made me uneasy. His eyes never left my face.

"Killing for money." Kowalczyk stood and walked along the glass wall that looked out to the hall. "You want to get rid of someone for money, you don't show up at the scene. You hire someone else to get rid of them, and you try to make it look like an accident. This was a violent murder. This kind of thing, either it's a crime of passion—a heat-of-the-moment situation with a long history of turmoil leading up to it—or the perpetrator has some kind of psychopathology, has a history of violence and at least a few priors. What's the name of this supposed sister?"

"Maggie Smith."

"Oh, great. You know where she lives?"

"No."

"What about her dad?" Kowalczyk continued. "I mean, assuming there's even a shred of truth to what you're telling me."

I could tell by his tone and his worried face he feared there might be more than a shred.

"He lives in Potomac."

"Does he know where to find his daughter?"

"No," I said. "And that right there tells you something about the family."

Kowalczyk scratched his neck and scowled, seemingly annoyed at his own thoughts.

The prosecutor continued to stare at me. There's a line between curiosity and rudeness, and there's another line between rudeness and aggression. In my mind he had already crossed the first and was heading for the second. If I wasn't in the position I was in, with all my money and worldly possessions, everything I'd pledged for bail at his mercy, I would have confronted him directly. I would have called him out for staring, made the other men in the room stare at *him*, put *him* on the spot in front of his colleagues, made him explain himself. But as things stood, I could do nothing. I had to bend over and take it, as Anton said.

"What's the father's name?" Kowalczyk asked.

"Lehmann," I said. "Roscoe."

"Lehmann? Like the appliance guy?"

"That's the one."

"Huh." Kowalczyk seemed to being trying to fit the pieces together in his mind. "Lehmann was Reisman's employer."

"He'll talk to you," I said. "I just came from his house. He thinks his daughter did it, though he's reluctant to say so without physical evidence to back him up. If he submits to a DNA test—and he will—and if the DNA shows he's the father of both the victim and the suspect, that's all the evidence anyone needs."

"You pay for Lehmann's DNA test," Kowalczyk said to Durant. "That's on your dime."

Durant smiled. "You have to wring some concession from me, don't you, Dennis? You have to score at least one point every time we meet."

"If you can prove the three were related," Kowalczyk said, "then I'll talk to Lehmann."

"You don't want to talk to him now?" I asked.

"If he's reluctant to talk without physical evidence, we'll be in a better position after we have that evidence. What are you smiling at, Anton?"

"You said *we*."

"By *we*, I mean the department. The state. The prosecution."

"Sure you do, Dennis."

"Shut up, Anton." Kowalczyk turned to me. "This sister, this *supposed* sister, you know what she looks like?"

"She looks a lot like me."

"Isn't that convenient?" he said sarcastically.

"Isn't it?" I asked.

"Both of you in the same apartment on the same night." Kowalczyk made no effort to hide his distrust.

"The fact that I was hired to go there," I said, "hired to get close to Reisman, a nervous, guarded man... No woman would naturally approach him, and if she did, his weird nervous energy would have warded her off. Someone wanted me to be near him. Someone needed the cover."

Kowalczyk said, "Let's see you prove that, Anton."

"Talk to *me*," I said, "not him. It's not a matter of law at this point, it's a matter of fact. And goddammit, stop staring at me."

That was to the prosecutor. Finally, he spoke.

"You don't know where Maggie Smith lives," he said. "Do you have any idea where she might be?"

"No. But I know who she might be with."

He nodded silently. "That's what you got from your meeting with Robert Smith yesterday in Las Vegas?"

"That's what I got."

"Claire!" Anton practically jumped out of his clothes. "You don't admit—"

"Oh, shut up, Anton. He already knows."

The prosecutor put his hands in his pockets and paced in front of the whiteboard.

"DNA is a lot more convincing than circumstantial evidence," he began, "and a lot more reliable than eyewitnesses. Any lowlife defense attorney"—he glanced at Anton—"can sow seeds of doubt over those."

"I have more for you," I said. "Her companion has a conviction for forging identity documents, and apparently he's still at it. They're both traveling under false names, with IDs good enough to fool TSA. Anton said there's video of the killer leaving Reisman's building through a rear exit. She gets into a BMW like mine and peels out..."

I stopped as a new realization struck me.

The day Reisman was killed, he had lingered almost two hours in Best Buy, agonizing over the purchase of the iPhone. I waited outside, looking at the BMW idling in the next row of the lot. Blue like mine, the air conditioning dripping water onto the pavement beneath. I had made up a whole story in my mind about the woman in that car. A woman waiting for her husband to buy a computer. I imagined she was thinking about dinner. How long had she been following me, waiting for her opportunity?

"What?" asked Kowalczyk. All three men were staring at me.

"You remember I told you I went to Lehmann's house? That he hired me to investigate Reisman?"

Kowalczyk nodded.

"Have you examined my phone?"

Kowalczyk and the prosecutor exchanged glances.

"Oh, you know where I'm going with this, don't you? You saw the photo of that SUV I took in Lehmann's driveway the day I went there. Your forensics guys would know exactly where and when it was taken because it's timestamped and geo-tagged. And you know as well that I've been visiting Lehmann since the murder. There's a cop in his driveway. Don't tell me he hasn't mentioned that your murder suspect keeps showing up at the house of the man who hired her. The man you didn't believe hired her. Let me ask you this: Did you go to Dulles Airport to check up on that SUV? Find out who rented it?"

Kowalczyk sat stone-faced. I couldn't tell if he had or hadn't.

"Because I did. It was rented by a man named Buzz DiNardo, who doesn't exist. He lives at an address in Illinois that also doesn't exist, and he was travelling with a woman named Anna Graham, who doesn't exist either. The day he returned the SUV, the day before the murder, she rented a blue BMW that looked like mine. She returned it the day after the murder. Are things falling into place now? Do you get it?"

Kowalczyk was unreadable, but the prosecutor's eyes showed it all. If looks could kill!

I didn't like the way that man had glared at me earlier, or the fact that I couldn't say anything about it at the time, so I couldn't resist a dig now that I had the upper hand.

"Oh, you don't like this, do you? You brought me here to twist my arm, and now I'm twisting yours."

Anton said, "Ease up, Claire."

"Look, you know that's not my DNA under Reisman's nails." I turned to Kowalczyk. "And you saw my hands and arms the day after the murder. You grabbed them without asking, remember? Reisman scratched someone in the altercation, but it wasn't me.

"I have copies of the car rental contracts. Freddy Furguson has access to flight records—"

"He's working on this?" Kowalcyk interrupted. The question was directed at Anton, who smiled and nodded.

"How does a guy like him do work for a guy like you?"

Anton rubbed his fingers together. Money. Kowalczyk shook his head in dismay.

"I'd be happy to give you what evidence I have," I said. "And you need to talk to Roscoe Lehmann. There's more to this story than meets the eye. Just, please, drop these charges. Please release my bail. Let me get back to my life."

The prosecutor motioned to Kowalczyk, and the two of them stepped into the hall.

"What do you think that's about?" I asked.

"Mommy and daddy have to make sure they're on the same page," Anton said. He was watching them through the glass.

When they returned a minute later, Kowalczyk spoke.

"The charges remain."

"Why?" demanded Anton. "You know you can't win this case."

Kowalczyk leaned back and stroked his chin. "If the killer went to these lengths to plan all this, there's more to the story that we're not seeing."

There is, I thought. But you'll never get it out of Lehmann. I can't get it out of him even though he hired me. And he's terrified of you.

"It's also likely," Kowalczyk continued, "that she's watching the case. If she sees the charges are dropped, she'll know we'll be coming for her. Let's not tip her off. For now, the charges remain."

"Drop the bail restrictions," I said. "I want to be able to move around freely."

Kowalczyk looked at the prosecutor. I tried not to. My dislike would show, and this wasn't the time to antagonize him.

"How do I justify that to the judge?" asked the prosecutor. "I'm basically saying, yeah, she's still violent, still a murderer, let's turn her loose, let her go wherever she wants."

"Come on, Bill," coaxed Anton. "You're as good at making up stories as I am."

"But I stick to the truth."

"I'd like to hear you say that under oath."

"Shut up, Anton."

"Can you swing it for us?" Anton put on his best car-dealer grin.

The prosecutor thought for a moment. Finally, reluctantly, "Your client will be free to travel. You might want to keep her on a leash though."

39

Durant was quiet when we left the building. Strangely quiet. I could tell he had something to say. He just didn't want to say it within earshot of the building.

A block from the office, he pulled up short and blurted, "You are the worst client I have ever had. *Ever!*" He was trying hard to suppress a smile.

"I'm innocent."

"All my clients are innocent!" he bellowed.

"Do you actually believed that, or is it something you tell yourself so you can sleep at night?"

"Claire, you wound me!" He clutched his heart in dramatic illustration.

"Innocence isn't the point," he explained. "The first thing you need to learn as a victim of the criminal justice system is to shut the hell up. Let your attorney do the talking."

"Whether what comes out of his mouth is true or not," I added.

"Everything I say is true," he insisted. "Okay, everything I say has a grain of truth. Or at least cannot be disproved beyond a shadow of a doubt."

"If you didn't want me to talk, why did you bring me here?"

"I wanted the prosecutor to threaten you, bring you in line so you behave. Because you sure as hell don't listen to my threats."

"Did you honestly think I could stand there and not say anything? Do you know me at all, Anton?"

He gripped his temple like he had a migraine coming on. "I know you well enough, Claire. Better than I want to at this point. I just thought that with a bail violation, with everything you own on the line, you could hold your tongue for ten minutes."

"You thought wrong."

"Obviously."

"But it all worked out."

"And what if it didn't? What if you took that gamble and it didn't pay off?"

"I was willing to risk it."

"Well that's something a good attorney will not do on a client's behalf. Take a risk like that. I like to have all my ducks in a row before the battle starts. I want to know where the ground is firm and where it's weak. I want to know the strategy, what evidence my opponent has, how he thinks."

"Anton, an innocent man was murdered."

"Yeah, yeah."

"And I don't want someone getting away with that. Plus, she framed me."

"Ha!" he snorted. "Now we're getting to the heart of the matter."

"What's that supposed to mean?"

"It means don't mess with Claire. Claire won't put up with anyone trying to screw her over."

"That's right, Anton. I won't."

"That's a lesson you learn the hard way. Don't mess with Claire."

"And you wanted me in sundress, smiling for the jury."

"How could you have stood me?" he asked with feigned mortification. It was the sort of mock drama I imagined he employed often in the courtroom.

"You're a good balance to my temper," I said. "I take everything seriously. You take nothing seriously."

"It only looks that way," he said. "Smiles on the outside, ulcers on the inside. Especially with a client like you. Where'd you park again?"

"Further up."

Anton was sweating in the mid-morning heat, though I think it was as much from frustration as from the weather. He kept quiet for the next block and a half until we reached my BMW.

A quiet Anton, I knew by now, was not a happy Anton. When we got to my car, he told me what was on his mind.

"Kowalczyk was right. The way Reisman was killed, that kind of violence doesn't come out of the blue. A murder like this has a past behind it. Do you know how long Reisman and his sister knew each other?"

"Maggie didn't know he existed until a few months ago. They talked on the phone before he left California, and then she visited him in a psych hospital here in Maryland."

"You dug all that up yourself?"

"You think I just sit on my ass all day?"

"Sometimes I wish you would. Keep you out of trouble. Still, it doesn't make sense. If they only had a few interactions, how could she have developed the kind of hatred that would lead to such a violent murder? Unless maybe the hatred wasn't for him. Maybe she hated someone else."

"I think you're right."

"What? You're talking like you know something."

"I didn't want to say it in front of Kowalczyk because if he talked to Lehmann... Well, Lehmann is delicate enough as it is. If Kowalczyk even looks at him funny, Lehmann will clam up."

"You didn't want to say what in front of Kowalczyk?"

"What I told you on the phone the other night. Lehmann thinks Maggie killed her other brother, her full brother, in a boating incident four years ago."

"What happened? You never gave me the details."

"The son was waterskiing. Maggie was driving. He fell. She turned around to get him and hit him with the boat, apparently at high speed. He died of head injuries."

"Was she charged?"

"It was ruled an accident. But think about it. Lehmann's son dies of head injuries. A few years later, a new son appears. He dies of head injuries too, but this time it's obviously a murder. Like an echo killing. Like, look what I can do, daddy. Show me another heir and I'll do it again.

"Lehmann was grooming his first son to take over the business. He still has photos of George in his office, but no photos of his wife or daughter anywhere. He doesn't talk to Maggie, but he takes in a son he's never met, gives him a job, pays for expensive psychological help, gives him an apartment, new furniture.

"I think you're right, Anton. The hatred wasn't for Reisman, it was for daddy. Which makes me wonder..."

"Wonder what?"

"What happened to Maggie's mother."

40

Vanessa Ridge, retired nurse from Our Lady of Mercy, lived in a single-story brick rambler in the woods off MacArthur Boulevard. When we spoke on the phone, her voice was clear, modest, and assured. She seemed to take the world in stride. I told her I wanted to talk about a patient from many years back, long deceased. She said simply, "Well, why don't you come over and I'll see if I can help you?"

The front yard was planted with azaleas, viburnum, and hydrangeas. A woman in khakis was watering the viburnum with a hose as I pulled into the drive. If not for her grey ponytail, a person watching from behind might have guessed she was in her thirties. She moved with ease and grace, turning only at the last second at the sound of my car.

"You're Claire?"

She had an easy manner.

"Let me turn this off and we'll go inside. I keep watering the hydrangeas even though they don't need it. This heat is killing the blooms." She twisted the spigot shut and dried her hands on her pants.

"The flowers will come back when the weather cools. Come inside, will you? The mosquitoes are out at midday! Can you believe it? The savages! It's what you get for living in the woods near a canal. Would you like some ice water?"

"That would be great."

She led me to a glassed-in porch at the rear of the house. The back yard was an explosion of white peonies and red roses. In the center was a round patch of grass, and in the middle of that, a marble birdbath. A hummingbird hovered at a feeder outside the window.

Inside, the room had a couch, coffee table and two cushioned chairs. The remains of her breakfast—a plate with crumbs and an empty mug whose sides were stained with coffee—stood on a table by the side window.

The table opposite held a record player and a stack of classical records. Books were strewn everywhere, many open and upside down. She seemed to be in the middle of reading a dozen different volumes.

"You wanted to ask me about a patient?"

She sat on the couch. I was in one of the cushioned chairs.

"Maggie Lehmann."

"Mmm." She closed her eyes and nodded. "There's not much I can say about her."

"You remember her?"

"She was with us for many years. But, you know, she never moved or spoke. She had brain damage. If you want me to tell you what type of person she was, I'm afraid I can't help you."

"Do you know what happened to her? How she was injured?"

"Yes. Yes. She had gone into shock from an allergic reaction. I remember there being some fuss when she arrived. Her doctors were upset, no... Someone was upset, I don't remember who, about there being penicillin in the house. Why would you have it in the house if you're deathly allergic to it? Ah—it was the daughter! Mary. She was the one who was upset."

"Maggie?"

"She was just a girl. Five or so. You can't blame her for being upset."

"What do you remember about her?" I asked.

"She visited often. Almost every week, it seemed. She sat at the bedside and, when she was older, she read to her mother. One of the nurses had told her early on that her mother might be able to hear what's going on around her, despite showing no outward signs of consciousness. We never really knew for sure. But the girl held onto that, the idea her mom could hear her.

"She was young when her mother came in, and she had witnessed the tragedy, the anaphylactic reaction. It's a frightening thing even for a seasoned medical professional to see a person in that kind of distress. The face can swell with hives. They struggle to breath. You can feel their terror. I can't imagine a five-year-old watching her mother go through that.

"But she visited almost every week. That girl was reading to her mother at age eleven, twelve, sixteen. All the way to the end."

"Did Mrs. Lehmann's husband ever visit?"

She thought for a while. "In the beginning, yes. But only to bring the daughter. When she was older, he'd drop her off, leave her in the room, and then go out with the boy. I don't remember his name, but I remember the father was very fond of him."

"Do you know how Mrs. Lehmann happened to take penicillin? It doesn't seem like something a person would do by accident."

"No," she said sharply. "It doesn't, does it?" I sensed a hint of suspicion in her words.

"From what I recall," she said, "they both were sick. The husband and the wife. It was some seasonal thing. Bronchitis? Walking pneumonia? I don't remember. He got penicillin, she was allergic, so they gave her something else. He left for work early one morning, but first he gave her a pill. One of *his* pills, which she wasn't supposed to have. I don't know how a person makes a mistake like that. I don't know if you've ever taken the time to notice, but medicines are designed on purpose to look different, so you won't visually confuse them. But somehow, he did. He gave her the wrong pill and then he left."

"How do you know he gave it to her?"

"Mary told me."

"You mean Maggie. The daughter."

"I mean Mary. She went by Mary then."

"But she was five when it happened. How could she be sure her father gave her mom the wrong pill?"

"You can't trust the memory of a five-year-old. I shouldn't repeat it as fact, but that was what she said and believed.

"The Lehmann's doctor told me that the parents kept an EpiPen in the bathroom. The mother had a penicillin allergy, which wasn't likely to ever get triggered. But the father was allergic to nuts. Deathly allergic. The pen was for him, because that kind of allergy can be triggered very easily."

I remembered something then. When I first met the real Roscoe Lehmann in the office of his appliance showroom, he was carrying a tin of cookies, a gift that had been waiting for him on his secretary's desk. He read the ingredients and then told his secretary, "He knows I can't eat these." That would have been because of the nut allergy.

"They had taught the son," Vanessa continued, "to use the EpiPen. He went to the bathroom to get it when he saw his mother struggling to breathe. The girl, I can only imagine, watched in terror.

"The pen wasn't there. The boy looked and looked. Maybe for too long. It may have already been too late for the mother when he called 911. The medics gave her a shot as soon as they found her, but by then, she had gone too long without air. She lived, but she wasn't ever really alive after that."

I asked her what she remembered about Maggie, the daughter. She told me she was quiet and withdrawn until adolescence, and then she became angry.

"She had this sort of brooding hostility. You could see it in her eyes. I worried about her mental health. Toward the end of her mother's life, her mother began to make some sounds. Not words. Not that we heard, anyway, but she was vocalizing. I do think she understood her daughter was beside her.

"But Mary, the daughter, was convinced her mother was trying to communicate. Maybe she was. I don't know.

"Her mother eventually died of heart failure. We could see it coming. It's not a sudden thing. We prepared the family. The father and son seemed to take it in stride. They had moved on in their lives. They knew for years this day would come, and I think they saw it as merciful relief.

"The girl took it badly. Some people rage in grief. I could see it in her eyes. But she wouldn't let it out. It was this black whirlpool swirling inside. I told her father she needed counseling to work through this. She was deeply attached. And when her mother did pass, she said something very disturbing to one of the nurses.

"She said her mother told her, just before she died, that her father had poisoned her on purpose. That he had taken the EpiPen before giving her the penicillin, so it wouldn't be there to save her. I am certain her mother told her no such thing. I am certain her mother couldn't and didn't speak.

"But the girl was convinced, and at that point, it doesn't matter if it's true or not. All that matters is that, in her mind, it's a fact.

"I ran into her, to Mary, in Whole Foods on River Road a year after her mother died. I said, 'Hello, Mary.' She remembered me. She told me her name was Maggie. It had been Mary Margaret, I knew that. But now she was Maggie.

"I got a strange feeling from her, like she was locked inside. Like she had retreated deep into herself and was peering out at the world from the dark. I told myself she was still grieving. She must have been seventeen then. Teens have enough emotion to deal with, just being teens. This was taking her a long time to process.

"But this is all heavy talk. I'm sorry to weigh you down with it. In all my years as a nurse, my biggest take-away has been that you can't solve anyone else's problems. Most people can't even solve their own problems. I don't like to dwell on the world's hurts. There are too many of them. This—"

She pointed to a bird hovering at the feeder outside the window.

"This is a ruby-throated hummingbird. He drinks nectar, which is really just sugar water. This is what I like to look at in retirement. The birds, the flowers, the Monarchs in the butterfly bushes. When all we think about are our troubles, we forget these things. We forget that God made this world a lot more beautiful than it needed to be. He could have gotten away with a cursory job, left us with rocks and water and just enough to eat. But he put color everywhere, the marks of his love on everything. Only we forget to see. We don't take the time for it. Well, now is the time."

She raised her ice water to her lips, took a sip and set it down.

"All the years I put into nursing were a down payment on this. This time of real living. What is it you do, Ms. Chastain?"

I had fallen so far under her spell, I was embarrassed to tell her. I wanted to *be* this woman who had found her garden and wanted nothing more. I wanted to be at peace with myself the way she was, and I wondered if I'd ever make it to that place.

"I wrap myself up in the troubles of the world," I said. "In my own, and in other people's."

"For money?"

"Yes."

"The person who chooses a life like that has something to work out of her system."

"I suppose so."

"I did at your age. And I think I pretty well worked it out. If you have a passion for what you're doing, you're on the right path."

41

At home an hour later, I stood at the bathroom sink thinking about the timeline of events in the Lehmann's lives. Maggie, the daughter, was now thirty-two. Jacob Reisman was twenty-five. If he was born when Maggie was seven, Roscoe's tryst in the hotel must have happened when Maggie was six, just a year or so after her mother was silenced forever and hidden away in a nursing home. Roscoe himself told me it was sixteen months, but it may have been less.

Maggie would have done the math on that when she first learned about Reisman. That could only have been fuel on the fire of her hatred for daddy.

I thought about her ex-husband's story. Was the strangulation in the bedroom a reenactment of what happened in Maggie's home when she was five? A reenactment where this time she was the powerful one, the one who walked out indifferently on the victim who couldn't breathe?

Robert Smith had said, "I still don't know what I did to set her off."

Maybe you didn't do anything, I thought. Maybe the offense had been committed decades earlier, by someone else. Maybe, as you said, even she didn't know she was going to do it. The opportunity arose, and the feelings slipped out. She re-enacted an ancient scene etched into the psyche of a child in the primordial language of terror, helplessness, and rage.

I felt a sudden pang of sympathy for that young girl and for the woman she had become. Looking at my own face in the mirror, I wondered how close I had come to being like her.

Not a murderer, but bitter, keeping score, seeing myself as a victim.

I had those same feelings in me all my life, but somehow, when my own crisis came, I turned the other way.

I wrecked what could have been a good marriage because I trusted no one. I wasn't comfortable at work unless I knew people were scared of me. I told myself it was wariness, precaution against being victimized, but really it was hostility. I had to ward people off or they'd find some way to hurt me, take advantage of me. My preemptive bitchiness, my porcupine's armor, came as much from fear of appearing weak as from real strength. That's as much a victim mentality as Maggie's, isn't it? Letting fear rule your life, letting it shape the way you treat other people.

I wrecked my life in New York, burned my bridges, then came home to something worse, to the festering nest where it all started. What stopped me from becoming Maggie? From becoming more hostile, harder, more bitter, like my grandmother who raised me? Why did I turn around when I did? Why not go one step further and wreck everything?

I don't know. I honestly don't. Is there such a thing as grace? And if so, why do some people receive it while others don't?

I want to put her away, I thought. Because of what she did to Jake, what she did to her brother, what she put her father through, what she put me through.

I don't like her.

When I look at her, I see the part of *myself* that needs to be put away, the destructive part that can no longer be abroad in the world.

You were right, Roscoe Lehmann. The investigator is more motivated when she has skin in the game. Once and for all, I want to put away that bitter person who can't get past her victimhood. She has no place in this world.

42

The phone woke me at eight the next morning. Anton.

"Were you asleep?"

"Yeah." I rubbed my eyes. "God, I never sleep this late." I was on the couch too. Fully dressed.

"Kowalczyk talked to Lehmann. At his house."

"How'd it go?" I stood and walked unsteadily to the kitchen.

"Not so good. Kowalczyk admits he screwed up the interview. Lehmann needs a light touch. Kowalczyk can be aggressive when thinks he's onto something."

I pulled the coffee pot from the burner, dumped the remains into the sink.

"Please tell me he thinks he's onto something."

In the cabinet above the coffeemaker, I found a filter.

"All he got out of Lehmann was that Reisman was his son. But that's all it took. Kowalczyk pounced, started asking about the daughter and Lehmann clammed up. Like a petulant child, as Kowalczyk put it. I didn't know that word was in his vocabulary, and I'm not sure he used it correctly. Anyway, his manner intimidated Lehmann. But he did get one thing out of him."

"What?"

I dumped extra beans into the grinder for a strong pot.

"A DNA swab."

"Who told you all this?"

"Kowalczyk."

"Since when do cops talk to defense attorneys?"

"Since he hates my guts and you being off the hook means I'm out of his hair. Plus, I think the guy actually respects you. You at the sink?"

"Filling the coffee pot." I yawned. "Sorry, Anton, I don't even remember falling asleep last night."

"You have a lot going on right now. It takes a toll, even if you don't want to admit it."

"How long do you think it'll take to get the DNA results from Lehmann's swab?"

I dumped the water into the coffee maker and returned to the grinder.

"I don't know. But once they're in, if everything you say is correct, the evidence shows Lehmann is the father of both victim and killer, and there's only one living person who fits the bill for the assailant's DNA. There'll be a warrant out soon enough. If—*if*—this all pans out."

I put the lid on the grinder but held off on pressing the button. The noise would have drowned out the call.

"You say 'if' like you don't believe me."

"I'm a defense attorney. My job is to cast doubt."

"It's a habit of mind, Anton. Like Kowalczyk thinking everyone's guilty."

"Makes us good at what we do. Look, I gotta go. I have a client accused of burning down his own business just to get the insurance money. These damn insurance companies will slander anyone to keep from paying. So what if the place was soaked in gasoline? Coulda been vandals."

"Go fight for justice, Anton."

I put the phone down, leaned on the grinder and watched the beans whirr into dust.

The red badge on the bottom of my phone screen showed I had missed a call. I dumped the ground coffee into the filter and tapped the phone icon. Roscoe Lehmann had called last night. At seven-thirty. And I was asleep.

I put the phone down, went to the bathroom, made toast, waited for the coffee.

Lehmann's behavior with Kowalczyk made sense. He couldn't bring himself to say what he believed. He needed the evidence to say it for him. The physical evidence, the DNA against which no one could argue.

Vanessa Ridge had given me a new perspective on the source of Lehmann's reticence. I didn't believe his excuse for not talking, his fear that the murder accusations against his daughter would damage his family. What did his family have left to lose? His paralyzing fear was deeper than a mere wish for privacy, and stronger, it seemed, than his sense of justice for his sons.

His fear was personal.

Maybe there was some truth to Maggie's belief that he had deliberately poisoned her mother. Maybe his daughter had been goading him all these years, daring him to go to the police, to throw everything wide open to public view, to have a full reckoning of the family history, knowing that his guilt over what was at the bottom of it all, his fear of *that* being exposed, would stop him. She could prod and provoke, push him ever further into the fire, and he would make no effort to get himself out. Let him roast in his own cowardice and guilt and shame. Could there be a more just punishment for a man who killed his own wife, who killed the mother of his children?

But no one can endure that forever. Eventually, it becomes intolerable. Eventually, you ask for help. You acknowledge you are a sick and broken family. You can no longer go on as you are, so you reach out to someone who can end it. Someone who will expose the truth you're too scared to reveal.

I picked up the phone, tapped voicemail and listened to the message.

I didn't hear a voice at first. Just a thwack, followed by three loud cracks echoing in what sounded like a cavernous space. Then the murmur of oohing voices. Thwack! Two echoing cracks. A cheer from a small crowd. An announcer's voice: "Outside the line. Etch-a-berry serves." Then a rustling sound, something rubbing against the phone's mic. Then the call cut off.

Lehmann must have butt-dialed me. I called him back.

"Were you at a tennis match last night?"

"I was in no state to go anywhere last night. I had a visit from the detective investigating Jake's murder."

"What did you tell him?"

Long silence.

"I'm sorry, Claire. I'm not in the habit of telling people things. I gave him a swab from my cheek. Or rather, I allowed his assistant, whoever she was, to take it. I want this all to be over. I want someone to tell me it will all be over soon. But it will never be over."

"Would it help, Roscoe, if I wrote up a statement of what you and I believe to have happened? Then you wouldn't have to say it yourself. You just sign and attest."

"I'm busy, Claire. I'm working. Leave me alone." He hung up.

His excuse sounded weak and pathetic, and I think he knew it. I think he was finally coming to terms with the fact that he neither liked nor respected himself.

I listened to his message again. And again. And again.

It wasn't a tennis match. A tennis ball makes a *puck* sound. Whatever Etch-a-berry was serving made a thwacking, cracking sound, like a hard ball hitting a hard surface at high speed.

And the message didn't come from Lehmann. I had two Roscoe Lehmanns in my contacts. The real one, and the fake number that belonged to Buzz DiNardo, aka Dice Colson. I had entered the fake number into my contacts at the start of the case and had never deleted it.

Lehmann didn't butt-dial me. Dice Colson did.

I thought he would have ditched that phone, but apparently not. The whole point of a burner is you get rid of it after the crime.

At our lunch in Vegas, Maggie's ex, Robert Smith, had told me Dice wasn't as smart as Maggie. It didn't look like he was even smart enough to be in this line of work.

I listened to the message again. Twenty more times.

By ten a.m. I had figured out who Etch-a-berry was. At 12:30, I was on a plane to see him.

Ilari Etxeberri had a 180-mile-an-hour serve. The bettors in South Florida loved him, even if every now and then he served outside the lines.

43

"Okay, so let me get this straight. He's not your husband?"

Ashlynn didn't dress like a prostitute. At least, now how I pictured one. Black tights and a white t-shirt with a big red lipstick kiss, white sunglasses in her left hand, Marlins cap over straight dark hair. A college kid's clothes, only she was close to thirty.

"No," I said.

"Not your boyfriend?"

"No."

She looked uneasily around the hotel room. My bag was on the bed, half unpacked. I'd stopped here briefly after landing in Fort Lauderdale, threw the suitcase on the bed, and then took a Lyft to the casino at Dania Beach.

I'd seen the Jai Alai court on YouTube. I had watched a few examples of Ilari Etxeberri's fearsome serve. Tall and lanky, with dark eyes and chiseled face, he wound up with an exaggerated pitcher's motion and launched the ball from his cesta at impossible speed.

Thwack!

It ricocheted off the front wall, and from there, the man behind him tried to corral it in the long scoop affixed to his right hand and send it back.

It was mid-afternoon when I got to the casino. The next game wouldn't start till seven. I didn't have to look long or far for Dice Colson. He was at the slots, drink in hand, looking bored.

He must be down on his luck, I thought. Playing quarter slots and eating ice from the remains of a gin and tonic. At least that's what I guessed had been in his glass, given the wedge of lime he kept spitting out.

I watched him lose a few rounds. When his ice was gone, he chewed the lime, made a sour face, then headed to the bar. The bartender's greeting told me Dice was a regular. The greeting, and the fact that he refilled the gin and tonic without asking or being told. Not yet four o'clock, and Dice was on at least his second drink.

I remembered what Robert Smith had said about him in Las Vegas. Dice would bet on anything, even horses and dogs, because he liked the two minutes of suspense where he thought he might win. A Jai Alai match lasted much longer than two minutes, and if you're short on cash it's a good way to stretch out the suspense.

I made a guess he'd be there at seven, when the match began. And then I almost made a bad mistake. I should have waited till I got back to my hotel to use the bathroom. But he was wrapped up in conversation with the bartender, and the restrooms were far from where he was sitting.

I was wrong to take my eyes off him, even for a minute. I almost ran into him on the way out of the women's room. If his head hadn't been turned the other way, eyes glued to the ass of a women in a tight red dress, we might have come face to face.

I went straight for the exit and never looked back.

I can't go near him, I thought. No way.

So, what to do?

Robert Smith had told me more in Vegas than he realized.

We have a difference in philosophy. I don't go to hookers...

The woman who was going to help me flicked her sunglasses nervously in her hand. She shot a glance past the bed, toward the bathroom, as if she were half expecting someone to come out.

"Are we alone?"

"There's no one else here," I said.

"You sure this isn't for you? Like, you wanna…" She said the rest with her eyes.

"Not for me. For him."

"Okay," she said. I could tell she was nervous. "I'm going to have to check in with my agency. Before and after. This isn't usually…" She stopped, made an inventory of my clothes on the bed. "This isn't usually how it works."

"Bring someone with you if you want."

"A threesome?"

"No, I mean, like a bodyguard."

"Do I need one?"

"If it makes you feel safer. Someone to wait outside."

"If I do, you'll have to pay for his time."

I told her I didn't mind.

"Your friend isn't into S and M, is he?"

"I have no idea. If you don't feel comfortable, just get out."

"I know how to read a guy, and I know when to leave. Just the more I know up front, the better. This is in a hotel, right?"

"You pick the place." I handed her a pre-paid Visa card. "You'll need that to check in. There's only two hundred on there, so don't aim too high."

"I mean, as long as he's not a creep, it's just a question of, well…" She studied the card for a moment. "Special requests cost extra."

"You don't have to do anything with him."

"I do if you want me to put that app on his phone. Why do you want to stalk him anyway? If he's not your boyfriend and not your husband? That's creepy."

"I can't follow him myself. He knows what I look like."

She stared at me blankly for a second, and then seemed to decide she didn't want to know any more.

"Pay up front."

"I'll pay you now. And more on the back end if it works."

"Okay, walk me through this." She sat on the edge of the bed. "What's the app? How do I get it onto his phone?"

I showed her what Freddy Ferguson had showed me on a Zoom call while I waited for my flight at Reagan National.

Where to download the app, how to set it up. Click install. It asks for permissions. Click yes on everything. The whole process takes thirty seconds.

"It'll ask you for a code, so it knows where to send information." I handed her a slip of paper. "Type that in. Then it goes into stealth mode. He won't even know it's on his phone. No icon or anything. It just runs invisibly in the background."

"What if he has a password? What if I can't get in?"

"See if you can unlock it with his finger."

She smiled.

"What?" I asked.

"Just thinking how I'd do that without him knowing what I'm doing."

The rules of evidence say none of what I gather will be admissible in court.

I don't care. The evidence that matters is back in Maryland, in the hands of the Montgomery County Police.

I just want to know where he goes, and if he can lead me to her.

44

At six, we drove to the casino in Ashlynn's car. Dice was planted at the bar, same stool as before. His slouching posture told me he was off his guard. He'd probably had a few drinks since I'd last seen him.

I scanned the room for Maggie Smith. I was more nervous about running into her than him. From the way her ex-husband described her, she didn't seem like the type who would ever be off guard.

"That him?" Ashlynn asked. "He's older than I thought. You know what games he likes?"

"Craps, slots, dogs. Anything."

"Give me some cash to gamble with."

"What's your plan?"

"Strike up a chat. Lead him to blackjack. Play dumb. Get him to coach me." She smiled like she was looking forward to the game.

I left her to her job.

45

Work doesn't make me nervous, as long as I'm the one doing it. What makes me nervous is depending on other people, especially people I don't know.

I went to a grill on Hollywood Beach and waited. The bar was long enough to seat thirty, though this evening it was mostly empty. Behind the bar, a wall of glass looked out on the sand and surf. I imagined the windows would be open in winter to let in the warmth, but in July it was just too hot.

The concrete floors and glass walls would have made the place loud if it had been more crowded, but in the low season, there were only six people at the bar and three tables of two. The bartender, a dark-haired woman with a Cuban accent, asked if I'd like a menu.

"Yes, please." The smell of seafood sharpened my appetite.

Something behind me caught her eye as she handed me the menu. I instinctively turned to look and wound up locking eyes with a young blonde-haired guy whose white shirt was unbuttoned to show off the pecs he'd spent all summer pumping up. He was sunburnt from head to toe, one of those awful burns that stretches the skin taut and makes it shine. He had a broad, round face and the cocksure confidence you only see in men who are too stupid to know they're stupid. He couldn't have been more than twenty-five.

Oh, God, I thought. Just once, let me have a quiet meal in public.

The bartender shot me a look and tried hard to suppress a smile.

He was on me before I could even look at the menu, slid onto the next stool without asking if I minded, and said, "Let me guess. New York." He put his finger to his lips in emulation of a thinking being and added, "Lawyer."

Then came the smile. Big, impossibly white teeth. Just the thing to charm a drunk twenty-one-year-old on spring break.

He didn't seem to notice I was eleven years older and a hundred percent more sober than his usual target.

"I nailed it, didn't I?" His red face lit with pride.

"Let me guess," I replied. "Gold's Gym. Bus boy. Fell asleep and roasted on the beach because you were hung over."

"Shit! You're, like, psychic or something. Except a barback is not a busboy. What are you drinking?"

"Do you see a drink in front of me?"

"No, but I can fix that. Ever had a sex on the beach?"

"Tell me you didn't just say that."

The bartender watched with amusement. "Tripp? You want a beer?"

"Yeah sure. And for the lady..." He pointed at me.

"Pinot grigio," I said.

Tripp's breath told me this wasn't his first beer of the evening. His burnt red skin was hard to look at. It hadn't begun to peel yet. The sun had bleached his thick blond eyebrows and now they looked like two white caterpillars facing off above the nose of a giant talking tomato.

"What are you doing in Hollywood?" he asked.

"Trying to have a peaceful dinner."

My phone chimed. First text from Ashlynn. Thumbs up emoji and a quick note. "He's half-cocked already. Players are taking the court."

"Tripp." The bartender made a subtle cutting motion with her hand. "Chill."

"Just trying to have a conversation. Pretty lady sitting all alone, no one to talk to. Hey!" He clapped and pointed at me. "Save this spot, I'll be right back."

As he headed to the restroom, the bartender leaned in. "He'll leave after he has his beer. He has no work in the offseason, and I never spot him more than one draft. Unless you want me to get rid of him now."

"It's Okay," I said. "At least he distracts me from the other things on my mind."

If the plan with Ashlynn failed, what then? I couldn't try the same trick two nights in a row. Dice would catch on. He'd know someone was trying to play him.

The tomato came back from the bathroom and nursed his beer for thirty minutes. He ate half my calamari appetizer and probably would have eaten all of it if the bartender hadn't shoved a basket of rolls in front of him. I nodded a silent thank you for that.

Tripp asked if I knew that oysters were an aphrodisiac. He told me he knew where to have a good time in Miami. And in Lauderdale. And West Palm. Shit, if there was fun to be had in Clewiston, he could find it. Tripp was a globetrotter with a nose for the highlife.

His new motorcycle was faster than his friend's. And it didn't burn oil, and both turn signals worked, because he didn't lay the bike down on the A1A like dumbass Tony. It was a sport bike with no backrest. If I wanted to ride, I'd have to wrap my arms around his ribs and hold on.

"You're in no shape to drive," I said.

"And you don't even have the bike yet," added the bartender.

"When the season rolls around, I'll be making bank." He slapped the back of his right hand into the palm of his left to emphasize the word. "New Year's Eve, you and me will take a ride." He pointed back and forth between himself and the bartender. "Pay you back for all the beer."

"I'd prefer cash," she said.

I was grateful when she nudged him along.

"Go on," she whispered. "You're done for tonight."

He stood and stretched, elbows behind his back, puffing out his chest and rocking his head from side to side to crack his neck. "Hey, I didn't get your name."

"Claire."

He pulled out his phone. "What's your number?"

"Why don't we leave well enough alone, Tripp?" I smiled as politely as I could. "Thank you for keeping me company and helping me eat my dinner."

He just stared at me.

"Tripp!" The bartender shooed him toward the door.

"Yeah. Whatever." He slid the phone into his pocket. "Later, you two."

* * *

Two hours later, 9:30 p.m., I was walking on the boardwalk. My phone made an unfamiliar chirp.

The tracking app had registered a location. The Super 8 Motel, just down the road from the casino.

I tapped the microphone icon and waited. All I could hear was the breaking of the waves from the ocean beside me. I turned up the volume and put the speaker to my ear.

Someone was snoring.

Then came the text from Ashlynn: "Hotel bar? Twenty minutes?"

46

"That was quicker than I thought."

She smiled. "He's the easiest kind there is."

"What does that mean?" I couldn't resist asking. "Like, missionary position, thirty seconds and done?"

"Like, stewed prune. Couldn't get it up and passed out trying."

She gave me a quick rundown of their evening. An accidental bump at the bar. A chat, flirty laugh, friendly eyes. One touch on the shoulder and he was hooked.

Her: *Teach me blackjack?*

Him: *Teach you to be a champ, baby!*

"I let him lead me to the tables. He wasn't very good. We ran through most of the money in thirty minutes. He told me to save some for Jai Alai. Then he nodded off during the match. In the hotel room, he was eager at first, but his eyes were bleary. He passed out on the bed.

"I did what you said. Unlocked the phone with his finger. I sat right next to him while I installed the app. He smells like a rotting still. Ugh, I hope I never come to that. Where's the rest of my money?"

I paid her.

47

I spent the next hour in my hotel room browsing Dice's phone through the spy app. It's sobering to know how much you can learn about a person from their phone.

Start with his browser history. He does lots of research on the horses running at Hialeah and Gulfstream. He watches girl-on-girl porn, lots of it. He searches daily for "Jacob Reisman murder". He looks at Airbnb rentals in the Miami-Fort Lauderdale area.

And then there's this cluster of searches: "Aries-Gemini chemistry." "How to make her want you." "Relationship counseling." "Restoring healthy communication." "Ten Signs You're an Alcoholic." "Viagra."

I go back further in time, see he searched for flights from Vegas to DC three and a half months ago. That would have been when Reisman was in Cortona. Mixed in with those searches, the stories The Washington Post ran about the drug ring I'd stumbled into last winter. One of those stories had a photo of me.

Dice's phone battery is at nine percent and falling.

I check his call history. Most of the numbers aren't in his contacts. I look up a few of them. Restaurants. Some look like takeout, the rest are too expensive for that. He must have been calling ahead to make reservations.

A couple of calls to Nevada. Those two are in his contacts. Someone named Larry. Someone named Jezz. Beyond that, he doesn't seem to talk much. Maybe he's laying low for a while. Maybe he just has no friends.

No calls to or from my number. That means this isn't the burner phone.

What's in his texts?

Confirmations that his Lyft is on the way. One-time passcodes from websites he logs into. Banks, maybe? There's no way to tell from the numbers.

As I scroll, a new message comes in from "Mags."

"Where the fuck are you?"

You should have put this app on his phone, Maggie. Keep better tabs on him.

I scroll back through their messages, the ones between Dice and Mags. All the ones from the past few days are about food. What takeout to pick up. Where to meet for dinner.

Then there's a gap. Nothing for months. Did he delete some chunk of their communication?

Then this:

Mags: What's my name?

Dice: Angela.

Mags: What time?

Dice: 12:30. Denver layover. Arrive Dulles 9:15.

Those were dated early April. Reisman was in Cortona then. This must have been a flight to visit him. She was flying under the name Angela, the same name she used on her July flight with Dice. The thread continued.

Dice: What's he like?

Mags: Brittle little tard. Fat, weak, pathetic, clingy. Makes me wonder what Roscoe fucked to make him. Some fat alley whore.

Dice: Think he's playing the old man? Trying to cash in?

Mags: He couldn't. Too stupid. Doesn't have to anyway. Roscoe throws money at him. The nuthouse is two or three grand a day, easy. That's 90K of MY MONEY down the drain every month.

Dice: Maybe you should go nuts. Get daddy to pamper you too.

Mags: Maybe you should go fuck yourself.

I scroll back another week.

Dice: Check it out. Twinsies!

The text has a link to the Washington Post story with my photo. I hadn't looked at that photo since the day the story came out. It brought back unpleasant memories. I look hard in that picture. Unfriendly. I remember everything I was feeling then. The gut-wrenching paranoia that comes from being stalked and physically attacked by men. The anger. It was there in my face.

Maggie must have taken some time to study the photo. Her response came twenty minutes later.

Mags: Hmm... Gives me an idea.
Dice: I don't like the sound of that.

Maggie replied with a grinning devil emoji.
Dice's battery icon flashes red. Three percent.
I lose contact.

48

I was drinking coffee in the hotel restaurant at 7:30 the next morning when my phone rang. I didn't recognize the number. For a second, I had this flashing fear that Maggie Smith had traced me through the spyware app on Dice's phone.

But the call came from the 301 area code. The Maryland suburbs.

"Hello?"

"What are you doing in Florida?" It was a man's voice.

"Who is this?"

"Dennis Kowalczyk. Where are you?"

"Hollywood, Florida. I'm allowed to travel now, remember?"

"Yeah, I know. Who did you talk to in Vegas?"

He knew who I spoke to. He had said so in our meeting with the prosecutor. I think he just wanted me to confirm it.

"A guy named Robert Smith," I said. "The ex-husband of Roscoe Lehmann's daughter."

"Yeah, the guy's got a record. And a reputation for a lot more than what they actually convicted him of. How the hell did you find that old man on the boat in Deale?"

"Rook? Did you talk to him?"

"I did. You know, the fact that Lehmann's got his house under twenty-four-hour guard, it made me wonder what he's so scared of. His son died in an accident and the only witness is his sister, the other heir to Lehmann's fortune. Why the fuck did the cops out there... Fuck it, never mind. Lehmann likes his peace and quiet."

"That he does."

"Everywhere I go, I find you've been there before me. And this is your first case?"

"Let's just say I'm very motivated."

"Yeah. It shows. You know where Maggie Smith is?"

"Not yet, but I think I'm getting close."

"Don't approach her on your own. Don't even show your face."

"I know better than that."

"Her husband was a rough character, and the cops in Vegas told me when she wanted to wear the pants, she did. What makes you think she's in Florida?"

"Woman's intuition."

"Bullshit."

"Her partner slipped up. Gave me a clue."

"The way things are going here, we may be able to get a warrant in the next day or two."

"What's the holdup?"

"The DNA test. If the skin under Reisman's nails belongs to a daughter of Roscoe Lehmann, that's enough for a warrant. Once we have results and a warrant, we can have someone down there take her into custody. We don't want to scare her off before then. Vegas tells us she has other identities. Fake papers. She's taken out credit cards in other people's names. That makes her hard to track. If you find her, call me. Don't try to do this yourself."

"I'll let you know when I find her."

For the next five hours, I stayed put in my room. Dice was probably still passed out at the Super 8 motel less than a mile away. Maggie could be anywhere in the vicinity. I wasn't going to risk going out in public. As far as they knew, I was in DC, charged with murder, restrained on bail, and no one knew where they were. No one was even looking for them.

49

Finally, at 1:17, that strange little chime. Dice's phone was back online. The battery was at 67 percent, but there was no location. Had he turned off the GPS?

I tapped the mic icon. Nothing. I turned up the volume, strained my ears. Nothing.

I set the phone on the nightstand, went to the window and looked out over the rooftops, the palms, the streams of traffic rolling silently down the gleaming avenues. Shadows of cotton-puff clouds raked the sidewalks and drifted out to sea.

Then at last came the sound of movement behind me. A rustling. Someone entering a room, perhaps. Then a knock. No, louder and harder than a knock. Something being put on a table. And a clink. A cup on a saucer?

Then a voice.

"Stop pacing, will you?"

A woman's voice. Sharp, irritable.

"I'm nervous." That was the voice of the man who had hired me at Lehmann's house.

Her: "You're weak. Learn some self-control."

Him: "I think you acted rashly."

"I'm not the one who can't remember who they fucked last night."

"You didn't need to do it that way. You should have stuck to the original plan. No contact. Hire a professional."

"How much did she cost, Dice? You're always so worried about money. Then you go and—"

"There was no reason to do it that way. No reason to take that kind of risk."

"What do you know about my reasons?"

"I know you're fucked. You're fucked in the head. This whole plan is fucked."

"Then why'd you go along with it?"

He didn't answer

"Why'd you go along with it?" she repeated coolly. She waited a second then said, "You'll get your money. Just relax and wait. Do you see me losing my cool?"

"No, because you're a fucking psychopath. That's what you are."

"Get a grip, Dice. Be a man."

"You're telling *me* to get a grip! I'm not the one who has to work out her daddy issues by bashing people's heads in, you psychotic fuck. Jesus, how long do we have stay down here?"

"Not much longer."

"What's taking him so long?"

Brief pause, then him again. "What? What's that look? I don't like that look."

Her, cool and easy: "No. You don't, do you?"

"Quit with the look, Okay?"

"Why don't you go to the casino? It's past noon and you haven't had a drink yet. Baby needs his bottle."

"You know, Bob was right. You are a cunt, you know that? A nasty fucking cunt. No wonder he beat your face in."

Her: "At least he had the balls. Get out of here, will you?"

A scraping sound. Maybe him picking up the phone from the table.

Then movement. Walking?

A few quiet huffs. I picture him putting on his shoes.

More walking. The ding of an elevator. In a minute, the sound of cars passing on the street.

Him muttering, almost drowned out by the wind and traffic. "Why's it so fucking hot down here? Vegas is an oven and this place is a steam bath. I swear, I'm in hell. Everywhere I go is a roasting, burning hell. How long do we have to stay in this goddamn place?"

His tone matched his words. He was a man nearing the end of his rope.

For fifteen minutes, I listen to him walk. Traffic is light, one car every few seconds. He's not on a major avenue. Where is he going? How far is he from where they're staying?

The spyware tells me he just opened a new app. Lyft. That turns on his GPS, so the driver will know where to find him. Now I can see where he is.

Coconut Grove, south of Miami. Wherever he's staying, it's within a fifteen-minute walk of where he's standing right now, on Grand Avenue.

In a few minutes, he's headed north on I-95. Back to Dania Beach for a gin and tonic, the quarter slots, and Ilari Etxeberri's hundred and eighty mile an hour serve.

50

Ten minutes later, I was talking to Freddy Ferguson.

"You're back in DC?" I asked.

"Anton told me they're dropping the charges against you."

"How long did you follow Smith?"

"Two days. When he's not washing dishes, he's at the table. Guy doesn't sleep. And he was up about eleven grand last I checked."

"Did you get a chance to meet any of his friends?"

"He doesn't talk to anyone. Not even on the phone, as far as I could tell."

"What does that make you think?" I asked. "A con man who likes to talk, and he's not talking to anyone."

"What are you getting at?"

"Can you go back to Vegas? To keep an eye on him?"

"Why would I?"

"You remember what you said about how you wanted to punch Smith's face in? How he looked like the manager who ruined your boxing career?"

"Don't remind me of that."

"It's natural, right? When you have unresolved feelings, when you hate someone and you never had a chance to get back at them. You see someone who reminds you of that person and the feelings come up again."

"So?"

"So, for all Robert Smith's complaints about his wife, he sure was happy to touch my thigh under the table. To hold my arm on the way to the ATM. To brush against my—"

"Yeah, I get it. You find who you're looking for down there?"

"I'm close. Dice Moran is in Coconut Grove with a rude, snippy woman who got her face beat in by Bob Smith. Dice doesn't call anyone except restaurants, doesn't text anyone except her. He's basically incommunicado. They're laying low, waiting for something."

"You get that app on his phone?"

"I did."

"How?"

"I'll tell you later. But it bothers me that Maggie and Dice are laying low down here and Robert Smith is doing the same back in Vegas. Wouldn't you want to talk to people after getting out of prison?"

"Maybe he wants to keep his nose clean, stay out of trouble."

"Does he really strike you as that type?"

"No."

"I'm not totally convinced Smith hates his ex-wife. I also don't believe that Dice Moran had the character to plot any of this out. He came off as weak, almost begging, when he hired me that morning back at Lehmann's house. He's a document forger, a small-time gambler, and a drinker.

"I'm not convinced Maggie hates her ex-husband. Her father told me they were equals. Dice is not her equal, and she doesn't respect him. Right now, she's putting up with him, but her patience seems to be wearing thin."

"So why do you want me to go back to Vegas? What am I looking for?"

"Dice said something funny to Maggie. 'What the hell's taking him so long?' I don't know who he was referring to, or what they're waiting for, but keep an eye on Smith. See what he does with all that money he's been winning."

"Alright," Freddy said. "I'll look into flights."

"Look into one other thing while you're at it."

I was thinking back to the texts on Dice's phone.

Mags: What's my name?

Dice: Angela.

Mags: What time?

Dice: 12:30.

"You remember Angela M. Ginhem, from Spokane? She was on the flight with Dice, aka Buzz DiNardo, to DC?"

"What about her?"

"Can you confirm that she flew to DC in early April?"

"I can give it a shot. How are you holding up?"

I let out a long sigh. "Bored. So much of this job is just sitting and waiting."

"Go out and get some air. Your phone will tell you where Dice is, so you won't cross paths. Unless you think you might run into Maggie."

"I don't think so. She's down in Coconut Grove and I can't see her having any reason to come up here."

I wanted to get out of that room, feel the breeze on the boardwalk, hear the crash of the waves. Maybe I'd get lucky at one of the local lunch spots, have another scintillating conversation with Tomato Head and his caterpillars. We could go for a ride on his imaginary motorcycle, hit the hot spots up in Clewiston.

51

Three p.m. - Me, on a sweltering bench in a sticky salt breeze. Dice telling the dealer he wants to double down.

Four p.m. - Me in a coffee shop drinking iced tea. Dice still at the table. His voice loud and clear among the welter because he's on a winning streak. Or maybe because the phone is in his shirt pocket.

Five p.m. - Hotel lobby. I can hear the liquor in Dice's voice. The spyware streaming audio from his phone is killing his battery. I make a decision. Turn off audio. Just send his location every ten minutes.

Five forty-five. I buy a straw sun hat in a beachwear shop, floppy and broad-brimmed. All the better that it's not my style. Cheap sunglasses—bad Chanel knockoffs—and a generic Miami Beach t-shirt.

Seven p.m. - I go to a Thai restaurant a few blocks off the beach. It has only tables, no bar. Tripp and his caterpillars aren't likely to wander in, and Dice is still at the casino.

Seven twenty. I turn on the mic for a few seconds.

Thwack! The cheering of the crowd. Whatever he won at blackjack, he's betting it on Jai Alai.

Nine, ten, eleven, twelve. He's still at the casino.

At one, I set my alarm for six a.m. and go to sleep.

Next morning, six o'clock, his phone is stationary and fully charged. I turn on the mic, listen to him snore.

I put on the shirt I bought yesterday, a pair of faded jeans, grab a cup of coffee in the hotel lobby, and order a Lyft. I carry the broad hat in my hand because I feel stupid wearing it. The cheap sunglasses block out the morning glare.

At seven twenty a.m., I'm within blocks of the building from which Dice's phone sends a signal every few seconds. On my phone, it appears as a pulsing green dot. Five minutes of walking and I'm across the street from his building.

It's an apartment or a condo, not a hotel. Maybe they own the place. Maybe someone they know owns it. Maybe it's an Airbnb.

I know she's in there. Everything Dice said in that apartment yesterday tells me it's her.

But I want to see the woman. In the flesh. I want to see the source of all this trouble.

I put my earbuds in, turn on the mic. Dice is still snoring.

I can't see those two sharing a bed. She must be in another room. I can't hear her. If she comes out, I can't track her because he's got the phone. All I can do is keep my eyes on the front door of the building.

But where to watch from? There's a bus stop, but if I let too many buses pass, that won't look right. There's a Starbucks at one end of the block, and a bakery-cafe at the other. If she does come out, it will probably be for her morning coffee. Which one would she go to?

Actually, a better question is which one has outdoor seating in the direct sun? If I'm going to sit with hat and glasses, it can't be in the shade at Starbucks. It has to be in the sun at the bakery.

Seven forty-five. I'm seated at a metal table with a croissant and coffee, the Miami Herald laid flat in front of me. I call Detective Kowalczyk. He's not in yet, so I leave a message.

"Hey, this is Claire. I think I found her. Let me know about that warrant."

My worry is that if Kowalczyk sends a cop to talk to her and there's no warrant, he'll have no grounds to hold her, and she'll flee. Best to have all our ducks in a row, as Anton likes to say.

Eight eleven. I hear movement in the apartment. The snoring stops.

Then a groggy man's voice. "What?"

Rustling sheets, then the voice again, sleepy and confused.

"Why'd you—what? Christ, what time is it?" Pause. She says something, I can't hear what. She must be outside the room.

He responds, "Yeah, a large." He grumbles and I hear the sheets again. He must be turning in the bed.

I scan the front of the building. The curtains slide open behind the glass doors of a third-floor balcony. Then the doors, and there she is, dressed sharply in coral slacks and vest with a long-sleeve white shirt. Where is she going in that outfit?

She spreads her hands on the rail and looks down the street, away from me. As her head turns in my direction, I look down at the newspaper. All she'll see is my hat.

I wait a few seconds, look back up and she's gone.

What to do next?

I check my phone. Eight sixteen. Come on, Dennis Kowalczyk. Come in early today. Give me the word and I'll—

Dice is up. Oh, God, he's peeing. Why can't he shut the door? The audio of the earbuds is so crisp, I feel the inside of my ear getting wet. Nasty!

I turn the volume down, wincing, and instinctively look to see if anyone else heard the sound, even though I know they couldn't have. I'm the only one out here on the patio. Inside, the couple behind the counter—an old man and his wife, who I take to be Cuban—go about the business of preparing for the morning customers.

From the phone, I hear the flush, then a sharp rasp that hurts my ear. He must have slid the phone off the nightstand.

He's moving now.

Her voice: "What do you want to eat?"

Him: "Ham and cheese croissant. Why'd you wake me up so early?"

Her: "So you'd be awake."

I know that tone. Short. Impatient, like she doesn't owe anyone an explanation for anything. I used to talk to people that way. I used to think I had to, or they wouldn't respect me.

It's not a pretty thing to see in someone else. Less pretty still to know how much it's been a part of you.

Dice steps out on the balcony in boxers and a t-shirt, turns his face sharply, as if the daylight smacked him. He goes right back in. Probably hung over.

Why *did* she wake him so early?

I know her type. Like me, she doesn't do things arbitrarily. She does things for a reason.

What is happening on this day that he needs to be up early for?

And why the suit, Maggie? Where are you going in that?

The scent of ham and butter and fresh-baked bread wafts through the open door of the bakery onto the patio where I sit. I look up as the woman removes a baking sheet from the oven.

Ham and cheese croissants. Just what Dice ordered.

Oh, no! She's coming here. She's coming here now!

The woman slides the hot tray onto the counter. The old man lifts a jar of coffee beans from beneath the register, sets it down, removes the lid.

Across the street, the doorman holds the door open and she steps out onto the sidewalk. She stops, talks to the doorman, points upstairs. He nods and tips his hat. I can see the whiteness of his smile from here, bright teeth contrasting with dark skin.

She turns and walks toward me on the far side of the street. She walks *like* me, with purpose and determination. With anger almost. Her heels stab the pavement.

Dice is breathing into the phone. A little chirp tells me he's opened an app.

The old man inside the bakery reaches below the counter, pulls out a percolator and an ancient hand-cranked coffee mill. He sets them down, scoops some beans from his jar, drops them into the mill and turns the handle, taking special care, I assume, for the cup he'll drink himself.

The spyware tells me Dice has his browser open.

She's here. She's in the bakery. I remove my earbuds, pull the wire from the phone jack and drop the earbuds on the table. I want to hear her, not him.

The woman behind the counter greets her. "Good morning, Miss Hine."

Hine? Where'd she come up with that one? I picture Dice forging a driver's license for her. Is Miss Hine a real person? An identity they needed to borrow for some special purpose? Or is it just a random name?

"Buenos días, señora." That's the closest I've heard her come to being polite.

"Two coffee, large?" asks the woman behind the counter.

"And strong."

Listen to her. Right to the point. I could like her if I didn't hate her.

I'm staring. I can't help it. Her back is to me and my eyes are burning a hole right through her. You feel it when someone stares at you like that.

I knew she was going to turn. I knew she had to, even before the old woman shot me that look, that what-are-you-staring-at look.

She turned and looked right at me without a hint of recognition or interest. What was I? Some idiot tourist with a cheap sunhat and knockoff Chanel sunglasses. I was less important than whatever happened to be on her mind at that moment. Which was something. In the second before my phone rang, before my eyes went down to the screen, I could see that something occupied her mind enough that the sight of me didn't seem to register.

That was me at my old job, consumed with details, mind going all the time on what I should be doing next. The world around me, the people, were all distractions, intrusions on my all-consuming thoughts.

I look at my phone to see who's calling. The little green bar hovering over the spyware screen tells me it's Dennis Kowalczyk. Below his name are the words Dice is typing into his browser search:

Roscoe Lehmann obituary.

A jolt shoots through me. My eyes go back to the counter where Maggie has just turned back to face the old woman. Beside the two women, the old man cranks the coffee grinder. Dice's question from the other day comes back to me.

What the hell's taking him so long?

I see Lehmann's kitchen again. The day Dice hired me, we'd signed the contract there on the kitchen island. He'd gone upstairs to get the money. An old hand-cranked coffee grinder sat on the counter. Beside it were several open boxes of cereal. There was no coffee maker, no percolator. The real Lehmann later told me he didn't drink coffee, couldn't stomach it.

Kowalczyk is ringing my phone.

Maggie says to the old woman at the counter, "One ham and cheese croissant and a blueberry muffin."

Kowalczyk keeps ringing, and I need to warn him— Lehmann has a nut allergy. And that day, the day I first went to his house, Dice was grinding nuts in the coffee mill. Beside the grinder were three open cereal boxes. Maggie probably told him which nuts her father was most allergic to. Dice would have put the grounds into the cereal boxes, Maggie orchestrating it all from her invisible perch on the second floor, the only hint of her presence the scent of her shampoo on the stairs. Oribe.

Roscoe's allergy was bad enough that he needed an EpiPen. Where would he keep it? Where did his son look for it that day when Maggie was five, when Maggie watched her mother choke and gasp for air? Where had her brother *not* found the pen? In the bathroom, right? In the bathroom upstairs.

What the hell's taking him so long?

Dice was asking why Roscoe hadn't eaten his poison yet.

When Roscoe kicks off, the money goes to Maggie. The house, the business.

He hadn't eaten it because his stomach was bothering him. When I visited Roscoe's house on the morning after my return from Vegas, he ate dry white toast for breakfast instead of his usual cereal.

But now? What if...

I have to tell Kowalczyk, tell someone up there who can stop this before it happens.

He's still ringing. He's right there on the other end of the line.

But if I answer, she'll hear my voice and she'll recognize it. She must have been listening that day in Roscoe's house. A controlling type like her, she's not going to just sit back and trust. She'd eavesdrop on the conversation below, to make sure it all went right.

I know because I'm the same way.

Another ring.

The old woman, the old man and Maggie Smith all turn to me at once, all with the same question in their minds, I'm sure. Why don't I answer the phone when it's right here in my hand?

I tilt my head down, hide beneath the brim of my hat before Maggie can get a good look at my face. I reject the call. Keep my head down. Type a furious text to Kowalczyk.

"She's here. Send Gutierrez or whoever's on duty into Lehmann's house now. Make sure he's Okay. Don't let him eat anything!!"

I hit send, then type some more.

"I'll call you in a minute."

Send.

The first message doesn't go through. This must be Kowalczyk's work number. His desk phone.

And what I said about knowing when someone is staring at you—I knew. I could feel her watching from the eerie silence inside the door. Someone should have been moving in there. Somebody should have been tapping the order into the register, or picking up a paper bag, or stabbing their heels into the stone floor. But no one was doing anything.

Except me. Typing an urgent text to an ancient land line a thousand miles away, a text that would never arrive. Me with my head tilted down, trying not to be seen by the people who are looking right at me, knowing how unconvincing this looks.

Feeling thirteen again, under the mean girls' glare in the cafeteria, wishing I had somewhere to hide.

If she paid, I didn't hear it. If the bag with the croissant and muffin made a sound, I didn't hear. All I heard was the click of her heels approaching, pausing in front of me, waiting. The light coral fabric fluttering around her ankles, the scavenging sparrows skittering away, the light gray pumps with the ankle straps. Toenails painted to match the slacks.

One second that felt like ten, and then off she went, across the patio to the sidewalk.

When at last I looked up, she was crossing the street, her steps purposeful and violent, each one sending a jolt up her spine that shook the ends of her hair.

Did she recognize me? Or was that just her habitual aggression?

52

"I found her."

"You sure it's her?" Kowalczyk asked.

"A hundred percent. She was standing right in front of me."

I'd walked a block down the street. I wanted to keep an eye on the building without her being able to watch me.

"Does Roscoe still have a guard outside his house?"

"Yeah."

"County Police? Any way you can get a hold of him?"

"What's up?"

I explained the situation to him: Dice, the nuts, the allergy. I don't think he took it seriously. He might have if I had gone into the backstory, told him about Maggie's mother, but I didn't have time for that.

"We have the paperwork all set for the warrant," he said. "But we still have to wait for the DNA results. We're hoping that happens today, but there are no guarantees. Assuming there's a match, that Lehmann is the father of both, we can get the warrant signed as soon the results come in."

"That could still be hours. Or worse."

"You nervous?"

"Yeah."

"Did she recognize you?"

"I don't know."

"Let me call—wait, where are you?"

"Coconut Grove."

"Let me get in touch with someone down there. We can keep eyes on her until the warrant comes through. Tell me where you are, what you're wearing."

I told him.

It was forty-one minutes before anyone showed up.

Forty-one minutes for Montgomery County to contact Dade County through whatever channels they go through, to explain the situation in whatever way they have to explain it, to get a dispatcher to send two plainclothes detectives in an unmarked car.

Forty-one minutes is a marvel of efficiency in government. To an anxious woman haunting an empty street, praying her prey doesn't escape, it's an eternity.

I paced the street, watched the curtain flutter by her open balcony door, watched the building entrance, my heart leaping every time someone came out.

The sun was getting hotter, and the humidity penetrated everything. My armpits were soaked with sweat when a black Camaro slowed in front of me. The tinted passenger window slid down. A stocky Latino man with close-cropped hair said, "Claire?"

"Yeah."

He nodded toward the corner. The car pulled around and I followed, grateful for the help, but not wanting to lose sight of the building.

53

The back seat of the Camaro is small. I sit in the middle, unbuckled, answering questions.

What does she look like?

"She looks like me. Only she's wearing coral."

"Coral? Like—" Detective Suarez, the passenger, points to the light tan of a coral stone building.

"No, like orange. Pink-orange. Sort of—like that." I point to a dress in a shop window. "That color, but pants and a vest. Not a dress."

We've been circling side streets for a few minutes. When a parking spot opens up on her block, the driver, Hickson, pulls in.

"What about the guy with her? You said there's a guy."

"Colson 'Dice' Moran. He has a record."

Hickson is already looking him up on the laptop mounted between the seats.

"He dangerous?" Suarez asks. "Any reason to think he has a gun?"

"I don't know. I don't think so, but—"

Hickson turns the laptop to Suarez. "Forger. He's done time. Not violent, but if he's with her..."

The photo shows Dice Moran in a blue prison jumpsuit with full beard. His eyes are lined from squinting in the Nevada sun.

My phone rings. Kowalczyk.

"Get ready," he says. "They're about to go in."

"How do you know? Did you get the warrant?"

"Lehmann's guard found him face-down at the bottom of the stairs. Couldn't do CPR. His throat was so swollen, he couldn't get any air in. We have a crime—Lehmann—and we have a witness—you—and that's enough for probable cause. We just put the word through to Dade. They're gonna move."

And they do.

The driver, Hickson, gets a call. Says three OKs, hangs up and cuts the engine.

He turns half-way around, looks at me from the corners of his eyes.

"We have a document forger and maybe a murderer. Maryland says they're probably travelling under false papers, so don't trust the IDs. You can identify them? Visually?"

"Yes. Dice no longer has the beard."

As we cross the street, he asks me to point to the apartment.

"That one," I say. "On the third floor, with the white curtain fluttering out through the open door."

54

Inside the building, Hickson shows his badge, gives the doorman a description of Maggie Smith.

"She's in three-ten," he says nervously.

Suarez presses the elevator button, turns to Hickson with a smile. "Left or right?"

Hickson looks at the two elevators.

"Left."

The light above the right elevator flashes and dings. Suarez smiles. "You owe me a coffee."

Before we get on, Suarez looks to his left, points to the door of the stairway.

In the elevator, Hickson tells me to stay by the stairway door. If there's any noise, any hint of resistance or altercation, go down immediately, exit the building, wait inside Starbucks. If all goes well, Suarez will bring me in for identification.

The doors slide open. Hickson takes my arm. Unnecessary. I'm an adult, goddammit. He points to the stairway, nudges me along. He's tense, overprotective. I don't like being pushed around and he doesn't like the look of annoyance on my face.

"Go!" he hisses.

I stand by the stairway door. Hickson and Suarez go around the corner, down the carpeted hall along the front of the building. I can't see them or hear them. Lions silently stalking.

I turn the lever on the stairway door to make sure it opens. The click startles me, a spark of nitroglycerine in my heart. I let go and the wind sucks the door shut hard.

I listen for the knock down the hall.

I wait and wait, but there is no knock. Just a hello. A questioning hello repeated twice.

Why?

"Police," says Hickson. "Mind if we come in?"

Air whistles through the crack beneath the stairway door, caresses my feet on its way down the hall, toward Hickson, Suarez, Dice, and Maggie. I see it in my mind's eye, the white curtain billowing out onto the balcony.

The apartment door is open. That's why they didn't knock.

And then, softly, in a tone of surprise, from down the hall I hear one of the detectives say "Shit!"

The other voice repeats the curse three times.

I wait through a long, long silence—forty, sixty, ninety seconds—and then at last, Suarez appears at the hallway corner. He waves me toward him. Doesn't say a word.

I follow him into the apartment.

A man is slumped over the round breakfast table, the back of his head to us as we enter, dark brown hair flecked with gray. Hickson kneels in front of him, examining the face.

Suarez turns to look at me, catches my nervous glance toward the open bedroom.

"There's no one here," he says.

Hickson motions me to join him.

I go around the table, look into the dead man's half-open brown eyes.

"This Moran?" Hickson asks. "Colson 'Dice' Moran?"

"That's him."

His face is starting to turn blue.

Hickson stands and I survey the table. The dead man's coffee, half empty, smells sweet, loaded with sugar. Ham and cheese croissant half eaten.

This is why she woke him up early. She wanted him to eat. She wanted to get some poison into him because... Because why? What's her plan?

The blue of his face is ghastly.

His phone is still in his hand. Underneath, a pad of paper. In a woman's hand, blue ink:

Login: mml52988@gmail.com
Password: inheritrix

MML. Mary Margaret Lehmann. And her date of birth.

"Don't touch anything," Hickson says.

Like I was going to.

A suitcase stands beside the stools at the kitchen island. Black and badly scuffed, with rollers and an extending handle. Dice's, probably.

Hickson goes into the bedroom, the neat one that smells like her, not the messy one that smells like a bar. He slides open an empty dresser drawer. After telling me not to touch anything.

I walk onto the balcony.

On the street below, a silver Prius, rear door open, woman in coral about to get in. She stops and gives me a look. No expression.

We've come full circle. Now I'm the woman in the window. She's the one leaving.

"Dresser's empty," Hickson says. "Bathroom too. She packed up."

As the Prius rolls away, the doorman huffs at the hallway door, announces in a breathless Haitian accent, "She got a Lyft."

Suarez: "You saw her?"

"She came out of the other elevator when you went up."

"Why didn't you—"

"I put her bags in the car."

I'm back inside now, looking at the doorman's face. He's sheepish, apologetic, staring at Dice face down on the table. I get the feeling the doorman was scared of Maggie.

"Goddammit. Get someone to MIA," Suarez says. "She made a mistake, wearing that suit."

"Check Lauderdale too," Hickson says. "It's only thirty miles up."

55

After I gave Hickson and Suarez a description of the Prius, the doorman described the driver, and they asked us to clear out. This was a crime scene. The fewer people inside, the better.

So that was it. All that work to get this close and then we lose her.

What if she was leaving the country? How would I ever find her again? Part of me just couldn't let go. I didn't have to catch her myself—honestly, I wouldn't even try, given what she'd done to Jake—but I wanted to make sure someone got her.

If I were her, I would have gone to Miami, not Fort Lauderdale. More direct flights to far-away places. Flights to Europe, South America.

Fifteen minutes after she'd gone, my own Lyft was pulling up in front of the building. Miami International is fifteen minutes up the road. Which means she's getting out of her car as I'm getting into mine.

Suarez called ahead. Miami-Dade County would send a contingent and TSA had a description of her, but what good was that? A white woman in her mid-thirties, five-foot six, with brown hair and brown eyes. How many passengers fit that description?

Oh, and a coral suit. Just look for the suit. If the male officers even know what coral is.

I tell my driver to hurry up I-95, past the heart of the city. I'm late for my flight.

He turns his dark, tired eyes to the rearview. "You flying without a bag?"

"Flying by the seat of my pants."

TSA should know her aliases. She's not going through security as Maggie Smith. She'll be Anna Graham, or Angela M. Ginhem, or...

I pick up my phone to call Kowalczyk, make sure he has the names to pass along to—to whom? To some central office in Dade County? And they'd relay it to the teams at the airport? And someone would pass it on to TSA? By the time they get the message, she will have boarded.

But I have to try.

When I pull my phone from my bag, it's already ringing.

Freddy Ferguson.

He says something, but I can't hear. The plane passing overhead drowns him out.

"What?"

"I said your buddy Robert Smith is on the move."

"What does that mean?"

"He left his apartment forty minutes ago with a shoulder bag. Took an Uber to the airport. But he didn't go into the terminal. He picked up a rental car. He's heading out of McCarran now. He's got a travel restriction on his parole. Want me to call his officer?"

"No. Follow him. Maggie's gone."

"Where?"

"I don't know."

"You saw her?"

"In the flesh. Keep following Smith. At least we have one of them in our sights."

"You think they're going to meet up?"

"It's all we've got right now. Let's not let go."

I hang up and call Kowalczyk, give him the list of names Maggie has used. He thanks me as we roll up to the terminal, but he doesn't sound too hopeful.

I leave my driver in the knot of traffic outside Departures and walk into a terminal teeming with people of every color, from every nation. Muslim women in modestly colored headscarves, Caribbean women in brightly-colored scarves.

Men in suits, men in shorts. Children clumped around their parents, international travelers with mountains of baggage, solo travelers checking themselves in at the kiosks.

What would I do if I were her?

I would have checked in ahead of time. I would arrive as close to boarding time as possible. I might ditch the suitcase and only take the carry-on. If she was lucky, she might have made it through the entrance before Dade County had a man on the scene. She could have made it through security before TSA was alerted. And then what? Then they'd have to walk all the terminals, scan every gate. Or use the security cameras. Look for the woman in coral.

Speaking of—my heart jumps at the sight of that bright color. The dark-haired woman in the security line!

She turns as if she felt me staring, and...

No. A wide-eyed Indian woman in a bright sari.

I can't get past security, so I have to leave the bulk of the airport to the police and TSA. And what am I looking for? I mean, really? She's not going to be in the check-in line. She won't be standing at a kiosk.

All I can do is walk from one security checkpoint to the next. If I see her in line, I can point her out to TSA. From there, it's out of my hands.

I scan the first, second, third, fourth checkpoint. She's nowhere to be seen.

I walk back the way I came, scan checkpoints three, two, one.

Nothing.

I'll go back to my hotel, pick up my bag, fly home and hope Freddy has better luck. I do think there's still something between Maggie and her ex. The oily con man and high-stakes gambler would be more likely than Dice to plot the murder of a man with a multimillion-dollar estate. Dice was a small-timer who couldn't stand up to Maggie.

I walk past baggage claim, out through the doors into the humid cloud of exhaust from taxis and limos idling in the South Florida sun. Pull the phone from my pocket, open the

Lyft app, and... What's this? A police car behind a silver Prius. An Arab-looking man, the driver, perhaps, talking animatedly, gesticulating to the three uniformed officers. They wear brown shirts, not blue. They're not TSA. They must be County.

I pick up my pace, head straight for them.

The driver's face lights up when he sees me. He points, and they all turn at once.

I want to ask if they've found her, but the way they come at me, the intent I see in their eyes—the question catches in my throat before I can ask.

One of them twists my arm behind my back. The fat-bellied man with crystal blue eyes in a mean, angry face.

"Let go of me!"

"You want to make a scene?" he growls. "We can make a scene."

I know I look like her but... "You have the wrong person." It's all I can say.

He puts the cuffs on tighter than he needs to.

In a minute, I'm in the back of his cruiser, watching him paw through my bag.

He looks at my license, then at my face, snorts, and tosses the license on the passenger seat. He empties my wallet, probably looking for other IDs with other names. When he finds none, he picks up the license again and says, "You want to go with this one? Claire Chastain?"

"Can I make a call?"

"Later."

He types my info into the laptop between the seats and my photo appears. He reads for a few seconds, then turns and looks back at me with a wicked smile.

"You have a pending murder charge." He couldn't be more delighted. "I bet the Maryland prosecutor would like to know what you're doing at the Miami airport."

He shifts the car into gear and we roll away.

56

Kowalczyk picks up on the second ring.

"Will you get me the fuck out of here?"

He starts laughing.

"What's so funny, Dennis? This isn't fucking funny."

It takes him a few seconds to get a hold of himself. Then he explains. He got a call from Miami-Dade. They picked up the target, Maggie Smith, travelling under the alias Claire Chastain. She had an outstanding murder charge in Maryland. Why hadn't Montgomery County mentioned the murder charge from the start?

"I knew right away what happened. I already talked to someone down there. You should be out soon."

He told me something else too. Maggie's choice of clothing was not a mistake. She changed in the back seat of the Lyft on the way to the airport. The driver almost wrecked the car, watching her in the rearview instead of watching the road.

"When the Florida detectives first put the word out, everyone was looking for a woman in bright orange," Kowalczyk said. "Meanwhile, she enters the airport wearing jeans and a t-shirt."

Same thing I was wearing.

"Do you know where she went?" I ask.

"No clue."

"What about security footage?"

"We're having trouble with TSA. They don't seem to see the urgency here."

"So, what do you do?"

"Find someone higher up who can apply more pressure."

"Who?"

"I don't know. We're still looking."

"And in the meantime, she gets farther and farther away. I bet she's leaving the country."

"That's what I'd do," Kowalczyk says.

57

Ninety minutes later, I was checking out of my hotel in Hollywood. The Miami-Dade police department was kind enough to drive me there, though they never did apologize for the aching red marks their cuffs left on my wrists.

I ordered one last Lyft, this time to Fort Lauderdale. I'd return to DC from the airport I had flown into.

Freddy texted as we were driving up Route 1.

"We're an hour from L.A. on Route 15."

I thought back to Dice Colson sitting dead over his breakfast. His phone was in his hand. On the notepad beside him, a login and password. For what? To check in for a flight at MIA? Was it for a bank account? Or some communications app so he—or she—could pass secure messages to Robert Smith in Las Vegas?

As we rolled into the airport, I watched the blur of exhaust trail a silver plane as it climbed into to the humid summer sky. Up it went, detached from earth for the next few hours. Where would it come down? Where would *she* come down?

Exiting the car beside the sign for Departures - American, I got a text from a 301 number. Given the message, it had to be Dennis Kowalczyk's cell.

"No Maggie Smith. No Anna Graham. No Angela M. Ginhem on any flight out of MIA. No luck. :("

I walked to the self-check-in kiosk, still scanning the crowd for her, even though I knew she was gone. Even though I knew she hadn't come to this airport. My mind just wasn't ready to let her go.

I breezed through check-in. No bags to check, just a carry-on. Walk to the TSA checkpoint, just like she did.

I'd push through security, walk right to the gate, board a plane, and disappear. How was it that easy?

Maybe we could trace her through that Gmail account. mml52988. Mary Margaret Lehmann, the inheritrix who got away.

The TSA agent waved me toward her, but I stopped short of the podium. Stopped and thought.

"Ma'am?" The agent beckoned me forward.

We don't always think straight when we're caught up in the bustle and commotion of a busy day.

"Ma'am? Boarding pass and ID."

I had missed something.

"Ma'am!"

The Cuban woman in the bakery. *Good morning, Miss Hine.*

"Yes. Sorry." I gave the agent my boarding pass and driver's license.

Anna Graham. That's a funny alias.

In my mind's eye, I saw the book of word puzzles in Lehmann's basement. The one Maggie had filled out and initialed.

Anna Graham.

Anagram.

Angela M. Ginhem was an anagram for Maggie Lehmann.

The agent initialed my boarding pass. "Line to the left. Next! Please step forward, ma'am."

I grabbed a bin, slid it onto the metal table, took one shoe off and called Dennis Kowalczyk.

"Can you check another name for me? With TSA?"

"What?"

"Hine. H-I-N-E. Or possibly H-E-I-N. First name Trixie."

"Where'd you come up with that?"

"Inheritrix."

"Huh?"

"That's what Maggie Smith is now that Roscoe's dead. The inheritrix of her father's estate. I saw it on a pad of paper beneath Dice Moran's dead hand. If Miss Hine is fond of anagrams, her first name must be Trixie. Let me know what you find."

58

I took my phone out of airplane mode as soon as we hit the ground in DC.

There was a voicemail from Freddy.

"We're getting close to LA and traffic's getting thicker. Listen, that question you asked, did Angela Ginhem fly anywhere in April. She did. Vegas to Denver to DC. Flew back ten days later."

That confirmed what I'd read in Dice's texts. Maggie had been to DC in the spring. She had probably visited Reisman then.

I also had a bunch of unread texts. The first was from Freddy, sent about forty minutes after the voicemail.

"Smith returned car to LAX. I missed the shuttle. Lost him."

Then a series of updates.

"Still looking."

"Still looking."

"Still looking."

"Can't find him."

There was also a text from Kowalczyk.

"Bingo. Trixie Hein, Miami to LAX to Tokyo to Macau. We'll have agents at the gate in LA."

I texted back. "Robert Smith is there too. Be sure to pick him up."

The flight from Fort Lauderdale to National took about two and half hours. Miami to Los Angeles was about five and a half. Maggie left Miami well before me. If she hadn't landed yet, she would any minute.

I called Freddy, told him not to worry.

Half an hour later, as I entered my apartment, I got the text from Kowalczyk.

Two smiley faces and two thumbs up. They had them both.

59

Two days later, we're in Anton's office. Freddy, Anton, and I.

"How'd she find you anyway?" Anton asks.

"Her friend Dice saw that article in the Post about the PharmaCore mess I got tangled up in last winter. There was a photo of me. Dice said I looked like her. Twinsies.

"She flew here in April to meet with Reisman at the psychiatric hospital. From what the staff there told me, it sounded like she tried to intimidate him. She stayed in the DC area for ten days. She didn't need ten days to mess with Jake's head. My guess is she took that time to do her homework, find out more about me. How I dressed, what kind of car I drove.

"I had told the Post I was thinking about detective work. What does that tell her? She can hire someone who looks like her to stalk the guy she wants to kill, because that's a detective's job, right? To follow. I get paid to be in the wrong place at the wrong time, and I don't think anything of it, because it's my job."

Anton can barely contain himself. He's pacing, rubbing his hands in delight.

"Okay, let's walk this through," he says. "Let's say it plays out the way they expected. Roscoe Lehmann returns from his trip. Next day, maybe the day after that, he eats from one of the cereal boxes, gets a mouthful of ground nuts, triggers his allergy. He goes upstairs for the EpiPen, but it's not there because his daughter took it. He kicks off. End of Roscoe.

"Twenty-four hours later, work reports him missing. The cops find him dead in his home of natural causes. Natural, mind you. So there's no crime there. No investigation."

Anton turns at the window, paces back toward us, his voice loud and clear, as if addressing a packed courtroom.

"In a separate incident, Jacob Reisman gets his head bashed in. No one knows Reisman is Lehmann's son except Reisman and Lehmann, and they're both dead, so no one ever *will* know. There's nothing to connect the crimes.

"Claire's on the hook for Reisman's murder. She just had a bit part in this play. She just had to be there long enough to provide cover. If there are any eyewitnesses to the Reisman crime, they'll identify her, and if that doesn't seal the case, it at least gives Maggie time to get far away.

"There's nothing tying Maggie to either crime. Nothing."

"Except the DNA under Reisman's fingernails," I say.

"I know, but no one knows whose DNA it is. She's never committed a violent crime, so her DNA isn't on file. Normally, it takes a long time to get DNA test results. If I hadn't pulled some strings to rush the tests along, you'd have been locked up for weeks before they realized the skin under Reisman's fingernails belonged to someone else.

"In that time, you can't investigate because you don't have your freedom. You're *not* snooping around Reisman's storage space. You don't know Reisman has a sister. You don't know Lehmann has a daughter because Lehmann's dead. How could you have connected the three? There's no way. And her! Maggie, traveling with fake IDs! No one would ever know she had even been here. There's no record of Maggie Smith leaving Vegas, so the cops couldn't tie her to anything."

"I would have gotten off," I say. "I would never have been convicted."

"You would have gotten off because I would have hammered home that DNA evidence. Whoever Reisman struggled with wasn't you. If the prosecutor had brought you to trial, I would have had him squirming to explain the DNA. Part of me regrets losing that opportunity.

"But again, the criminal justice process would take a long time. Meanwhile, the estate goes to the daughter. By the time you're free, she has the money, and she's off in—where were they going?"

"Macau," Freddy says.

"Macau," Anton says. "Full of casinos, like Vegas. Back to the old life with her scammer husband. The high-stakes gambling. The boom and bust. That's an addiction, you know. That's a—she might be co-dependent. You ever think of that?"

He didn't wait for Freddy or me to answer.

"Now where she screwed up was in this whole getting back at daddy thing. If you want to commit a crime, get your motives straight. Are you doing it for money, or are you doing it for revenge? Pick one. The Mafia knows that. The gangs know that. Act with a single purpose. Don't let your emotions get in the way of business. God, I would love to defend this case!"

"You would actually defend her?" I ask incredulously.

"Oh, yeah!"

"But she's guilty!"

"Yeah, but you have to look at it from a strategic perspective."

"No," I shoot back. "You have to look at it from a moral perspective."

Anton, still pacing, shakes his head. "In my line of work, it's strategic, and I already know how I'd get her off."

"How you'd get her off?" I say. "God, your enthusiasm when you say that makes it sound obscene."

Anton stops at his desk, turns dramatically, and raises a finger to make his point. "The prosecutor has a very complicated case to lay out. The inheritance, the family history, all this flying around under fake names. That's a lot to ask of a jury. My story is much simpler. Claire did it."

"Come on, Anton."

"She did. She went into Jake's apartment, he made a pass at her, and she bashed his head in."

"That's not what women do. We deal with those situations all the time without resorting to murder. Though maybe we should start. It might be an effective deterrent."

"A normal woman knows how to deal with that situation, but not you."

"What? Anton!"

He was working up a head of steam now. "Because you're a hot-headed bitch with an uncontrollable temper! This is the second guy whose skull you've fractured."

"That's not fair, Anton."

"Ha! And now look at your face! You're angry. You *look* like a bitch!"

"How do you expect me to react when you talk about me like that?" I could feel the color rising in my face.

"You have to hold yourself together, Claire. This is a trial."

"No, it's not. We're in your office."

"You're on trial, and you're losing!" He pointed at me. "Because you can't control your temper. The jury is watching you and they see a very hostile woman. The way you glare at me, Claire! That angry scowl! You're proving my point for me!"

As I shoot up off the couch, Freddy grabs my arm and pulls me back down. "Let him have his fun," he says.

"And then!" Anton stabs a finger in the air and starts to pace again. "Then I'd start hammering on the names. Every time I cross examine, every time I ask a question about the defendant, I change what I call her. Trixie, Anna, Angela, Mary, Maggie. Confuse the jury. Every time the prosecutor tries to straighten out the story, I muddle it.

"Because I don't have to convince the jury of anything. All I have to do is prevent the prosecutor from convincing them. All I have to do is sow enough doubt and confusion to make the jury hesitate, make them ask if they're really sure, beyond a shadow of a doubt, that my client, my very attractive client in her lovely sundress—"

"I'm going to strangle you, Anton."

Finally, he breaks character. "See, this is why I didn't like having you as a client. I mean, I respect you, Claire, but when your attorney asks you to look demure, you need to follow his advice. You do not announce in court that you're going to strangle *anyone*."

Freddy's laughter annoys me.

"Why are you laughing at that? It's not funny. *He's* not funny."

"He's just playing devil's advocate," Freddy says.

"No," I say, "he's serious."

"Of course I'm serious," Anton declares.

"Oh, shut up," Freddy says. Then he turns to me and explains. "See, the value of this guy is that he shows you what you're up against. You keep him in mind when you gather evidence. He'll cast doubt on everything. He'll taint every fact. You recover a murder weapon, he'll object to the chain of custody, say the evidence was tampered with, get it thrown out. You have to always remember, as a detective, you're fighting two adversaries. The criminal and him." He points an accusing finger at Anton, who makes a pouty face and puts his hands to his heart as if wounded.

"How can you say things like that?" Anton whines. "Don't you think I have feelings?"

"You need to work on your act," Freddy says.

"Nah. I just have a hostile audience. Now—the DNA evidence. The DNA evidence placing Maggie at the scene presents a real problem. *If* it's admitted. *If* it's not contaminated."

"Here he goes," Freddy says with a roll of his eyes.

Anton begins a monologue about cops planting evidence, samples improperly bagged, items mislabeled, mix-ups at the DNA testing facility, painting the cops as inept, or worse, malicious.

"Not that I really see it that way," he says. "But I believe a jury has a right to be informed of every *potential* fact that *might* be true."

Freddy leans in and says softly, sincerely, "You did a good job. You did a really good job."

"Thank you," I say. "That's all I wanted to hear."

"Are you looking for work?"

"With him?" I point to Anton. "No."

"I heard that!" Anton barks. "Just so you know, I could also argue the prosecutor's side of this case. Then you'll see my other side. I'd have the jury stringing her up before they even went in for deliberations."

"With us," Freddy says. "In DC. It's a separate firm."

I pull back, look at him quietly for a second.

"You're serious?"

"I'm serious."

I take a moment to think it through. On the one hand, I see the windowless office I had once inhabited at the Securities and Exchange Commission, the computer with ten thousand files. Hours and hours beneath the fluorescent lights, combing through the output of electronic discovery software.

On the other hand, I see Maggie Smith in the court dock with some other Anton defending her. Some other Anton twisting the facts to undo all the hard work that Dennis Kowalczyk, Freddy Ferguson and I have done.

And him, Freddy…

I like that he looks me in the eye when he talks. I like the quiet confidence, the intelligence he doesn't feel the need to broadcast. Just scratch the surface, and it's there.

I like that he's not intimidated by my own intelligence and confidence. People often resent those qualities in a woman who doesn't try to soften them. They try in their subtle ways to deprive you of the traits that make them uneasy. They try to take away your power. Men talk over you, or ogle you, or dismiss you outright. Or they tell you, like Anton did, that your best chance is to look pretty and demure.

That's not me. That was never me.

All I've ever asked is to be accepted as I am. Not perfect, but getting better. Not always advocating the comfortable perspective, but the honest one. Not always right, but never willing to accept what I know is wrong. Bold enough to make mistakes and honest enough to own them.

I am competent, capable, and doing my best. Whether the world likes me or not, I want that much to be acknowledged. It means a lot to me when someone sees the person I work so hard to be, and when they take the time to say it.

"Yes," I say. "I'm looking for work."

GATE 76

Mystery/Thriller

A mysterious woman fleeing an unknown terror boards the wrong plane at San Francisco International and disappears into the heart of the country. Freddy Ferguson, a troubled detective with a violent past, believes she's the last living witness to a crime that has captivated the nation.

Sifting through the wreckage of her past, he begins to understand who she's running from, and why. Now he must track her down before her pursuers can silence her for good.

A modern crime thriller with elements of Raymond Chandler and the classic pulp mysteries of the 1950s, *Gate 76* weaves a deeply personal tale of witness and investigator, loss and redemption.

"A consummate thriller with some of the best characterization you'll see all year." —*Kirkus Reviews (starred review)*

"One of the year's best thrillers." —*BestThrillers.com*

- Named to Kirkus Reviews' Best Books of 2018
- Named to BestThrillers.com's best thrillers of 2018

THE FRIDAY CAGE
Mystery/Thriller

Someone new has taken an interest in Claire Chastain. He circles her house when she's alone and follows her on errands across town. He tours her home while she's away, leaving little things disturbingly out of place. He may even be involved in the recent death of her childhood friend.

But who is he? And what does he want?

Claire soon discovers that, like Cary Grant in *North by Northwest*, she's caught up in someone else's dark conspiracy, and she has no choice but to play the game. The only exit from her troubles will be the one she makes, if she's smart enough to figure out when and how to make it.

A suspenseful crime thriller in the tradition of Hitchcock and Ross MacDonald, *The Friday Cage* features an exceptionally tough, sharp-minded protagonist who must do some soul-searching in the midst of her quest to survive.

"Fast-paced and exciting… ingenious and gloriously unpredictable…. one of the most compelling and odd private investigators in literature today." - *Jack Magnus, Readers' Favorite*

"Anxiety, fear, grief, regret and the quest for survival and justice are constantly simmering under the surface… A deeply psychological crime thriller that perfectly captures the terrors of both murder and life itself. Highly recommended." - *BestThrillers.com*

TO HELL WITH JOHNNY MANIC

Psychological Thriller / Noir

John Manis, aka Johnny Manic—charming, stylish, impulsive, and reckless—is racked with guilt over the secret he doesn't dare tell. Marilyn Dupree, passionate and volatile, has too much money and the wrong husband. Johnny and Marilyn have a chemistry like nitrogen and glycerin, and that makes Detective Lou Eisenfall very uneasy.

"Poor Lou," Johnny muses as his mind begins to unravel. "There's a madman running around his town, and who knows what he'll do next."

This riveting tale of deception, murder, and psychological suspense was named one of the best of 2019 by BestThrillers.com.

"A feverishly readable psychological noir."—*Kirkus Reviews*

"Diamond cultivates an engrossingly dark vision of a protagonist whose alter ego takes over in many different ways. The build-up of psychological suspense and the evolution of evil is truly compelling… highly recommended for crime readers who like their stories introspective, brooding, and psychologically astute." – *Midwest Book Review*

"Truly riveting… One of the year's best thrillers." — *BestThrillers.com*

IMPALA
Thriller

After four years on the straight and narrow, Russell Fitzpatrick has a boring job, the wrong woman, and an itch for something more. All he needs to get his life going again is a nudge in the wrong direction.

When he receives a cryptic email from a legendary and slightly deranged fellow hacker—his old friend Charlie, whom he knows to be dead—he tries to tell himself it's none of his concern. But the guy who stalks him across town at night, the two thugs waiting in the alley, and a ruthless FBI agent let him know his days are numbered if he doesn't turn over the money Charlie stole.

The problem is, Russ doesn't have it. As his enemies close in from all sides, Russ slowly unwinds the mystery of his old friend's paranoid mind and finds that Charlie left behind something worth much more than the money. And no one but him is on to it...

- A Kirkus Recommended Review - September 2016
- An Amazon Best Book of the Month - Sept. 2016 - Mystery/Thriller
- An IndieReader Best of 2016 Selection
- First Place Winner - Genre Fiction - 24th Annual Writer's Digest Awards
- Gold Medal Winner - 2017 Readers' Favorite Awards

WARREN LANE
Mystery/Comedy

Susan Moore is about to hire the wrong man to investigate her philandering husband, Will. There's something not quite right about that detective. "Warren Lane" drinks too much and has a hard time staying out of trouble. He's just the kind of guy Will's mistress can't resist. And everyone is starting to figure out that Will is hiding a lot more than his affair with a reckless young woman. With a bit of mystery, romance, crime, and suspense, Warren Lane has his hands full.

WAKE UP, WANDA WILEY

Comedy/Romance/Satire

Hannah Sharpe has been written out of all eighteen of Wanda Wiley's romance novels. A runaway heroine who won't conform to the plots laid out for her, Hannah has been consigned to a realm of fog deep in the recesses of the author's imagination.

Trevor Dunwoody, the protagonist of a macho action-thriller that Wanda has regrettably agreed to ghostwrite, is single-minded and obtuse, understanding only what he can beat up, shoot, or screw. Like Hannah, he's a character Wanda doesn't know what to do with. When he appears one day in Hannah's fog world, she can't convince him he's in the wrong story.

Hannah knows she'll be stuck in the limbo of Wanda's subconscious until the writer can find a suitable story to cast her in. But Wanda, trapped in a disastrous relationship with the philandering narcissist Dirk Jaworski, is sinking into a deep depression. The pot she smokes to self-medicate impairs her ability to write and thickens the fog of Hannah's timeless isolation.

As Hannah explains her predicament to the thick-headed Trevor, she begins to realize that she knows her author better than her author knows herself. If she can only break out of the limbo of Wanda's subconscious and nudge the writer in the right direction, she can free them both.

But how can Hannah penetrate the fog of her creator's mind from within? The answer is right in front of her in the form of the big, dumb, action-ready tool, Trevor Dunwoody.

"Diamond's prose is funny and barbed, particularly the dialogue between Hannah and Trevor... surprisingly compelling." —*Kirkus Reviews*

ABOUT THE AUTHOR

Andrew Diamond writes mystery, crime, noir, and an occasional comedy. His award-winning books feature cinematic prose, strong characterization, twisting plots, and dark humor. You can follow Andrew on Goodreads or on his blog at https://adiamond.me.